LADY WITH
A LAPTOP

BY THE SAME AUTHOR

Fiction
The Flute-Player
Birthstone
The White Hotel
Ararat
Swallow
Sphinx
Summit
Lying Together
Pictures at an Exhibition
Flying in to Love
Eating Pavlova

Poetry
Two Voices
Logan Stone
Love and Other Deaths
The Honeymoon Voyage
Dreaming in Bronze
Selected Poems

Translations
Pushkin: The Bronze Horseman and Other Poems
Boris Godunov
Akhmatova: Selected Poems

Memoir
Memories & Hallucinations

LADY WITH A LAPTOP

A NOVEL BY
D. M. THOMAS

Carroll & Graf Publishers, Inc.
New York

Copyright © 1996 by D. M. Thomas

All rights reserved

First edition 1996

Carroll & Graf Publishers, Inc.
260 Fifth Avenue
New York, NY 10001

ISBN 0-7867-0308-3

Library of Congress Cataloging-in-Publication Data is
available.

Manufactured in the United States of America.

ACKNOWLEDGMENTS

Most of Lucinda's improvization on pp. 25-27 first appeared in the *Observer* Magazine (London), as part of a game of literary Consequences.

The quoted extracts on p. 93 and pp. 141-142 are from *The Marriage of Cadmus and Harmony*, by Robert Calasso (Jonathan Cape, London). The extract on pp. 107-108 is from *Rupert Brooke: a Biography*, by Christopher Hassall (Faber & Faber, London).

For the past few years I have been fortunate enough to be invited to lead writing workshops at the excellent and highly professional holistic holiday center on Skyros—never on its neighbor, Skagathos. I dedicate this novel to the Skyrians, and particularly to those I have been privileged to meet in the writing workshops. I am grateful to them for their good fellowship, inspiration and help in the writing of this fiction. No tutor has ever lost a student on Skyros, but all who go there lose their hearts to the beautiful island.

DMT
Truro, Cornwall
1995

I

ONE

The Corrupted Mayor

"Welcome to Skagathos! The sky is not always this blue at this time of year, but it mostly is! I hope we're lucky. My name is Stephanos. I live here and look after the place. I was able to talk to a few of you last night, but it was late, and you'd been traveling one helluva long time, almost two days in some cases. But the sun and the sea breezes will soon revive you!" Standing barelegged on one of the long outdoor tables, he flashes a smile as bright as the morning, and raises an arm to salute the sky. "Are your rooms okay?" He waits; there is a low murmur, implying uncertain approval. "Good. This Center will be closed at night but the kitchen is kept open; you can come here and make tea or coffee if you want at any time of the night. There are also a couple of showers. I know it's not much among fifty people but . . . some of you have showers where you are staying."

I look at the people who are drinking in this Greek, then look at him again myself—gazing up, because he has been sitting with me—his bony brown John-the-Baptist legs inches from my eyes. He has a long, refined face with curly shoulder-length brown hair; he wears pince-nez. Naked to the waist, he has a snake, "the snake of healing" he has told me, tattooed around his shoulders.

"Well, I'd just like to say something about this house." Fifty pairs of eyes swivel to observe the graceful, bouganvillead curves and balconies of the white two-storied villa. "It was built by a Turkish pirate in last century. Earlier this century it was owned by an American mayor, Mayor Lansky, I think he was mayor of New York but I'm not certain—"

"It was *Meyer* Lansky," interrupts an angular female East Coast American voice; "he wasn't a mayor he was a Mafia boss."

"Yes, Mayor Lansky," confirms Stephanos, unperturbed. "It was a holiday home, and lots of rich, famous Americans came to stay. President Roosevelt, Henry Ford, the young President Kennedy before the war, Goldwyn of the movies . . . lots of others. It's still in the family, we lease it, so in a sense you are Mayor Lansky's guests! Anyway, it's an interesting house. Enjoy it. But if the weather is good like this, you'll want to stay outside as much as possible."

On one side of the long tables are pomegranate and fig trees; on the other, a stone wall, part of which is on the edge of an almost vertical rockface, falling a hundred feet to a dry, stony riverbed. Stephanos refers to this now, warning us to be careful at night if we come here after drinking too much retsina, ouzo or Metaxa. If we wish to gaze at the moonlit sea, we should take care we don't stumble.

"We could do with big Mafia boss to run Greece, believe me! As you know, there is big one-day strike, shut-down, in Greece on Friday week, when you should be flying home, so you have extra day; and those who follow you will have a day less. Well, that's nice for you, but it's been a big headache rearranging flights. I don't know what the strike is for; something to do with Macedonia; I don't know. Some sort of demonstration." He rolls his eyes.

"Now, when you clear up your breakfast dishes, please put any scraps in the bin marked 'Donkey,' because we help to feed our neighbor's donkey. We try to help each other on this island. And now I want to say something about the plumbing . . ."

* * *

"We are as the gods. Whatever we wish to create, we create."

I sit on the upper terrace, with a circle of "students." They have briefly, and mostly shyly, introduced themselves.

These eleven strangers, all sensitive and vulnerable, most of them vegetarians or Vegans and certainly friends of the earth, have booked with Skagathos Holidays because they're looking for something different. They want to be changed, transformed, healed. I am offering them the Therapy of Fiction Writing, a morning workshop. Breakfast and either lunch or dinner are taken communally. Sue, who greeted us in Athens, has already organized work groups to help prepare and clean up; it's not, Stephanos has made clear, a way of getting free labor but to help provide the experience of a symbolic community, so lacking in modern life.

"I'd like you to chant that after me," I urge them.

"We are as the gods," they murmur in a ragged, tentative unison. "Whatever we wish to create, we create."

"Good. Believe in that."

It's a load of crap, of course; but in a sense that's why they're here. At least it's *different* crap from what they get at home. The cold relationships or none at all; the work without spiritual value, or none at all; the junk on television. They don't mind— indeed they positively love—living in inadequate "ethnic" rooms in Skagathos village. They don't mind placing their used toilet paper in bins, instead of flushing it away. Stephanos has given them instructions on "number one" and "number two."

John, a stunted, bandy-legged Liverpudlian, says he heard the aged widow who is his "hostess" call out to a boy playing football on their lane of many steps: "Achilles!" It showed him how close we were, in Skagathos, to the ancient Greeks.

"That's right, John," I say; "we are." And I quote Tennyson: " 'It may be we shall touch the Happy Isles, / And see the great Achilles, whom we knew . . .' " I repeat the last phrase, with emphasis. *"Whom we knew . . . "* They could picture his face; the wart on his chin perhaps; the livid scar on his brow; his habit of picking his nose. They'd *seen* him, talked with him a thousand times. And if you look out there—" I indicate the

5

shimmering blue sea, and their faces swivel—"you can imagine those thousand ships heading for Troy, can't you?"

They nod, uncertainly. I suspect some of them (the grey, hunched, bewildered little American widow, for sure) have no idea who he was, except that he was, or had, a heel.

But, for myself, I am moved, and fall silent for some time, gazing at that sea, those sails. This is why I came. In addition to the fee, which is not lordly, not Olympian. And to see the grave of a modern warrior, Rupert Brooke, the Georgian poet who was a youthful god of mine—buried on neighboring Skyros. I am between novels. It's a blessed relief to be able to live again, to breathe freely! Though there is already a slight nag of anxiety: when will the next one be? Will there even be another one?

But did Achilles even exist? Did Homer create him? Does it matter? "From this moment," I say to them, "you must eat, drink and breathe *fiction*. Everything can be transformed, re-created, translated. Even ourselves."

A tall, sunglassed, laptopped lady from New Zealand breaks an awkward silence to say that she saw, in an Italian museum, a statuette of the young Achilles, wearing women's clothes. A large man with a proportionately even larger red face and a grey ponytail explains in contorted public school English that Achilles' mother hid him among the females to try to save him from his predicted fate on the field of battle.

A man sitting to my left, who smokes through a cigarette holder, asks me if I think a male writer can write in a female voice, and vice versa. I say it's difficult but one can and must try. We're all human. The man with the cigarette holder—Harold—says in his opinion it's easier for a male to empathize with the opposite sex, since he's been inside a woman for nine months and after that close to her, nurtured by her. Girls, he says, have no such early identification with their father.

Lucy, a slim, fair London girl, explodes with anger. A lively debate follows. I keep glancing at raven-haired Natasha, not only because of her Slavic beauty but because she obviously can't follow our rapid, emotional talk. A similar strained look is on the face of Jeanne, a middle-aged French lady. But they both know it's going to be hard for them, struggling to keep up with the Anglophones.

When three or four are arguing at once, I step in and ask for a moment's silence. The red-faced man with the ponytail says we are sailing between Scylla and Charybdis, through the narrow strait of political correctness. Someone asks him to explain his allusion; after he's done so, to bring us back to a cooler subject I speak of the sound-symbolism of words beginning *sk-* or *sc-*, as with Skiathos, Skyros, Scylla, Scillies, Skagathos, Skopolos, Skye. "It's a very cut-off, islandy sound," I suggest; "scissors is another."

"Scimitar, skein, skim," says the ponytail, Angus. "Also skelf, a dialect word in my native Scotland, meaning splinter."

"Sklaniatos," says a boyish Welsh-sounding woman; "he's the doctor here on the island; I've heard he loves cutting people open."

"Well, perhaps . . ."

Over the limestone wall an elderly Greek, black-suited, his face a labyrinth of creases, is calling out to us and waving his arms alarmingly—indicating (according to the boyish Welsh woman—Emily—who has been here before) that the island council has ordered the water to be turned off. He is, in fact, the mayor, as "big" on Skagathos as "Mayor" Lansky was in New York. Waving our thanks, we leave our notebooks and hurry down the steps to the "communal" terrace and the house. The Reiki and Gastric Dancing groups are already standing or drifting around the terrace, drinking their herbal tea; but orgasmic moans and sighs from the bowels of the house tell us at least one group is still busy. We spread the news that the water is about to be turned off. There is a frenzy of filling urns, saucepans and buckets. The three large bowls, one containing disinfectant, another soap, and the third clear water for rinsing, are emptied of their breakfast waste and refilled. I head, meanwhile, for the coffee urn.

A cockerel crows, and a donkey brays; the latter adding a bestial and ejaculatory impetus to the moans and sighs emerging from the Orgasmic Consciousness group in their womblike, blacked-out room.

"How are we supposed to crap," a mousy-haired woman asks in clipped Home Counties tones, "if the water's off?"

No one offers her an answer; all are intent on getting a drink

7

while they can. It's rather sad to hear a grown Englishman, bearded like Livingstone, heir to Drake and Nelson, call out a request—verging on a demand—for elderflower tea to be made available.

A tall, skinny man with an Afro hairstyle and a long neck gobbles at me as if he's a mute trying to speak. His Adam's apple bobs. I recognize the typical stiff, inarticulate, emotionally stunted male, and help him out by saying, "Hello."

"Hello! You know Alan Jackson, I think. Geography teacher at Marlborough."

The unexpected question blanks me out for a moment, then I reply, "Yes! He's a very good friend; how do you know him?"

"We're on an educational working party together. I happened to mention I was coming here and he said you were coming here to teach creative writing. He said you did some part-time teaching there and your wife is—assistant bursar?"

"That's correct, yes."

"He expected me to know you. I'm afraid I didn't, I don't get much time to read fiction, though I did read a Ludlum on the way over and quite enjoyed it. You writing anything at the moment?"

He doesn't really want to know; his eyes are as glazed as mine, he's totally uninterested and we shan't speak again during the fortnight.

"I've just finished a novel."

"Oh, what's it to be called?"

"Probably *Infidelity.*"

"I must look out for it."

He fills his mug from the urn, nods at me, and walks off. I take his place. Is it finished, though, my novel? Or am I just tired of not living, being so buried in fiction that I notice nothing, absolutely nothing that's going on around me? Like this summer: blind! She had to tell me, I'd never have guessed! Ah well, it goes to show Marie knows when to pull back. No great harm done. Embarrassing, no more.

Even from a brief acquaintance, which—though one looked out for *Guardian* newspapers, beards, beads, ethnic skirts, etc., in the tourist-crammed Gatwick terminal—really only started yesterday morning in Athens, I know there are a few here I probably wouldn't throw out of bed. Natasha has to be the out-standing one, though I suspect I'd be crushed in the stampede. I did manage to sit beside her in the coach from our Athens hotel to the coast, and astonished her with a few poor Russian phrases. Uncertain what workshop to join, she was persuaded to try Fiction.

Skagathos Holidays discourage their tutors—or facilitators, as we are known here—from romance, except possibly with each other. Their printed guide for facilitators says we should not form relationships with participants because it's bad for the communal spirit. That's fair enough. A less formal, typed post-script, however, introduces confusion, since it asks us not to have "very much sex" with participants.

As I recall saying to Alan, on a pissy-awful June day, when he was envying me my Skagathos contract, "Does it mean I can screw with one, grope three or four, or French-kiss with a dozen?" He chuckled. Bastard! I trusted him.

As we trail back up the rising, flagstoned path to Calypso, as our upper "writing" terrace is called, our thoughts I suspect are on something more basic even than sex—the shit that threatens to build up in toilet bowls.

I decide to have them write something. "You haven't had much time to get to know each other yet; but there's *someone* you've got to know a little, during the long journey. I'd like you to describe him or her, but without using physical description, just metaphors. For instance, if he were a tree, what kind of tree would he be? Focus your mind on this person. Jot down a phrase as I give you the metaphor."

They poise. The statuesque New Zealander, Lucinda, asks me to wait while her laptop warms up.

I murmur, at intervals of half a minute: Tree . . . animal . . . musical instrument . . . article of furniture . . . drink . . . city . . . article of clothing . . . vehicle . . . Greek god or hero. Now I ask them to take ten minutes to try to pull their phrases together.

It's good to sit in quietness, drinking the sun in, while they think, and scribble, or in Lucinda's case, tap away on the laptop. My God, though, I do miss cigarettes. Cigarettes are for relaxing as well as for concentrating, for boredom as well as for moments of high drama.

I think being a different, non-smoking self contributed to that strange moment of lost identity on my way here. My Intercity train was drawing towards Reading, where I'd have to change. I left it rather late getting myself ready to leave the train, since I was engrossed in Herodotus's *Histories*. I had to spring to my feet and move fast. I went down the carriage to pick up my suitcase from the luggage rack, and found it had gone. There was one case there (the carriage was almost empty), and it was similar to mine, but clearly *not* mine. It was far more frayed and battered. Someone at a previous station must have picked up mine by mistake.

I panicked over the next few minutes, rushing up to the next carriage and back, agitatedly questioning my fellow travelers and the guard. I had a few minutes of pure dementia, in fact; because when I studied the suitcase more soberly it turned out to be mine—of course. There was my name and address on the label.

Later, in the slow, dirty Gatwick connection, I looked at my reflection in the dust-grimed window and asked, "Who the fuck are you?"

"Okay, it's time."

They stop writing, stretch out on their seats.

"Who's willing to go first? . . . Harold? Thanks."

Afterwards I lie, "You've all written splendidly. You didn't think you could, did you?"

"No! No!"

"I think you're all so clever!" Krystal (weeping willow, truck, grey squirrel) says quaveringly. "I don't know any Greek gods; I haven't read anything. Well, only detective stories; I shouldn't be here." But her perfectly justified self-doubts are drowned by a chorus of praise for her humdrum attempt to describe Angus.

"You are as gods." I look up at the dazzling sky; out at the shimmering sea. A light breeze blows. The cockerel crows again. "At every moment the world begins afresh. At every moment, a million possibilities arise. Well, it's time for lunch. I don't suppose the water's back on."

I fall in with Natasha (silver birch, jaguar, balalaika,

waterbed, vodka, Petersburg—according to Welsh Emily) on the walk down, and ask her if she's going to the nudist beach.

"I don't think so. Are you?"

"Yes. I'm looking forward to a swim."

"I too, but I'll swim with the villagers and keep my swimsuit on. We Russians are romantics, and I prefer a private unveiling. I don't want to know what a man's penis is like before we've even held hands."

"I tend to agree with you, Natasha."

"Helpers" are laying out lunch dishes and glasses on the long tables. Natasha excuses herself to go and freshen up.

I watch her buttocks swing globally under her tight white shorts.

It feels good to be between novels; not to have to suffer, for a few weeks, the unreality of fiction. To be able to gaze at real buttocks, Russian buttocks, without distraction.

TWO

An Orgasmic
Prophet

"Hi, I'm Ezekiel Morgenstein!"

The voice jerks me from solitary erotic reverie back to communal living. He stands with his plate in front of me in the line for macaroni cheese. His accent is American; there seem to be four or five American participants. I'm a modest five foot nine, but he has to look up at me. If he were a tree he would be . . . He has a beard like a tree, a bushy golden tree; and bushy blond hair, fluffing out around his ears. His even teeth gleam with instant friendship. Between the glittering teeth and the prominent nose there's a mustache of the dated "handlebar" kind. "It's good to meet you, Simon!" He thrusts out his free hand.

"Hello." *Simon!* American participants are friendly, sometimes pushy; but *this* degree of self-confidence, when he can surely see I'm abstracted, tired from talking for three hours, is exceptional. None of the others in the queue, or wondering whether to join it, are so tactless. I thank Christ this brash participant isn't in my workshop. "Whose group are you in?" I inquire, without interest, feeling obliged to say something.

"No, no, I'm a facilitator," he replies, unperturbed by my gaffe. "I'm leading the Orgasmic Consciousness workshop."

"Oh, I'm sorry! Of course!" I've seen his name on the brochure. Not American, Canadian it said.

His radiant sunlike beard nestles against a black sweater decorated with interlocking yellow triangles. His brief white shorts scarcely visible, his legs look too spindly to carry his body, beard and hair. "I was here the previous two weeks also," he says, holding out his plate to have macaroni dumped on it. "So far it's been good. I couldn't make the welcome drink last night because of a slight stomach upset. But I'm fine now. You settling in?"

"Yes, thanks. Well, not entirely, not yet. It's all a bit overwhelming."

"I can resonate with that. I was bombed when I arrived. I don't think I've adjusted yet to the time difference. You ever been to Vancouver?"

"I'm afraid not." I add that I know the Pacific coast farther south, as I have a brother who lives in San Francisco.

"I prefer Vancouver, but then it's my hometown."

A gong sounds, quelling all talk, freezing the ladles in midair; Stephanos leaps onto a table and announces that there'll be a short meeting at five this afternoon to discuss something called *oekos*. Just five minutes. He won't bother us with explanations now. He jumps down and the noise resumes, the ladles move.

"I hope we'll talk a lot while you're here," Ezekiel says. "Have you seen Elke? We're to have a short staff meeting after lunch to discuss the water problem. I feel I've descended into the primitive here, and it's great. The whole atmosphere impacts me."

* * *

Elke, our Icelandic art therapist, is our "course director." She awaits us in the parqueted Lotus Room, cross-legged on a cushion (there are no chairs), fat and white, narrow-eyed, a Buddha. She exudes serenity; her white T-shirt disports a smiling dolphin. If she were a piece of music, she would be an endlessly expansive Bruckner symphony; if an animal, a woolly mam-

13

moth; if a picture (and this is probably the most apt comparison), a Rubliov icon.

We take our places, cross-legged, around her. She welcomes us in her gruff voice. This is a democratic meeting—even the old Greek widow, swathed in black, who empties the shit buckets, is present. Our cook, a Kojak-skulled, earringed young man, fresh this season from a London Polytechnic home economics course, tells us quietly that the water is back on, there's no problem.

Elke, gazing at him or through him, seems to take a whole minute to absorb the information; then she nods. "That's good. It was very brief."

"Yes. We can expect worse."

I'm ready to leap up and head for the nude beach, but Elke says, "All the same, this gives us a chance to get to know each other, and come out with any problems. Shall we go round the circle? Ezekiel? How are you feeling?"

"Oh, I'm almost better. Ninety percent well. Thank you. Even the ten percent that's still in sickness hangover feels positive now. I feel good in myself; very very good." He smiles and nods around at us all, his blond beard bobbing. "I have a nice group. I'm looking forward to getting to know them. I'm looking forward to getting to know everyone. The last course was great; I felt very close to them all by the end. Not merely those taking the Orgasmic Consciousness workshop but all the others too." He continues to nod. His voice is gentle, sweet. "I've only just met most of you, but I feel good with you already."

Elke nods. I nod. Elspeth, the slender fair-haired Gastric Dancing facilitator, nods.

Elspeth is pleasant. I talked to her on the ferry. Gastric Dancing is a way of focusing on one's stomach while one dances; and in so doing one gets into touch with the sacrificed being—vegetable or even animal—in mutual love.

"I'd like to thank you for the lunch, Peter," she says sweetly to the earringed cook. "It was beautiful."

Ezekiel echoes her. "It sure was! The cooking here is wonderful. The rest of you will find out. We had some unforgettable meals in the last course."

Peter, his face reddening slightly, I guess knowing the praise to be wildly over the top, says thank you.

"It couldn't have been easy for you and your helpers, preparing lunch when the water's been turned off. I know how well you cope when that happens; as if it's the easiest thing in the world. Thank you—all of you." His gaze takes in the two sleepy-looking English girls, Sue and Tamsin, who have enjoyed a Greek summer in return for doing humdrum chores.

The Greek widow is nodding, her eyes closed. She is squatting uncomfortably, her black skirt stretched taut, her spread thighs reveal a generous length of laddered black tights. She's probably only about forty, I reflect, though looks much older, heavily wrinkled, her hands calloused. She looks closer to Cassandra and Clytemnestra than to Elke and Elspeth.

"Simon?" Elke asks.

"I feel fine." I nod several times. "I've a good group too, I think."

"It's good to have you here."

"Thank you."

"Yes, it's really good to have you, Simon," Ezekiel echoes. "Judging by the last fortnight, when we had Tim O'Brien here, the writing workshops really add something to the holistic process. Tim did a wonderful job; gave endlessly of himself." He glances for confirmation at Stephanos, Sue and Tamsin. Awaking, they nod with evidently genuine appreciation.

"Those wonderful baseball caps!" Sue recalls, smiling.

"You know his work, Simon?" Ezekiel asks.

"Not well. A few of his Vietnam stories."

"Right! he was there. He's good. And much in demand. National Book Award winner. Skagathos was lucky to attract such a writer."

Actually, says Stephanos, he came thinking we were Skyros. But he loved it here. A lovely man. His students adored him.

Silence falls after this encomium of my predecessor. I lick my dry lips. Ezekiel, at length, murmurs at me pleasantly, "I'm sure you'll be just as popular. I want to read your books."

I nod. Silence hangs over us again, as Elke seems lost in a trance. Ezekiel murmurs, "Yes, he was a great guy, and so intelligent. It was hard to imagine he was once a grunt."

15

"What was that?" Elke asks.

"A grunt."

"Yes, we could do that. There's some tension here. Not much but a little." And she grunts, from deep inside her powerful belly. Ezekiel follows suit, and then, more feebly, the rest of us.

"That feels a lot better," she says; "thank you for suggesting it, Ezekiel. And now let's go on. Brenda? How are you feeling?"

Brenda, a Reiki healer, is a grey-haired retired social worker from Tower Hamlets. She reports, in a quiet, slightly cockney voice, a minor problem with a disturbed student.

"You get many disturbed people coming here," says Ezekiel; "one has to keep an eye on them."

Elspeth, having been in an earlier course, is very worried about this problem; she already knows of one participant, Sandra, a tall, plain, painfully shy girl, who's on a powerful antidepressant. The secret, Ezekiel says, is crisis intervention at the first sign of disturbance. Any problem—hammer it: he bangs his fist into his palm. He's willing to announce at *demos* that he's available for private consultations on emotional problems. And he'll keep an eagle eye out for Sandra. "Thanks, Elspeth."

The discussion of what to do about disturbed participants drags on for half an hour. It's not going to be worth making the long trek to the beach. Ezekiel says the last director had a staff meeting every morning, before breakfast, and that had seemed to work well. Could we not do that? In Vancouver, where he runs a clinic called Joy of Living, he always gets together with his staff every day. You would know where everyone was at.

I sense dismay on every face except Elke's. It must be after breakfast, she says, because of the domestic staff, but she thinks it's a good idea. We'll start tomorrow.

With a few words of a Sanskrit meditation, our eyes closed, she brings the meeting to an end.

"You going to swim?" asks Ezekiel, as we emerge into the sunlight.

"I think I'll give it a miss for today."

"I know. It went on too long. But it was worthwhile."

"Yes."

"Are you writing a novel at the moment?"

16

"I've just finished one. I'm between novels."

I ask him to explain his Orgasmic Consciousness workshop, and he tells me he gets people to lie facedown, in the darkened room, and he plays to them subliminal music, very carefully chosen. Also he asks them to breathe very deeply. "After a while they get the impression they're outside time. It's an extraordinary experience. Three hours seems like twenty minutes. They have an orgasm that's somewhere close to the Big Bang."

Promising to catch up with me later, he heads off for the beach. The terrace is deserted, except for Pasha, our second Russian holiday-maker. An ex-cop, so he tell us, and a keen amateur violinist; Natasha guesses he plays for KGB Philharmonic. He sits in his grey slacks and short-sleeved blue shirt, looking sad and lost. I join him. *"Vam khorosho?"* I ask him sympathetically.

He shrugs dolefully. *"Da. No mnye golodno.* I'm hunger." He doesn't understand; in Novocherkassk, back in the sixties, thousands of miners downed tools and went on strike, just for meat, butter and soap. Soviet troops shot and killed twenty or thirty of them. "Yet here, my friend, you *want* there not to be meat, not to be butter!" His eyes roll uncomprehendingly, drolly; he waves an arm. "And there's not merely no soap—well, just a sliver, among fifty people—but some of the time no water!"

"Are you in a group?" I ask him.

"Nyet. My hobby photography," he says mournfully, picking up an expensive-looking camera from the seat beside him. "No photography groups here, so I—freelance!" He offers a gloomy smile.

* * *

The moon, at night, is just a sliver like Pasha's soap, and the stars shine brilliantly above the terrace. There's an autumnal nip in the air, and I'm glad Marie had the sense to make me pack a thick sweater. It's noticeable that Pasha and Natasha have made an effort to dress up a little for dinner under the stars, but no one else has bothered. But then, no one else won this holiday in a quiz show on Moscow TV, and thought they were coming to a first-class resort hotel. The mood is subdued. Our Greek manager, the pince-nezed Stephanos, tries to get

17

some dancing going, but it quickly subsides. Pasha stands under the lanternlit trees, playing a melancholy violin.

Natasha is smiling though, deep in conversation with a rather handsome young man. How can I—conceived, my father says, on VE Day—compete? Of course, being a published western novelist gives me a certain cachet; but it doesn't equate with a smooth young face, perfect teeth, bulging muscles. Natasha, I can see, goes for men younger than herself.

"When business is slow in the pub I do some reading," says a middle-aged woman in purple leggings and yellow T-shirt, a part-time barmaid in Brighton. "Oh, can *I* have one?" asks her neighbor at dinner. "Of course, Val; I'll bring the cards tomorrow."

I retire to my bedroom, above the Lotus Room, early. For a while, lying in the dark, I plan what I will do tomorrow morning, ("We are as gods"), then masturbate imagining Rupert Brooke's curvacious Tahitian bedmate.

* * *

"My country is in state of madness," says Natasha at breakfast; "you can't begin to imagine what it's like, Simon." My name, the way she speaks it with a slight accent, has a certain charm.

"Mine too," I say, thinking of the tarot lady. Natasha pushes her bowl of muesli away uneaten, screwing up her face. "We are desperately searching for some meaning to life." Her big black eyes, untroubled as yet by the mild sun in the cloudless sky, search mine as if she will find meaning there. A mistake, of course. "And so we turning to all sorts of charlatans. Do you hear of Moscow's Institute of the Brain?" I shake my head. "Well, it's a big building, and it holds lots of dead brains. They're all sliced up, preserved. It was founded in order to study the size and shape of the brains of our great Communists . . ." She smiles ironically. "Lenin's is prize possession, naturally. Well, there is a man who used to work there, who now goes around claiming he's able penetrate into Lenin's thought processes, and transfer them onto computer, then onto tape! He gives stage performances, all over Russia. Lenin, and also Trotsky, Bukharin, Mayakovsky . . . Reflecting on present life! Well, most people see it as weird entertainment; but I've heard Ph.D.'s argue that our Soviet technology was capable of anything."

She asks me if I mind her smoking. She's finding the West's anti-smoking crusade difficult. I don't like having to breathe in smoke, myself, since I'm becoming addicted to nicotine patches, but I tell Natasha it doesn't bother me. She clicks a cheap lighter. Two other members of our workshop join us with their mueslis and oranges—Harold, wistful, fiftyish but still a minor public schoolboy; and Jeanne, a tutor in economics at the Sorbonne, our other non-Anglo. Of fading attractiveness, she is flattered by Harold's attention, which is already apparent to everyone. She wants to write poetry in English, for some reason. Natasha and I say hello to them. Harold, who only wants coffee, brings out that black holder I thought had died out thirty years ago with black-and-white films and Noel Coward.

He takes his first deep draw, raises his eyes to the sky and intones, "What a wonderful morning! Sitting here, with two such charming and beautiful ladies, it makes me feel it would be good to become an eternal student, as in Chekhov. Don't you think, Natasha my dear? Do you like Chekhov?"

"Yes, I love him."

"I love him too. He's so *wistful*. I adore wistful writers." He focuses his attention on Jeanne. "That's what I like about your French films, Jeanne; they have a wistful, romantic quality. Not like the brutal Yanks. Though I saw an excellent American film recently in New York. *The Bronx Tale;* has anyone seen it? Then you should. De Niro directed it; it's flawless."

Jeanne has her notebook of English words out. "Lawless?" she asks. I've noticed already she's slightly hard-of-hearing.

Harold gives a kindly chuckle. "No, I said the direction is flawless." Jeanne writes the word down.

"Is he a new young director?" she asks.

"De Niro's an old established actor, my dear."

"She means Flawless," I say, guessing.

"Yes, Flawless."

I laugh. "But how wonderful to have a director called Flawless! Think of the reviews outside the cinemas—since all the reviewers would be bound to mention his name, if only to say his direction was crap! 'Flawless . . . ,' *Washington Post;* 'Flawless . . . ,' *Daily Telegraph;* 'Flawless . . . ,' *Express;* 'Flawless . . . ,' *Figaro . . . !"*

Harold smiles wistfully. Freckled Welsh Emily, followed by a fellow les, sidles past with her piled plate. She has cropped hair and the legs of a runner. "Allo!" she cries, like a parrot's squalk.

"Allo, Emily!" I squalk back satirically.

Harold grabs Emily's large hand and murmurs, with a kind of self-parodic fervor, "Emily! I loved watching you dance last night—such wit, such energy, such bravura—and such a waste!"

I sit on the terrace wall, with its sheer fall to a dry riverbed, and gaze at the horizon. The sky is so clear today that Skyros is visible. I would rather have been on Skyros; mostly because of Rupert Brooke, buried there.

Stephanos tells me it is easier to take a boat trip across, landing on the deserted coast and walking up to the grave—silent, olive-shrouded, where even Echo never strays—rather than go across by ferry and have to haggle over taxis. Next weekend, he suggests.

I spoke to my group yesterday about that myth, the myth of Grecian England. The clean-limbed Housmanesque young men of before the First World War. I quoted—sudden memory surging up from my youth—Brooke's sonnet beginning, "Breathless we flung us on the windy hill, / Laughed in the sun, and kissed the lovely grass . . ." *Smoked* the lovely grass it would be, today, I guessed, and got a laugh.

When I think of Brooke I also think of Masterson, head boy to my deputy head boy at Nailsea Grammar. Handsome lad, and tossed a curly gold lock back from his eyes, as Rupert did. His father a postman, though Masterson pretended he was a tea planter in Kenya. Didn't explain why he was at Nailsea Grammar and not Rugby or Charterhouse. Bright lad, though; brighter than I, and got an Exhibition to King's, Cambridge. — Emulating Rupert Brooke, who was Fellow of the college at twenty-seven, just before war, and death. Of a mosquito bite turning septic. His death shocked England. Symbol of a generation of lovely, bright youths. Celebrants of English hedgerows and pastures, familiars of the Greek poets.

Brooke, Edward Thomas, Abercrombie, Marsh, Sassoon . . . Lovers of the lovely. Brooke a complex man, though; Fabian, tormented by sexual ambiguities; perhaps even welcoming death as a way out.

I visited Masterson once, in King's, after our "A" levels. He fed me toasted crumpets; clearly felt it was gracious of him to be nice to an ex-chum now at a redbrick university. He was in the College Eight. Became a lieutenant of the Gloucesters in his national service. Recently, fat and balding, took early retirement and a golden handshake from ICI, of which he was a director. I saw his photo in the *Evening Standard.*

> "Through glory and ecstasy we pass . . .
> And when we die
> All's over that is ours, and life burns on
> Through other lovers, other lips," said I . . .

Not sure how it goes after that; but I know it ends with: "And then you suddenly cried, and turned away."

Well, he's over there on Skyros, our golden Rupert.

      *   *   *

"Thank you for arranging the Greek dancing last night, Stephanos," Elke says, when we have squatted down in our staff circle and composed ourselves. Stephanos, his long wavy hair shimmering, his eyes mild and friendly as they survey us through or over his old-fashioned pince-nez, replies, "I enjoyed doing it; it was fun."

"Yes, it was. And thank you for the lovely meal, Peter, and Sue, and Tamsin."

The cook and his assistants lower their heads. Possibly in shame. Elke, swaying her bulk forward so that her blue sweat-shirted stomach overhangs her shorts, turns her gaze on Elspeth. "You look so pretty today, Elspeth! How did the early-morning meditation go?"

"It was fine. Seven people turned up." A dryad, slender, pale, spun-gold hair.

21

"That was good."

"Yes. I think they enjoyed it. Tomorrow we may go up to the Acropolis to watch the sunrise. You're welcome to join us, anyone, so long as you can stand getting up at five thirty!"

"I'd like to do that," says Ezekiel.

"Good."

"Should one eat something beforehand?"

"Some fruit would be good. It helps. Although if the stomach is empty it's still possible to do gastric dancing successfully. But some grapes or something: okay?"

A nod. "I only wish I could attend your workshop; I've heard such good things, Elspeth, about the opening session." He is silent for a few moments, continuing to nod. I watch, in a kind of trance, his pale floaty beard and pronounced nose outlined against the white wall below the broad window with its expanse of blue. The Lotus Room is indeed trance-inducing. All carnal thoughts fly away in it; and the Greek widow is absent, so there is nothing that seems out of keeping with the holistic harmony; no muffling black cloth nor laddered tights. "I feel very good this morning," he continues; "very good. Very calm in myself. I feel comfortable with you all. I think that covers it." He shrugs.

"Thank you, Ezekiel," Elke murmurs. "I feel good too. Tomorrow, I must tell you, I have a young friend, a lovely young man, visiting me for a few days. His name is Rollo. He's a brilliant student of mine in Reykjavik. He will be sharing my room while he's here. Well, it's no problem."

Ezekiel clears his throat then says, "And on Friday I have my assistant and lover coming."

"Is that two people?" I ask, and there is a mild chuckle round the room.

"Her name is Teresa Bombassoni. She runs a shamanist workshop in Taos, New Mexico. I'm sure you'll like her. She's a very beautiful person."

I feel a slight twitch of envy and resentment. I wanted Marie to come with me but she refused. I guess that was when she was otherwise engaged. She might have come if I'd asked her again in the past few weeks. It would have been good. The college would have given her time off, they're quite decent about that if you're in admin. Christ yes, it would have been good to show

22

her off; she's not Miss Natal anymore, but still bloody good-looking.

"Well, it's time for our workshops. If there's nothing else? . . . Thank you. Enjoy your groups."

THREE

A Liquid Sonata

My group is already gathered on the high terrace under the shady olive. Only Angus is absent, and it's rumored he has a stomach upset. They have been passing around snapshots of Emily's cottage in Snowdonia, and of her partner Bronwen, a forestry worker. Bronwen—who enjoys being left on her own occasionally—swings an axe outside the pleasant little cottage.

I plunge them into a game of Consequences. They are asked to write down ten adjectives in a vertical column, then fold the paper back to hide what they've written, and pass it to their neighbor. After that, ten nouns. "Fold back and pass on." Then I have to explain patiently what a transitive verb is—no one learns grammar at school anymore, and I know some will still get this wrong. After the verb, ten more adjectives, and ten more nouns.

We fling our folded-up papers into the dust in the middle of our circle. We pick one up at random, and unfold. There are little murmurs of amusement. I ask them in turn to read out their serendipitous sentences. Laughter greets such as:

"The serene tiger fucks the voluminous ashtray."

"The silken chocolate bar predicts a liquid sonata . . ."

"The virginal widow leaves the corrupted mayor . . ."

"A Rainy Inter City Mourns a Ghostly Hollandaise . . ."

A respectful murmur greets such as:
"A wasted mother dreams a bleeding college."

"A prosperous atrocity finds an admiring ghost." ("Why the preoccupation with spectres, I wonder?" Harold asks.)

"The mournful brook evokes an elegiac storm."

There are also, of course, the ones that flop because of bad grammar or wrong spacing:
"A sensuous tree lies the rare mountain."

"A Black Sea-dog . . ."

"A Flying Author Unravels . . ."

"Choose a sentence that intrigues you," I instruct them, "and make up a story about it. Remember, you are as gods." Stately, workaholic Lucinda warms up her laptop. Her fingers race. Almost before the others have opened their notebooks she is squinting at the tiny screen and announcing that it's not very good but would we like to hear it? She's chosen *"A sprawling gnat frightens the murderous sister . . ."*

She let herself into the silent cottage and—calling out "Nat, it's me!"—climbed the rickety stairs. Nat was still sprawled in bed, one naked, muscular leg outside the duvet. Smoking, reading a paperback, he gave her a cursory greeting: "Okay?" Then his gaze returned to the page.
"I'm drowned."

25

D. M. Thomas

"Fucking stupid to go out in this weather. We already know the right spot."

Mildred began stripping off her sodden clothes. His eyes, blue and cold, flickered with a touch of interest; but he had moved a million miles, she reflected, since the passionate lovemaking of a few hours ago.

There was a big house spider trying to climb the craggy sides of the stained bath, and she had to call Nat to remove it for her. He came and did so, edging it with his finger gently into a glass, then opening the small window to drop it out. He was so tender to all creatures except humans. "Stupid bloody bitch!" he said to her, but with an affectionate grin, and he hugged her. She felt embarrassed by her middle-ageing stomach against his youthful tautness. He let her go and shambled away to the bedroom.

She was glad she'd remembered to pack bathfoam. Submerged to the neck, she thought about the Welshman with his gun, and his stuttering companion carrying a spade, whom she'd met in the hills. Badger-hunting, they'd said. But it had seemed sinister, almost like an IRA killing, in which the culprit, the traitor, connives at his own killing and burying. From guilt, he consents to his death sentence. And she felt like that. Nausea again, churning in her gut. I'll go to the village, she thought, and ring my sister; tell her the roads are flooded and she's not to drive down and join us.

Agnes was so innocent; truly a lamb; it would never occur to her to distrust Nat, starting the holiday alone with Mildred while she sat her final law exam. She'd always left them alone together without a thought.

Nat—as if guessing her treacherous revery—stood over the bath. She reached out and touched his long, limp penis in its matt of black hair. The Dangling Man. *Bellow. College long ago. It haunted and obsessed her. A drug.*

"You won't cop out, will you?" he asked, staring down.

She lifted the yellow sponge out of the water, squeezed it and felt the trickle onto her breasts. "Couldn't we just tell her, and you get a divorce?"

"It would ruin us. We fucking can't live on air."

26

Her eyes closed. She drifted. It was one thing talking about it during sex, the rush of sadistic, murderous excitement as he brought her to the edge, then pushed her over—quite another getting ready to do it. The relaxed meal tonight, the last marital bedding, then tomorrow the hike in the mountains.

"It'll be dead easy," he said, stroking her wet shoulder.

But perhaps—perhaps he was still only fantasizing. He'd always loved fantastic, way-out sex. And it appealed to her too. That was probably what had drawn them together. At first it had been relatively innocent. He'd made her dress up tartily: spiky heels, black silk seamed stockings, red satin suspender belt; he had drawn up her tight skirt around her waist, and covered her from foot to waist in melted chocolate. "My silken chocolate bar," he'd whispered— licking it off from the toes up. And it had ended in an incredibly wet, orgiastic fuck to a Beethoven sonata on Nat's and Agnes's hi-fi.

Then, gradually, the sadistic touches. Like having her pull her legs right back and strapping her ankles to the bedposts; sitting by her, smoking, tigerish yet serene, flicking his ash into her stretched-open cunt, as though she were nothing but a voluminous ashtray. A spark on that vulnerable soft flesh had made her scream.

Yes, perhaps he was still only fantasizing. The blue eyes were faintly mocking. He was pushing it to the very edge. That stir of excitement in her. She caught hold of his hand, drawing him down.

When Lucinda has finished reading, I notice that unconsciously I have been sketching Harold, his eyes closed, head tilted back, cigarette holder between his teeth. He remains in the same pose as silence engulfs the group. Faces are lowered in embarrassment at the lurid sexuality.

Caroline, a big plain redhead from Luton, breaks the silence by exclaiming, "I think that's bloody brilliant!" And Jeanne echoes her: *"Oui, c'est* flawless!"

Lucinda, stiff-backed Artemis, wears a faint smile acknowledging the tributes. "I changed g-n-a-t to N-a-t, and I couldn't resist getting those other two in. Krystal, hope I didn't steal your line."

27

"No, honey, you didn't, I'm allergic to chocolate."

Harold removes his cigarette. "I feel distressed by it, Lucinda," he murmurs.

"Oh—why is that?"

"You're such a lovely, sweet girl. I suppose I shouldn't call you a girl. And yet to think you can write something like that! It pains me. There's enough violence in the world, without adding to it. Surely we're here on Skagathos to enjoy the sun and the sea, and beauty—such as yours—and to try to write beautiful, tranquil things according to our modest capacities—"

"—You speak for yourself, Harold," Lucinda says sharply. "I certainly don't think my capacities are modest, and I'm sure that goes for a lot of us."

"I'm sorry if I've offended you. Yes, I speak for myself. I don't feel anything for these people. Nat and Mildred. They leave me cold. There's no warmth, no love, no romance in them. Not to mention the fact that there are some words I simply couldn't use. It's my weakness, I suppose, I'm old-fashioned. But of course it's very skillfully written, very skillfully indeed."

"Well," I say, "the world is not a very sweet place. Jamie Bulger knows that; or rather, he doesn't." Jamie Bulger was a two-year-old boy abducted and murdered by two ten-year-old boys in Bootle. A few of us have chatted about the terrible case.

Natasha has not heard of Jamie Bulger, and Emily, in her strong Welsh, summarizes for her.

"Ah, that's terrible!" Natasha blinks her beautiful eyes, close to tears.

"Lucinda's piece doesn't distress me but it makes me very angry," says slim, quiet, laurel-like Lucy. Because of men. Their abuse of women.

"Of course. I feel the same," agrees her almost-namesake, laptopped besunglassed Lucinda.

Bandylegged spectacled John: "Ay, Lucy my dear, we can all say amen to that."

Andrea: "How the fuck did you think it up? Was it based on anything?"

"Not really. I thought of Emily's Welsh cottage. And there were two sisters involved in a murder case in Dunedin last year; a lust murder. But it wasn't really close. I don't know—where *do* these things come from?"

"I don't know either, Lucinda," I say. "But Nat and Mildred—and Agnes—now exist. We can't get rid of them."

Lucinda's sunglasses stare at me. I'm stirred by her erotic imagination. I haven't till now considered her as a possible lover, but she must be added to the list. Though she nearly always appears in a brown divided skirt, which doesn't turn me on, and her breasts, under a crisp white shirt, look somewhat flat.

And they *are* flat, seen naked on the nudist beach. Elke, a gigantic Aphrodite waddling out of the sea, stirs me more; and I fancy I can see even John's seventy-year-old wizened Liverpudlian dick give a slight twitch as she lurches past him, dripping wet. A woman-mountain.

* * *

In the late afternoon, when the volcanic mountain dominating the little white village spreads its shadow over our terrace, people start to regather, but in a subdued spirit. It's the time for co-listening, a daily event in which a different kind of stripping takes place. At the opening session Elke invited everyone to get into pairs, choosing a partner whom one didn't find sexually attractive. The idea, she said, was that in turn you poured out anything that was troubling you, for fifteen-twenty minutes, and your partner must listen in silence, sympathetically.

I think almost everyone here, staff included, is taking part in the co-listening, but it didn't appeal to me.

At the long tables or tucked away in corners, couple by couple, isolated, people are murmuring, listening, nodding. Already some have told me they feel as if they're married. This is quite normal, says Stephanos; and indeed there will be divorces. I sit alone, sipping mineral water. It is good to feel withdrawn. I think of my novel, just finished. Or *is* it finished?

The tall, sad figure of Pasha appears. He looks around, sees me, heads towards me.

"You are not co-listening?" I ask him as he sits beside me. He doesn't understand. I search for a clumsy phrase in Russian which will convey the meaning.

"Nyet-sovyershenno nyet!"

"I neither . . . I didn't see you on the beach. You weren't swimming?"

"No. I cannot swim. I've been walking a little."

He sees me looking towards where Natasha sits, hunched forward, elbows on the table, addressing Eddie, the attractive young man she has evidently taken to quite strongly. His entranced eyes are inches from hers. He is nodding slightly.

"Natasha," Pasha says: "don't trust her. Her father was Politburo apparatchik. Supported the *putsch*. You understand, Gospodin Hopkins."

"That doesn't mean his daughter thinks that way."

He spreads his arms. "Apples fall under the tree."

"She thinks you were in the KGB, Pasha."

"Hah!" A mouthful of silver teeth. "I police. Traffic offenses." We sit in silence for a while. Not far from us, Emily is giving Caroline a neck massage. Pasha says finally, "I go to village for Metaxa. You come?"

Later, I tell him. I'll join him. He nods, resigned to loneliness; rises, stalks off between the tables towards the gate. Rather a keen wind has got up; I climb the steps to my room to fetch a sweater. As I approach, the bathroom door opposite clicks open and Elke appears, wearing only pink knickers. Her breasts lie on her huge stomach like two beached whales on a sand dune. "Hi!" I say.

"The water is cold."

I offer a sympathetic grimace.

"Will you help me, Simon? Come to my room."

I follow her to her bedroom, wondering. She wants two single beds moved together. For Rollo when he comes tomorrow. I help her heave a bed across, her muscular arms and neck swelling, huge breasts flopping.

"Thank you." Her eyes seem to linger on me; almost as if she would like to try the beds out.

"Any time."

Outside again, having donned a thick sweater against the evening chill, I let sad widowed vulnerable Krystal bring me a coffee. She's combed Washington, D.C., for my books but can't find any. No, I say, irritated, I'm not yet published in the States. My irritation causes my mind to wander away while she talks about her husband, who seems to have been some kind of hypnotist entertainer (I confess I'm uncertain of this).

"I don't think I have much to give the workshop. I didn't get much of an education; you know, in my days girls were supposed to get married, and that's what I did. And then I got immersed in motherhood; not that I did a great job of it; my daughter Trixie hasn't bothered to visit since her dad died, five years ago. Of course she lives quite a way away, in Dakota . . ."

"I think you have a lot to offer us, Krystal. You bring your own experience, your own perspective."

"I hope so."

I stifle a yawn. A wind sneaks in from the sea. She speaks of Agatha Christie. I stifle another yawn. She excuses herself to go and put on a cardigan. Wind-ruffled people are beginning to set the tables for the evening meal; the co-listening is breaking up.

I shall draw a veil over the meal, the vegetarian mess that rapidly cools as one hunches shivering. The Skagathos Centre is in a natural funnel for the wind. It's called *meltemi,* Stephanos explains. It could last for days. I have almost to shout as Krystal and John discuss with me Lucinda's shocking piece. They're inclined to agree with Harold about its coldness, pornography, violence.

Krystal goes to bed early. Her stomach is playing up. There's a bug affecting quite a few people. Poor Angus hasn't appeared.

Later, several of us find a haven from the wind, and some necessary alcohol, outside one of the village cafes. The village, which concentrates around one steeply descending, traffic-free lane, is getting ready for winter. The jewelery and souvenir shops have put up sale signs. I sit with Andrea (Chicago bar stool, Gershwin, oak tree, according to Lucy), and her genial husband Danny; Lucinda of the statuesque pose and brown divided skirt; Natasha and her co-listener Eddie.

Andrea and I are praising Lucinda again for her piece. She responds with a faint smile and the comment that it was only an exercise. "But it had power, it let it all out," I assure her; "it didn't give a fuck about being genteel—that was what I liked. There's too much fucking niceness in that place." I nod my head up the steep lane.

Across from us, at another cafe, Harold and Jeanne are drinking. Behind them, inside, a huddle of Greek men surround a splendidly imposing Orthodox priest.

Getting tipsy on Metaxa, Natasha starts to talk about her country. "We were brutal, corrupt, poverty-stricken Communist state," she slurs, "and now we're going to be brutal, corrupt, poverty-stricken capitalist state. Oh, not brutal in the same way, there won't be sixty million dead as under Stalin, but in sense of greed, neglect of poor peoples, and culture. Well, in some important ways it will be worse. Under Bolsheviks we were at war. Party against the people. The *narod, da?*" She nods at me, dark eyes ablaze. "And war bring out nation's greatness. The intellectuals and common people were together, against oppressors. When our great Akhmatova died there are many, many thousands at her funeral—ordinary workers as well as writers and intellectuals. At Pasternak's funeral too. Sakharov—a hundred thousand at his grave! How many workers, Simon, were at T. S. Eliot's funeral?"

"I haven't a clue. None, I guess. Well, the gravediggers."

"So I drink a toast to Comrade Stalin!" She raises her glass and knocks back the Metaxa. "He give us one of our most glorious cultural epochs. Such Gulag literature!—Solzhenitsyn, Natalia Ginsburg's wonderful Siberian memoirs, Nadezhda Mandelstam, Shalamov! And don't let's forget that the *ideal* of Communism was something these writers shared with the *narod.*"

Her head slumps forward, her long black hair hanging over her eyes.

Danny asks, "What is it you do, Natasha? What's your job?"

She raises her head to stare at him almost aggressively. "I

used to be ballet dancer in Magnitogorsk. Now I train striptease dancers in Moscow." Her head slumps forward again.

Danny shakes his head. "Amazing!"

After a waiter has brought us another round of Metaxas, Natasha launches forth again. "Okay, so Stalin bumped off sixty million people. But in three hundred years the world will still be reading our great writers of this century—of Soviet epoch. They will say, this was great age. Shostakovitch! He too! The 'Leningrad.' The only art in history that seems to come straight out of common people, but in majestic language, and spiritualistic. And now? Nothing! Writers are free to write absolutely everything, so they can't write! Freedom is nothing; only hunger for freedom is noble. And perhaps the moment when it arrive us, like when the Berlin Wall come down and the people stream through so joyful. Well, and when the tanks turned back from the White House. *That* was wonderful! I dance in the street, I dance!"

She jumps up from her seat, clears the glasses to one side and climbs onto the table. She starts to dance, clapping her hands, white skirt swirling, and we clap too; and soon everyone is clapping approval, on both sides of the lane. She is dancing—it is clear from the language of her feet—for that illiterate bronzed hulk Eddie, a lifesaver from Newquay, gawping openmouthed up at her.

She staggers, almost falls; he helps her down. "I'll take you home," he says, and throws a few thousand drachs on the table.

They stagger off, arms around each other. "She's amazing!" Danny repeats, gazing after her. "And all they can find for her to do is train strippers! Wow!"

Soon he and Andrea, starting to yawn, put some drachs on the table and leave too. I summon one last drink for Lucinda and myself.

She has grown quiet; I sense I may have shown rather too much appreciation of the beautiful and dynamic trainer of Russian strippers. "Russian histrionics!" I say, rolling my eyes.

"She has a big mouth. I liked your irony, Simon—is it okay to call you that?—in suggesting to her she might do a striptease for us in the workshop, to inspire us. I was dying to laugh! But she took it so earnestly, didn't she?"

"It didn't amuse her, you're right."

And she seems almost a Fascist, she continues—almost suggesting that freedom was incompatible with art. Defending Natasha, I suggest the relationship between liberal values and literature is indeed complex. "For instance—do you know Chekhov's story *Lady with a Lap-dog?*"

"Of course."

"The two lovers meet with such passion, every few months, wondering how they can free themselves from their awful marriages so they can be together. Well, today there'd be no problem. Two quickie divorces and hey presto! And in a few years, if they start to get bored with each other—they can do it again! No problem—lots of happiness—and no art!" I grin, but see that Lucinda is unimpressed; her lips are a thin straight line. "Your writing today was quite stunning, Lucinda. I'm tremendously impressed. You *must* have published."

She shrugs. "A couple of short stories, in small magazines. Harold was right about it; and Natasha's right. We deal in frivolous trifles. Silken chocolate predicting a liquid sonata. The planet is going to be buried under pollution, and all we can do is play word games. No disrespect, Simon."

"No, I guess you're right."

"And look how we torture animals, through intensive farming. Excuse me."

She pushes her chair back; looks pale and as if she's about to throw up. "Are you okay?" She stands and moves towards the restaurant interior, then heads back to gather up a three-day-old *Herald Tribune* that Danny has left behind. She is away a long time. When she eventually returns and sits down she says, "I've drunk too much."

"Did you throw up?"

"No. But—there's not much of the *Herald Tribune* left!" She'd used, first, a review of a new CD of Beethoven sonatas. Very liquid chocolate.

"I hope you're not getting the bug that's going round."

"It may be just the retsina and Metaxa; I'm not used to it. But

I'll be okay." She gulps a glass of mineral water. Glances at her watch. "I must get some sleep."

"Me too."

The tables have emptied out, on both sides. Harold and Jeanne leave, waving to us. Our waiter dashes out at my signal. Lucinda insists on putting in her two thousand drachs. We get unsteadily to our feet.

I take her hand, mounting the dark lane. I'm looking forward to her private consultation with me, I tell her; I'd like to read her published stories. She's sorry, she has none with her.

Feeling better again, she becomes more communicative during our climb. She is spending three months in Europe; it's a kind of sick leave; she's had a sort of glandular fever, though she's over it now. She only saw this workshop advertized at the last minute. She is due to fly back to New Zealand in a month's time. Though she might come back to England for a while. Because she has friends there. But New Zealand is not so terminally sick, ecologically, as Europe. Since arriving in Europe, she says, she really grieves for the earth and her creatures.

These answers to my questions come in bursts, between taking care mounting and descending the dark, treacherous, slippery stone steps.

This is where our paths divide. She has one of the more self-contained units, she says, pointing down a winding lane. She'd asked for privacy. We stand close, motionless, our hands joined. I don't feel really drawn to her, sexually, yet the late hour and the brilliant stars seem to expect me to make a move. I kiss her. We put our arms around each other and kiss more passionately. She tenses, and pulls back. "I thought I heard footsteps," she says. But there's only the unnoticed chorus of cicadas. We relax, and now her tongue slides into my mouth, and my spine tingles. I think of touching her breast but instead slide my hand down under the waistband of her divided skirt. As my fingers reach her pubic hair she pulls away from my lips to say, "No."

Yet she kisses me strongly again, and allows my hand to stroke her belly. Her tongue churns in my mouth and I thrust my fingers down again; this time she pulls sharply away. "No!"

I remove my hand altogether and step back. "Sorry!"

D. M. Thomas

She kisses me lightly on the cheek, grasps my arm for a moment, then says goodnight. I watch her disappear and then turn right. As I reach the Centre I hear and feel the wind again.

FOUR

A Reminiscent Notebook

By morning—I'm late up, with a thumping head—the wind has dropped, it's another perfect autumn day. I hate having to come down the steps in full view of the breakfasters. Dishes are being cleared away. I head for the coffee urn.

The bearded man who likes elderflower tea exclaims in pleasure as he finds sachets of it have appeared. Also thyme and sage.

Sue the domestic, dipping her spoon into muesli, has a jaunty baseball cap, blue and gold, on her head. She tells me it's a good-luck gift from O'Brien. He gave away several. She thinks he said he'd left one behind for me, as the next writer. I shake my head; I haven't seen it.

"He was terrific," she says, her rather tired eyes glowing for a moment. "He took his students up Mount Atreus, at the other end of the island, so they could write about the view! It's five thousand feet high! Even a woman of seventy made it; they had complete trust in him."

Someone touches my arm tentatively and I turn. It's Krystal;

her face is wan, but she says she's feeling okay. Several people are down with the stomach bug, and she had a rotten couple of hours last night; however, she's escaped lightly. "I'm sorry to grab you right away," she says, "before you've had your breakfast, but Harold happened to mention that Ruth Rendell is taking a workshop over on Skyros. Since I love her books, and really want to learn how to write detective novels, I think it would suit me better."

She looks embarrassed, but I reassure her. As Stephanos tacitly admitted when mentioning that O'Brien had thought he was coming to Skyros, their holistic center is longer established and more prestigious. The island itself is more populous and has better communications with the mainland. We journeyers to Skagathos shared with the Skyrians a modern, comfortable ferry as far as that island; then we had to change onto Tugboat Annie to come the rest of the way. And it seemed to me that the most attractive and interesting-looking people—with obvious exceptions, such as Natasha—had disappeared. I wondered if O'Brien had felt the same.

"I've spoken to Stephanos," Krystal says; "and he very kindly called them. Someone dropped out at the last minute and they would be able to take me. Stephanos says I can go over on the ferry but it all depends on you. If you're not happy about it, I'll willingly stay."

"It's fine by me, Krystal. You go."

She beams. "Oh, I'm so grateful! There are such lovely people here, and I'll be sorry to leave them, but . . ."

"She'll give you what you want."

"I hope so. I'll tell Stephanos it's okay. I think the ferry leaves at ten."

She scurries off towards the kitchen. I shan't see her again, through all eternity, and I can't say I feel terribly upset.

My head throbs. It throbs still as, in the Lotus Room, Brenda suggests we start with some appreciations. She appreciates the way Ezekiel helped calm down a disturbed student. Elke appreciates my help in arranging her room for Rollo's visit. Peter appreciates the fine work of the shit-bucket-emptying of the Greek widow—who has appeared again. "It's not an easy job, emptying those bins when there's dysentery around." We all look at her; her eyes are almost closed and she is swaying. She opens her eyes when he addresses her in voluble Greek, and breaks into a smile. "Thank you, Maria. *Efkaristo!*"

She puts her plump hands together and makes a little bow. Her black-tighted thighs strain against her black skirt as she squats uncomfortably. I remember suddenly my brief erotic experience with Lucinda. I won't let it happen again. A foolish mistake.

She is completely out of my mind; yet I am a little haunted by her creations, Nat and Mildred. I think of them in that rainy Welsh cottage; Nat looming over her in the bath. Their plans for killing Agnes.

They—my fellow-facilitators, my comrades in arms—have moved on from appreciation to reflection. Where they're at at the moment. Brenda, Elspeth and the domestic staff feel good. I confess to a hangover but otherwise I feel fine. One of my group showed real talent yesterday. Lucinda. I explain who she is: tall, rather stately and self-possessed, wears a white shirt, New Zealander. Ah yes, they recall seeing her. "I'd guess she's far ahead of the others," I say. "One of the group, Krystal, is going to Skyros because Ruth Rendell is teaching there. It's okay by me." I glance at Stephanos, who nods. "Thank you, Simon." He explains that she doesn't expect a rebate.

"Well, that's it. It's all fine." I shrug.

"Good," murmurs Elke. "I'm fine too. I have a very nice group. And I shall have Rollo to help me for a few days, starting tomorrow." She nods pleasurably, and we all nod. She turns to Ezekiel, who has been abnormally quiet. "Ezekiel?"

After a slight pause, he says in a choking voice, "I feel *pissy.*" I pull myself up slightly, astonished, and sense that others do too. "As you know, I have my assistant Teresa Bombassoni coming at the weekend. I called my wife in Vancouver, and we talked, but . . . I think our marriage is at an end. She slammed the phone down on me. She doesn't trust me. She doesn't trust me." He chokes off. I recall his phrase "my assistant and lover . . ." It seems, in the circumstances, a bit rich to expect his wife to trust him. I feel embarrassed by his emotion. It all seems very personal, very theatrical.

Yet everyone looks sympathetic; except possibly Tamsin—a

girl who can look quite Sussexy uppercrust even when ladling out Peter's uneatable veg: she, I notice, can't conceal a swift look of distaste. She's not bad-looking. I'll talk to her sometime. Even though she and her coworker, Sue, seem distant and reserved.

That look reminds me I must ring Marie sometime soon.

"We've been married for twenty years, she's raised our five sons," Ezekiel laments; "can she really think I'd try to cheat her out of anything?"

Ah! the woman is talking alimony.

"She can have all I've got." He gazes with red, moist eyes at the parquet floor. Then he lifts his head and gazes at Brenda. The grey-haired, bespectacled Reiki healer from Tower Hamlets—with a wart on her nose I find increasingly irritating—compassionately observes the dwarfish, lush-bearded Canadian. "We'll have a talk later," Ezekiel says. "I very much need to talk to you." They are co-listeners.

"Of course. I'll look forward to that, Ezekiel."

At Elke's suggestion we stand and hold hands in a ring. She wants our strength to feed into Ezekiel. She offers up, in her baritone voice, an Icelandic healing song.

* * *

My head thumps with every jolting step of the way up the stony path to Calypso, in spite of the healing song. Even the purple blaze of bougainvillea, the gold cannonades of sunflowers, hurt me. I'm ten minutes late, yet there are several breaks in the ring of chairs. Angus is still ill; John, who has been taking drinks and medicine to him, says he's really suffering. Caroline (double-bass, maternity bra, king-sized bed) was seen at breakfast briefly, but then had to hurry back to her ethnic lodgings. I picture her heavy body, freckled face and the red hair bobbing as she hurries to the gate. No one has spotted Lucinda or Krystal this morning. I tell them Lucinda was showing signs of the bug last night; and Krystal has left us.

This news evokes a surprising regret, since Krystal has hardly made a dynamic contribution to these early stages of our workshop. "Oh, we'll miss her!" "Such a good writer!" "It won't be quite the same without her."

John worries whether the Centre's history, as a holiday home of a Mafia figure, might have upset Krystal.

These are sweet, kind people, I'm reminded.

Harold wonders whether he should be drummed out of the group, and from the island, for mentioning to her that Ruth Rendell was teaching on Skyros. He's an admirer of Rendell too, though she has a rather *dark* imagination, so that he wasn't altogether sorry when he tried to book up with Skyros Holidays and was told the workshop was full, more than two months ago. "Of course she's a great writer," he continues, "but being a great writer isn't everything; there was the danger of being too narrowly focused on the detective novel. And great writers can be very egotistical creatures; a lesser-known writer of good quality may have more to give." His cigarette holder emerges from a pocket of his floral shirt. "I like detective novels, but I'm not sure I wanted to spend a whole fortnight learning how to write them. But Krystal evidently did, and I'm glad she's found there was a cancellation. Nevertheless it's a sad loss. She has sailed away from us, she has deserted us, she has abandoned us, I almost feel I could cry." He lights his cigarette.

"Well," I murmur, "we must try to survive without her."

"Agreed. But it will be difficult, it will be difficult."

Lucy says Skyros looked beautiful, the brief glimpse we had of it. There are murmurs of pleasure when I say I'm hoping to organize a boat trip across, at the weekend, to the grave of Rupert Brooke. Harold lifts his gaze skyward and breaks into "Grantchester." Yes, he says, we really must make a pilgrimage, and expresses surprise that I, modern as I am, should like Brooke.

After the mid-morning break, I tell them I am going to read to them a passage from my most recently published novel, *Transplanted Hearts,* which concerns the kidnapping of, and enforced removal of organs from, street boys in Rio. Harold, who is clearly in a dominating, not to say mildly sadistic, mood, informs us he possesses that book at home, having managed to find a remaindered copy in a London discount shop. He enjoyed it very much.

I read a passage in the first person and in the present tense, to illustrate the importance of voice and tone in fiction. How a

D. M. Thomas

first-person narrative offers certain opportunities, by imposing certain limitations. As for the use of the present tense, it can add vividness at the risk of becoming tedious and awkward. They listen rather sleepily, I feel. Natasha almost nods off completely, and has to jerk herself awake.

* * *

I'd like to island myself totally from England, this two weeks. To be honest, though in a way it would be nice to have Marie here, I don't really want to phone her. We've had a few weeks of unusual intimacy, after her "confession," and the strain was telling. I'm not ungrateful that we're discouraged from using the phone in Stephanos's office, which in any case is locked whenever he's not working in it. I'm sure Marie doesn't want to speak to me either. But she'll want the *fiction* that I've tried to ring her, despite the awkwardness of the Skagathos phone system.

I use the phone in the beach taverna, at an hour when she *just* might be home (it's a morning only at College for her, today) if she's rushed back, but I'm assuming she's more likely relaxing in the office with a wee dram, having a chat; or perhaps calling in on my father to check he's okay; or at Tesco's. I'll hear my recorded message.

However, Marie answers. It throws me out of my stride. Like Natasha this morning she seems only half-awake. She's having a lie-down, she says in that voice that still has echoes of Natal and that I still find charming. If *we* can have siestas on hot nudist beaches, why can't she have one on a miserably wet afternoon in boring Wiltshire?

"No reason," I reply. I picture our bedroom; the Lowry print facing her; a confusion of clothes and magazines; probably pages of the *FT* strewn around the bed and on the floor. Marie is the most sluttish of my wives. She's lying down in her bra and pants; she'll have flung her navy skirt and jacket carelessly onto the cane chair; her straight blond hair trails over her white shoulder. I hear a gust of wind shake our window.

"What's your group like?" She asks the question as though it's a boring duty. She's always surly when awakened.

"They seem okay."

42

"Good."

"How's work?"

"Boring as usual."

Part-time work in the offices at a boys' public school is a big comedown from the glamour of her youth, the Miss Natal title; even from her more recent position in BBC Accounts.

I hear her yawn. "So they're okay—your group?"

"Yes, so far as one can tell. I hardly know their names yet."

I catch the faintest click-click. An ex-smoker finds it impossible to mistake the sound of a lighter not working the first time. She doesn't smoke pot during the daytime. "Have you got someone with you?" I ask.

"Why should you think that?"

"I heard him."

"Yes, there's someone here."

I swallow involuntarily. "Anyone I know?" I say in a light tone.

A muffled male whisper: "Sorry." She's no doubt pursed her lips and knuckled him in the ribs.

"I went to the Old Boys Reunion last night," she says.

"Ah! I see!" I keep my tone light, amused. "Well, I won't embarrass you by asking who it is. I'm sorry to have interrupted you, darling."

"You didn't. I'll drop in on your dad later; I've made a casserole for him."

"He'll appreciate that."

"And collect his washing. Our tumble-drier's finally conked out. It's a bloody nuisance in this weather. It's rained nonstop since you went."

"You'd better order a new one."

"I have, I'm afraid."

There's always something that needs replacing. If you divorce a couple of times, the good equipment gets left behind and you're left having to make do with secondhand rubbish.

"Well—enjoy yourself. I forgot—it's Founders Day, you didn't have to work." I wait for a response, but there's none. "Well, I'm running up the drachmas. You can ring this number in case. —Got a pen there?" She pretends to get a pen, and I read out to her the Skagathos Centre emergency number. "Take care, darling. I love you."

"Yes," she says.

As I put down the phone, and turn to pay the Greek crone who sits patiently by, I'm faced by Danny, Andrea's husband, in a Columbia University T-shirt. He's smiling, holding out my black notebook.

I'd left it around, he says; Andrea had picked it up. She's not feeling well and will have to skip her consultation today. "We thought you might be on the beach."

"Thank you so much." I'm sure my face is red. Andrea will have looked inside. Others probably have too; they'll have read what I've scribbled about them during our initial consultations. How stupid of me to leave it behind.

I know it's important to be able to address someone by name, but I'm extremely bad at remembering names. What I do, therefore, is jot down as soon as possible some distinguishing features, along with an early assessment of their writing, character impressions, snatches of biographical information, wild guesses, prejudices, verbal doodles and even sketches of prominent features.

Thus, on this occasion (my face burns as I sprawl on my unmade bed reminding myself of what I've written and what has probably been read by most of my students). Some remnant of BBC formality made me write down their full names, though surnames are irrelevant in this holistic heaven . . .

Lucy Crozier . . . Smouldering eyes, floaty walk. Fiddles with fine brown hair. Quit Univ., works as temp. in London. Broken romance. Attractive, pleasant voice, but rather Roedeany. Father complex probably. Writing pretty crappy, no color. Ariadne looking for a bull to fuck her.

Lucinda Gilbert . . . New Zealand, but little accent. Very tall, thin, scrawny neck, divided skirt, no tits. Always dark glasses. Laptop. Dunedin. Taking Ph.D. in anthropology. Older than she looks—late thirties. Intimidating manner, forbidding. Intense, wants no bullshit. Starchy.

Angus MacDuff . . . Red-faced, large. Wobbly jowls. Pompous and pontificating. Medieval historian. Talks nonstop.

Plummy Eng. voice though Scot. Writes poetry but has brought none, can't imagine the stuff he writes. Purple cravat. Gay?

Krystal Polkinghorne . . . Hunched over, small, Maryland, hands holding hanky, loves Christie. Widow of small-town hypnotist; daughter estranged. Appallingly lonely I guess. Excruciatingly dull, vapid stories. Charity work for black single mothers.

John Darby . . . Ill-fitting dentures, wrinkly, tiny, bandy *(Illustration)*. Primary teacher, retired. Wife dead. No kids. Relate counselor, wants to write novel about destruction of society under Thatcher. Boring, boring.

Natasha Rodlova . . . Very fuckable. Blonde. Magnitogorsk. Ballet dancer turned strip teacher *(Illustration)*. High tension. Well read, mostly poets.

Andrea Fritsch . . . Cheery American-in-Paris. Husband—trainee archiitect—here too. She pleasant but not very bright. Along for the ride. Not much interest in literature or writing. Boobs like marrows *(Illustration)*.

Harold Fallowes . . . Noel Coward (of Hemel Hempstead). Cigarette holder. Twee little stories. Loss adjuster for insurance co. Divorced. Terribly mannered. Ladies' man.

Caroline Bickerstaff . . . Forty-five, red-haired (dyed?); Duty Free perfume saleswomen; huge thighs and large stomach, double chin; humorous, doesn't take her writing seriously, but likes to try. In and out of relationships, one son. Pussy Galore?

Emily Williams . . . Jolly lesbian. Footballers' legs. Vegetarian reflexologist. Welsh cottage, with partner. Likable. Shrill voice.

Jeanne Cirot . . . Fading Frenchy. Economics lecturer. Wants to write poems in English for some reason. Very earnest. Likes men. Father in resistance in war, arrested, tortured, family suffered a lot.

I lie and reflect: I've fucked up, leaving this around.

* * *

Reflexology under the stars, after dinner. A quiet mood. No apparent anger in the members of my group I talk to; but pleasant smiles and conversation. A lot of tiredness from an afternoon's swimming, and from stomach upsets and perhaps the long exhausting journey from England or farther catching up with them. Angus has reappeared, but even he is quiet. Elke introduces me to Rollo, immensely tall and gangling, shy and friendly. Elke is obviously proud of her young lover.

Morning, however, brings news from her, at our staff meeting, that poor Rollo has been throwing up all night.

Stephanos asks us to make a list of those in our workshops who are off sick, so that he can keep a check of those who are in self-contained accommodation, and may need to be visited with medicine, food and drink. The whole village is suffering from this bug, he says; it's not only the Centre. We discuss hygiene and toilets.

"Hygiene is a Greek word," booms Angus; "Hygeia, as I'm sure you'll all know, was the goddess of health; Sheridan refers to her temple in his play *The Critic;* Guillemeau refers to Hygiena as early as the sixteenth century; yet hygiene is unknown to the modern Greeks. Which is why, my dear"—he plants a large hand on Andrea's knee—"for the past forty-eight hours I've been shitting through the eye of a needle. I'm rapidly coming to the conclusion that the Skagathos Centre is a quite extraordinary place. Perfectly genteel people, having breakfast together *en plein air,* fart openly and loudly, without apology, without turning a hair."

"That's certainly true," Andrea agrees with a chuckle. "Well, we're glad to have you back, Angus. And you too, Caroline."

We murmur our agreement. Caroline attributes her quick recovery to John's nursing care: he kept bringing her bottled water and medicines. John blushes, gazes at his scrawny knees, mumbles it was nothing. Lucinda is still away, and Jeanne is absent too. Harold says he will look in on her and make sure she's got everything she needs; she was feeling queasy last night, and missed dinner. No one is quite sure where Lucinda's room is; Lucy says she told her she'd deliberately asked for a room well away from the Centre and any other students, since she wanted to write without distraction. I'll tell Stephanos, I promise them; he'll check on her. "From what we've seen of Lucinda," says Harold, "I can't imagine she'll want to be checked up on! She's very much the modern independent miss. But of course she must be visited."

It can last for days, Angus points out; some people haven't left their rooms since they arrived. He and Caroline have been quite lucky. Caroline nods at him. "It's a foul bug, this one."

"Okay . . ." I say, after a few moment's silence. "This morning we're going to take on our game of fictional consequences."

"Oh what fun," says Harold mildly.

Ignoring his sarcasm, I speak of how fiction moves ahead and expands unpredictably, often surprising the writer. Lucy is, very appositely, reminded of a saying by Robert Frost, whom she studied at an evening class: "No surprise in the writer, no surprise in the reader." She also quotes his definition of a poem (new to me), that it "rides on its own melting, like ice on a hot stove." Fiction is not unlike that, I tell them; and one never knows when an apparently chance image or character, or both, can enter the scene and later become an important *motif* or symbol.

"So chance," I say, "is important. Letting one's thoughts drift like that ice cube on the hot stove. This consequences game is a way of practicing that technique. We're going to start from Lucinda's piece." I might, I explain, have chosen any of their own fascinating pieces, such as John's Liverpudlian council estate saga based on *A lonely jigsaw liquidates a red traffic warden,* or Natasha's surrealistic fantasy arising from *The perfect pen admires a juicy solstice;* but I threw the dice and Lucinda's number came up. (This is a lie: Lucinda's just happens to be far and away the best; it's in elegant typescript rather than an illegible scrawl; and it irritates Harold.) *Their* fragmentary stories would continue in the realm of pure imagination, somewhere; but life throws the dice at every microsecond, and in this case we are faced, like it or not, with Mildred and Nat. Harold utters a groan. The unseen donkey brays, as if in agreement; there are chuckles.

I hand around photocopies and invite them to reread Lucinda's piece. Beyond all the subtler critical points, I tell them, I find myself at its end wanting to turn the page. "Fiction's as basic as that, in a way. Only there is no page to turn, at present. Give me the next page. You have half an hour."

Harold, after a swift scan, says he likes the fragment no better on a second reading. He is sure Lucinda is a good writer, but this is unworthy of her; sordid, depressing. Yes, of course such cold, calculating, wicked people exist as Nat and Mildred, but life is short, and art should be elevating.

But there is Agnes, I point out. The sister taking her law finals; innocent, trusting. And I like the conflict in Mildred's mind; I want to know if she would really help to kill Agnes by pushing her over a cliff edge. And, after all, it *may* be just a violent sexual fantasy. I read aloud: "But perhaps—perhaps he was still only fantasizing. He'd always loved fantastic, way-out sex."

We drift into the subject of sexual fantasy. My agent, I tell them, a man called Jim Telford, has just taken on the British rights for an extraordinary Japanese author by the name of Issei Sagawa. Andrea gives a little shriek; she and Danny saw him recently on a French talk show, publicizing his new book. "Jeez, he's some weirdo!" Between us we tell the others about Sagawa. Grew up obsessed by his oriental puniness, and with a growing compulsion to kill and eat a white woman, so that he could draw her plumpness and beauty into him. While studying in Paris he was befriended by a Dutch girl, and was able to live out his fantasy. Gendarmes found his fridge stocked with her body parts.

He was returned to Japan after a couple of years' imprisonment, and there he was placed in a mental institution. But the doctors thought he had recovered his sanity, and released him. Now he is writing bestsellers about cannibalism and his own nature, and has become a celebrity.

"We have become sick, sick!" cries Harold, inserting a cigarette in his holder; and no one disagrees.

"If Oswald hadn't been shot by Ruby," says Andrea, "he would be out of jail by now and would be doing all the talk shows too, promoting his memoirs."

"And lots of people would be congratulating him on killing a warmonger and womanizer," Angus observes.

"And they'd be right," murmurs Lucy. (A laurel, a gazelle, a viola.) Her light-brown eyes, I suspect, are staring at the lover, owner of a Thai restaurant in Bermondsey, who betrayed her.

"That's one point of view," intones Harold, breathing smoke up to the brilliant blue sky. "I find the young are extraordinarily harsh in their judgments these days. Andrea, in the chat show you saw, did the audience clap Sagawa?"

"Yeah."

He shakes his head in disbelief. "Well, of course they were French. I can be a shade xenophobic in dear Jeanne's absence."

I draw them back to fiction; to the way in which every moment of a short story or a novel is a point of departure, a crossroads with a thousand possibilities. I speak of the theory of parallel universes. I ask them to take out their pens and continue the story of Nat and Mildred. They can give their efforts to Lucinda as a gift when she's back with us.

"You are as gods," I remind them once again.

Andrea interrupts my daydreamy state a few minutes later to ask quietly, "The main roads in England, you call them freeways?"

"Motorways."

"Okay." She scribbles.

FIVE

The Tangled
Soap

The rain started to lash the windscreen of the Porsche as Agnes headed deeper into the countryside towards Wales. She switched the wipers to double speed, and eased back on the throttle, drifting from the outside lane into the middle. She had been looking forward to the long drive down the motorway, after the concentrated mental work of the past week, but this was no fun. Fortunately there was only light traffic.

She was really looking forward to seeing Nat and her sister. Mildred was a good influence over him, the steady sort; and Nat, surprisingly, seemed to like her. Well, it was easy to like Mildred. As Nat said, she was a bit dim, but goodhearted and jolly. She'd have made a wonderful mother; it was a shame.

She'd mothered Agnes, in a sense.

How smoothly the Porsche ran! If only she didn't have to concentrate so hard on the road. Visibility was getting much worse; she slowed further, down to sixty.

She thought she'd done okay; though this last paper had been tough.

Wanting the seven o'clock news, she got the last few minutes of an arts program, a review of books and paintings by a Japanese cannibal. Agnes had read about his case; it had made her skin crawl. The thought of that poor girl! But a weird fascination too; and it crept over her again. "Oh, my God!" she exclaimed involuntarily, learning that Sagawa had been appointed food critic by a magazine; had described the Dutch girl's flesh as "melting in my mouth like raw tuna" and how "nothing was so delicious"; had produced an erotic video called Desire to be Eaten. *He was a popular cult object in Japan, she learned, partly because his victim, being non-Japanese, was considered less than a person. Agnes felt queasy. Out of the corner of her eye she saw she was low on gas, and would have to stop somewhere.*

When an expert from the Slade referred to a Sagawa painting in which female buttocks were depicted next to chopsticks, Agnes gagged, lost concentration for an instant, found a high-backed lorry ahead looming up close; she slammed on the brakes; swerved into the inside lane, just missing the lorry's back; skidded on the wet surface and, fighting for control, came to a halt on the hard shoulder. She was breathing heavily; scared shitless; she'd escaped death by blind chance. Her shaking hands reached for her purse and took out her cigarettes. "Sagawa now has a new Dutch girl-friend, an actress who takes part with him in soft porn videos, and who apparently does not know of his past." She switched off the radio.

Ten minutes later, having come off the motorway, she was drinking a whisky in a rustic pub-bedroom. It was a pity she couldn't ring Nat, but they would surely not expect her to arrive tonight in this weather. She could make a leisurely drive down and arrive for lunch. If the downpour kept on, there'd be no opportunity to walk and climb anyway.

Unzipping her case, she took out her nightdress and laid it on the bed. Under her toilet bag nestled a packet of tampons. But the likelihood of her using them was receding; it was already a week, and she was regular as clockwork. She stirred in excitement; she knew in her bones she was pregnant. It was that drunken night in Paris when Nat couldn't be bothered to find the rubbers. She would tell him tomorrow. He would be thrilled; Mildred might be jealous at first, but then she'd be thrilled too. Agnes had intended

51

not telling anyone until she had confirmed it; but the near-accident had caused her to change her mind. That brush with death had made her much more acutely aware of her condition, of the miracle of new life. An abstraction before, her pregnancy was now the most real thing in the world, infinitely more important than her law exams—or even dear Nat.

She called her mother in Berkshire. It was possible Nat would go to a phone-box and check with her mother to see if she knew what had happened to her. Her mother was having a vodka tonic; Dad was at the golf club. It was just beginning to rain there, her mom said; and Agnes heard a peal of thunder. After chatting for a while about trivia, Agnes couldn't resist saying, "Mom, I think I'm pregnant! . . . No, not yet, but I'm sure of it! If Nat rings, don't tell him! I want to tell him myself . . ."

* * *

They came together very quickly, but he stayed semi-hard in her vagina; she lay back in the water and he rested against her. Stroking his back she found, to her surprise, that she had scratched him quite badly. Agnes would see the scratches tonight, no doubt, and wonder what or who had caused them.

Blood passed from Mildred's finger to her tongue. Thatcherite fucking . . . That's what Nat called it; and he was a Thatcher child. Straight out of school onto the jobless heap—and yet he had actually admired the odious woman. Mildred, a committed Socialist, couldn't understand why their political differences increased rather than diminished the sexual pleasure.

"What music do you think Agnes'll want for her funeral?" Nat asked, kissing her ear.

"Don't," she whispered.

He started humming "Abide with Me."

Nat was the first man who'd given her as much sexual pleasure as her female lovers.

There was another big spider on the ceiling, fortunately not overhanging the bath. There flashed into her mind a poem from her student days, one that Sue Radford had read aloud, so compellingly, a few weeks before becoming her first lover. Mildred recalled only the title, Mr. Edwards and the Spider; *and the last line was something about seeing the spider death. It had chilled her because she'd always loathed spiders.*

Nat pulled away from her and, with a cascade of water, got out of the bath. Toweling himself vigorously he left the bathroom; he returned with a lighted cigarette and perched on the side of the bath. "The rain's easing," he said. "We'll take Agnes to the Prince of Wales and get her pissed out of her tiny mind."

"Why should you want to do that?"

"Because . . ." he rubbed his stubble with the thumb of the hand holding the Rothman; "I'd like to fuck both of you in the same bed tonight. I want to get that prissy bitch doing something dirty before she leaves this earth. Do you mind?"

She felt her lips dry and she had to moisten them with her tongue. Her throat connecting suddenly with her vagina in one erotic ache, she said thickly, unable to swallow, "Fuck the shit out of her."

"Yes!"

The motionless spider suddenly scurried like lightning across the ceiling and poised above her. "Nat!" she screamed.

* * *

Agnes settled herself in a first-class seat of the Inter City, laying Vogue *and* Newsweek *in front of her. She leaned back into the soft upholstery with a contented sigh, her eyes drooping closed. She recrossed her legs in their designer jeans. It was good to feel comfortable, out of the tailored suit she'd had to wear for the past week in the examination hall.*

Thank God she'd let Mum persuade her to go by train, after she'd drunk rather too much wine in celebration. And Olwen was thrilled she'd be spending the night with her. They hadn't had a real get-together since Cambridge; they'd get pissed as newts, like in their student days.

And tomorrow morning, Agnes thought, maybe she'd like to come with me, in her car. Nat and Mildred wouldn't mind. It would save me having to hire a car. Yes, I'll ask her!

Mrs. Williams, the owner of the holiday cottage, had said it would be no trouble to go and tell her husband and sister of her change of plans; and it was very wise, she'd said, as it was bucket-

ing down in North Wales; she might not even have got through, because of flooding.

Opening her eyes, she glanced at her watch. Two minutes to departure. There were only a couple of boring-looking businessmen in first class.

Just as the train slid smoothly out of Paddington, she heard a patter of footsteps and a small, unprepossessing Japanese man slid into the seat opposite her. It was an irritation, since he had plenty of empty tables to choose from; but, conscious of the need to be welcoming to foreigners—even of a slight tendency to xenophobia where Japs were concerned—she gave him a brief smile before opening Vogue. *He exposed small, uneven teeth in what was meant to be an answering smile, though there seemed no warmth in it. His eyes too: slit, expressionless, with their brown pupils as lifeless as raisins. But it wasn't his fault, Agnes reminded herself; it was cultural; no doubt his fellow countrymen and women would find his smile and his eyes warmly expressive.*

His small hands running over his black document case on the table before him, he gazed blankly out at the graffiti-scrawled tenements and high walls. He was impeccably dressed, in dark suit, white shirt and tie. Mid-thirties, she guessed.

She flipped through the magazine. The new Paris fashions. She didn't usually buy fashion mags, but she'd yearned for something frivolous after Torts and mens rea.

Her traveling companion stubbed a finger across, touching an elegant model. "Too thin," he observed.

She was startled, but replied: "Do you think so?"

"Yes. No flesh on bones."

Amused, she said she was glad not everyone liked tall, thin women. She glanced down at her own figure, which could be flatteringly described as "small, buxom and cuddly." Fat, she thought, was the proper word. "I just look," she said; "I know I couldn't get into them."

A muffled voice over the intercom announced the bar was open for snacks and afternoon tea. "You like drink?" the Japanese asked.

"Thank you. A brandy."

He nodded and went off. Well, why not? she thought.

He came back with two brandies, and poured them both.

54

He thrust his hand towards her. "I am Issei Kagawa," he said. She shook his hand. "Agnes Redland."

He was an author, he said. He opened his case and brought out his book to show her; a French translation. He was going to Cardiff to give a lecture. He asked her where she was going, and she explained the circumstances of her trip. She'd just finished some law exams, and was going to join her husband for a short holiday in Snowdonia, but had decided to stay overnight in Cardiff with an old college friend.

"I interested in law, very much. European law different from ours." Reading the word Paris upside-down, he touched her magazine and said, "I did time in Paris."

"You spent some time in Paris?"

"Yes. I like very much."

"It's a beautiful city."

They chatted about Paris for a while; but his English was not terribly good, and at last they fell silent. He gazed out at the countryside around Henley and she turned, with some relief, to News-week.

The sky outside was darkening, shrouding. It seemed not like an early evening in June but November. Very quickly the sky was black; the lights in the carriage came on.

Her companion, without asking, brought her another brandy. She thanked him. He said, looking at her intently, "I like have you for dinner."

She almost smiled. Silence of the Lambs, *she thought. "Oh, that's very sweet of you, but I'll be having dinner with my friend."*

"So sorry."

"Aren't you being met?"

"Yes, but . . ." He shrugged. "I like plump thighs, plump bosoms." He spread his hands.

Agnes was amused by his effrontery. But perhaps this was normal Japanese politesse. *With a bright smile she said, "I have a husband."*

"No matter."

"I'm afraid it does, to me. Sorry!"

"Just have you for dinner. No sex."

"It's sweet of you."

He delved into a breast pocket and produced a wallet. Opening it, he flourished two tickets. "You like opera? I two tickets, tomorrow night, for Welsh National. They good?"

"Yes, they're excellent. You'll enjoy it. What are they doing?"

He peered at a ticket. "Jenufa."

"Ah! Wonderful!" It was an opera she loved from records but had never seen performed on stage. She knew the Welsh National production had had rave reviews and tickets were sold out. She glanced out of the window, searching her conscience. The rain was sweeping against the window; Mrs. Williams had warned her the forecast for the next two days was terrible. She imagined a poky, damp, uncomfortable cottage, with the rain bucketing. In her imagination she was already phoning Mrs. Williams from Olwen's flat, asking her to let Nat and Mildred know she was suffering from a post-exam migraine and would be a day late. Why not let the persistent Nip "have her for dinner" and take her to Jenufa? She could lie in tomorrow morning, and have more time with Olwen.

Glancing back at him, she asked, "Who was the other ticket for?"

"For my host. Lecture to conference at university in afternoon, opera in evening. But he not know about plans for evening. You come?"

"Yes, all right! Thank you."

He smiled, and his slit eyes widened. She could almost glimpse joy.

"And I have you for dinner?" he persisted.

"Yes, you can have me for dinner! But only dinner!"

"Not for breakfast?"

"No, not for breakfast!" She chuckled, and he did too.

With the pen that had written about Torts she wrote down Olwen's phone number on the envelope containing the opera tickets, and told him to ring her.

"You not come to psychological conference," he said, shaking his head dolefully and discouragingly. "Boring."

She took it as a hint he would like her to be there. "I'm sure it won't be; I'm sure your lecture will be very interesting. But I do have plans for the afternoon."

"Good."

They were plunged into darkness as the train rumbled into the Severn Tunnel; they fell silent, and when at last they reemerged

Agnes quickly picked up Newsweek *and buried her face in it. She was aware, for the rest of the journey, of his eyes observing her, tranquilly, contentedly.*

As they slowed on entering Cardiff she said, "This is it," and stood up. Rising too—she found they were the same height—he offered another handshake and said, "You nice meat."

"It's been nice meeting you too."

"I ring you. Dinner first, then we go opera." He rubbed his white-shirted stomach. "Full up. Nice music. We enjoy."

"We enjoy."

"Yes, so important woman enjoy too!"

It was such a chauvinist comment she was lost for words; yet she realized that in Japanese society it would have passed for a very liberated remark.

* * *

Margaret Rainsford skimmed to the end of the chapter then snapped the book shut in disgust and stowed it back on the shelves. Was she so hopelessly old-fashioned? she wondered wistfully. Ten years ago she could still come to her local library and find a good detective story she hadn't read; an Allingham or a Sayer, for instance. She would know it would be a good read and, if her daughter happened to pick it up, it would not affect her adversely.

Now, when Marilyn came home from college, she brought even worse books that were considered by her scruffy tutors worthy of serious study. And she swore readily; not the F word in her mother's presence—though she had overheard her using it to her friend Jim—but "shit" and "piss off!" And thought her mother just an old fuddy-duddy, hopelessly square, for objecting.

After she had had her books stamped—two Agatha Christies that she had read before—she left the library and sat down on one of the benches outside. It was a beautifully fresh spring day, with a few fleecy clouds scudding across the blue sky. She breathed in the sharp air gladly, and tried to cast from her mind the sordid images of Nat and Mildred. But it was difficult. The corruption spread insidiously.

She heaved a sigh, stood up, picked up her shopping bag, and headed for Safeways, moving slowly because of her arthritic hip. In the crowded supermarket she felt, as always, a pang as she passed the stacks of crisps and other snacks; once upon a time, she'd moaned because she could never buy enough crisps for her daughter; and then the cakes. How David, her dear husband, had loved a nice madeira or rich fruit!

A trolley knocked against the back of her legs. "Forgive me!" said an apologetic voice; and she turned to see a tall, rather distinguished man in his fifties. He was trying to maneuver a loaded trolley and seemed unaccustomed to it.

"That's quite all right," Margaret said sympathetically. It bothered her to see men pushing trolleys in supermarkets. Men, she believed, should mow the lawn and do the painting and decorating, as David had always done, but shopping was women's work.

"I was looking for the cheeses," he said; "would you happen to know where they are?"

"I'm just heading there myself—you can follow me."

"That would give me the greatest pleasure," he said, with a gentle smile that lit up his blue eyes; and Margaret, for the first time in many years, felt herself blush.

They and their trolleys stood side by side at the cheese counter. "I don't usually come in here," the man said; "but I have my son and his family arriving from New Zealand tomorrow—three healthy, hungry young lads. Shopping just for myself, I use the corner store."

"You live on your own?" Margaret asked shyly.

"Yes. Since my wife died two years ago." His eyes had a wistful, faraway expression. "It's wonderful to see my son again, and grandchildren, but it's also going to be a sad occasion. Here— would you like a coffee after we've gone through the—what do they call it? check-out? It's good to talk to someone—someone so pleasant and charming." As she hesitated he added: "But you probably have to get back to your family; stupid of me. An impulse—forgive me!"

"I don't have to get back for anyone—and I'd love a coffee."

"Good! Now let's see . . . Cheddar . . . Red Leicester . . . I'm sure they'd like some good old English cheeses . . ."

Margaret felt, as she waited for him past the check-out, her heart expanding; and Nat and Mildred had receded a long, long way.

* * *

After they had made love in the bath, Mildred brewed a pot of tea and in front of a gas fire in the tiny parlor, they watched television—a quiz show, then the racing from Haydock. She knew she ought to be marking Latin exam papers: Mildred belonged to the dying breed of Classics mistresses at a girls' grammar. But in this break she felt deliciously irresponsible. She felt her lover's presence within her still, a lovely warm tender feeling all through her. She had wrapped herself in his thick blue bathrobe, and was curled up in a lumpy armchair; Nat, in sweatshirt and boxer shorts, squatted at her feet. With the rain rustling against the window, she felt at peace, held in a womb.

She thought of the generations of peaceful women, wives of quarrymen, who had sat in this room; and their calm, religious spirit still seemed to haunt it. Nat too seemed to have calmed down; he did not move except occasionally to run his hand affectionately over her thigh. His plans for murdering Agnes seemed laughable—merely a bizarre fantasy.

His father had vanished when he was five; his feckless mother had brought up him and three other kids on a brutal inner-city estate. His school had allowed him to play truant as he wished. He'd watched scores of horror videos at a friend's house. Social workers had threatened to remove him if his mother dared to give him a smack. No Christian values. He was, in brief, a victim of that socialistic progressivism and wet liberalism that was destroying England, Mildred considered. Agnes's mixture of condescension and starry-eyed submission to his "authentic" working-class nature made him worse. He needed an older woman, a mother-figure—needed Mildred.

She laid her head back, and drowsed.

The ringing of the doorbell woke her with a jolt. "Christ, she's fucking early," Nat muttered. He sprang up, with the agility of a monkey.

"Wait!" she whispered. "Don't you think you should put your pants on? Mightn't this seem just a tiny bit intimate?"

"Oh—yeah."

"You slip upstairs and I'll let her in."

But the two-thirty was just starting; it was a good race too, with

Fiery Fred and Greenpeace neck and neck to the line. As the tension relaxed, he saw Mildred was in the room, looking thoughtful, holding a damp piece of paper at which she was staring. "It's was a policeman," she said; "on his bike. You're to ring Fulham police station; Agnes is there."

"What the fuck . . . What's happened?"

"He wouldn't say; said he didn't know."

"Christ almighty, this fucks up everything. Got a couple of quid?"

She went to search in her purse and found him four pound coins. He jerked his anorak from a hook, opened the door, and ran off, hunched, against the rain towards the village.

Quickly Mildred slipped on jeans and a baggy sweater. As she was putting on some lipstick she heard the door open. Nat appeared in the doorway. "Well?" she asked.

He sat on the bed and put his head in his hands. "The bitch has got herself raped."

"What?"

"You heard. It was a fucking awful line, and she was hysterical; but from what I could gather there was a party last night after her exam and a guy raped her. I think. She wants us to drive back. I suppose we'd better. Shit!" He stretched out and pounded the pillow. "I'd like to have five minutes with that bastard! I'd kill the fucker."

SIX

A Burning Egg Yolk

"Thanks, Lucy," I say: "astonishing! Well, they're all astonishing! I'm sure Lucinda will be absolutely fascinated by the way you've—" I can't think of a word, so I demonstrate by spreading my arms like wings. "We'll hear the others tomorrow; sorry we couldn't fit them all in."

"Thanks, Simon," says Emily; "that was really good." Others make complimentary murmurs. We stand, stretch, move off at different paces.

Outside the shade of the olive trees the noontide is radiant, pure, blue, Botticellian.

"That was fun!" says Caroline, descending the stony path just ahead of me.

"Yes, wasn't it! Yours was excellent. Hilarious!"

"Really? I enjoyed writing it. I was sexually harassed on a German train once by a creepy little Jap tourist. I drew on that. A shame Lucinda wasn't here to join in."

"Well, she'll get her chance."

Caroline's tousled russet hair—natural, I now concede—

sparkles in the sunlight; her double-chinned fleshiness adds an appealing solidity to the transparency of our island atmosphere; her loose red shirt is almost off one freckled shoulder and reveals the shadowy cleft of her lightly bobbing breasts. Her nipples jut through the cotton. I've not yet seen her on the beach, but look forward to it.

"You've escaped the dreaded plague so far, Simon?"

"So far. It's early days."

We pass Elke's Art Therapy group, still sitting under a bamboo canopy, drawing boards on their laps, concentrated. There is a muted orgasmic cry from Ezekiel's indoor workshop. I've never understood this need to work up to and beyond the appointed end time.

I didn't, I murmur, understand the reference to *Silence of the Lambs*. She explains. *I* explain that if I'm writing feverishly I tend not go anywhere, and I haven't seen a film since *JFK*.

"I haven't seen it," she says; "I still get upset by his murder. I was studying for my O levels when he was shot. I'll never forget it. Christ, he was so bloody handsome! I had a poster-picture of him in my bedroom. He grinned down at me, my hand in my navy-blue school knickers! Soon as I came in from school, usually, I was at it! Thinking I'd be damned to hell for it."

"I know what you mean. But it made sex seem very powerful, didn't it?"

"Christ, yes!"

We've reached the terrace. She says she fancies a shower before lunch; and replies "Maybe" when I ask if I'll see her at the beach. Pasha, in his formal slacks and short-sleeved shirt is walking about between the tables, looking as ever sad and at a loose end. *"Zdravstvuite, Gospodin Hopkeens,"* he greets me eagerly.

"Zdravstvuite! Kak vy?"

His mournful shrug gives me the answer. He motions to me to sit down, so we can talk. I feel irritated by his presumption, and almost regret the smattering of Russian I picked up as a BBC drama producer. I've had enough of talking, despite the restful half-hour in which my students wrote. I'd rather sit quietly, absorbing the peacefulness, the distant sparkle of the sea, the warmth on my body. To think a little more about Nat and

Mildred and Agnes. I'm feeling good about the exercise; my students have done remarkably well with it, though their scribbled writing is very raw and ungrammatical. Students from the other workshops are beginning to turn up, and I see Caroline in conversation with Fred, a white-bearded pensioner who's doing Orgasmic Consciousness. She stirs me; I'm beginning to find her more sexy than the more exotic, toyboy-enamored Natasha, and certainly than the cool and workaholic, absent Lucinda. I have an image of Caroline coming home from school, flinging her satchel into a corner, sprawling on the bed, sliding her skirt up above the nylon stocking tops and strong white suspenders and delving her busy ink-stained hand into her navy-blue pants.

The last thing I want to do is talk awkwardly to a lonely middle-aged Russian male.

Ezekiel comes out through a door, that extraordinary biblical figure; Stephanos, armed with a list and a biro, approaches him. "My wife, you know," Pasha says to me, "she is—"

I clutch his arm. "I'm sorry, excuse me, I have to catch Stephanos."

Crestfallen, the Russian nods. I thread past Emily, who is doing a neck massage on Harold. "Stephanos," I say, "Lucinda. You wanted names of people who are sick and aren't being seen by someone."

He nods, scribbles the name on his list. "Lucinda. I'll check where she is, and go and see her this afternoon. Elke . . ." The Icelandic mountain-woman has ghosted up to his shoulder. She mentions two students who need checking on. I chat with Ezekiel, whose eyes look red as if he has been crying. But his group is going well, he insists; everyone orgasmed, at least briefly and shallowly, this morning.

Angus staggers out of the kitchen, humping a gigantic bowl of pasta. His ponytail sways in the wind, which has started to rise again. I reflect that middle-aged men with grey hair look ridiculous with a ponytail.

I climb the steps to my "quarters" for a shit. I'm loose, need lots of paper, and the bin is overflowing. Exiting, I meet Elke's friend, Rollo, in a white bathrobe. He looks green. I say I'm sorry he's not well, and warn him he should wait for the air to clear in the bathroom. He says, "I can't wait."

"I can't wait," Lucy echoes on the beach, having a private consultation with me. I have urged her to be patient with her writing; to explore different styles, learn from other writers, not seek to rush into print. I should be honest and tell her she'll never make it, but I don't want to spoil her holiday. Or rather, I'm too cowardly to face her despair.

I haven't realized before how much her writing means to her. She's started on a novel based on her broken romance with a Thai restaurateur, the only man she's ever loved. She is lonely in London, working as a temp in an office, writing in the evening and before breakfast. She is Ariadne abandoned by Theseus after she has given him everything, led him into her most secret and holy center. Someone described her on the first day as a laurel, a gazelle, a viola, Sorrento, divan, campari, sarong and ski lift; but right now, naked, skinny—her ribs showing through beneath the slight and sunken-nippled breasts—she appears none of those things.

She sits on her towel with her knees drawn up, exposing the dry, pink slit of her vulva; her arms around her knees, head bowed, and long, fine, brown hair falling over her knees and arms.

"I liked your piece this morning, Lucy. Quite a surprise, Agnes raped!"

She raised her head and opens her large, rather blank eyes. "Why should it be a surprise? Most women have been raped at least once." Her eyes close and her head drops again.

"Well, I liked it. But be patient. Now I'd better see Caroline."

Lucy rises and steps out towards the sea. Caroline, who has been sitting a few yards away, reading, closes her book, smiles, and heads across. Her breasts sliding and bobbing and slithering. When her large body slumps down at my side, her right nipple is within reach of my mouth, and I feel the temptation.

"You have a beautiful body, Caroline."

"You're mad! you've been drinking! I'm fat."

The stretch marks slide into the crevice between pads of flesh at her waist.

"But thanks! It's good for my morale."

"A lot of women don't like compliments anymore."

"I do. If they're sincere."

She doesn't really want to discuss her writing, which is just a hobby for her; she'd rather ask me about my life. I tell her about my working-class childhood in Bristol, my first marriage to a Swedish proto-bimbo I met while at Birmingham Uni, my second to a guilt-ridden Irish Catholic, and my third to Marie. My career in television, followed by modest success as a novelist.

She was married for seven years, before her husband left her for her stepsister—so she can sympathize, she says, with Agnes. Then she lived for ten years with a jazz musician. She ended that relationship, for a short and disastrous liaison with an alcoholic painter. "I've had problems with relationships."

Me too, I say; but my present wife and I keep each other on a very loose rein; which seems to work better. "If I'm working on a novel, which is most of the time, I hardly speak; it's bad enough having to teach, two days a week. So it's almost a relief if Marie indulges in a lighthearted fling now and then."

"I couldn't bear my husband to be unfaithful."

She is sifting the sand through her fingers; rises on her hands and knees to stretch for a sheet of paper that has blown a few feet away: turned from me, her fat thighs apart, her sandy cunt and asshole exposed for a moment. My cock fattens, stirs; as she sits back down, handing me the paper, she says, "I was wondering if you've read Kundera. I'm reading his *Eternal . . .* something or other."

"*Lightness of being.* Yes, it's a great novel."

She gazes out to sea, where the ships of Agamemnon gather. Where Lucy is swimming, her head a dot in the water. A few figures are tossing a ball around.

"I don't know what life is all about," she says.

She is orange tree, hippo, double-bass, Glasgow, king-sized bed, guinness, maternity bra, charabanc, Dionysus.

"I'm confused, like Mildred. But at least I have Andy. My son's a smashing kid. Bit wild; got himself arrested for joy-riding a couple of months ago"—she sighs—"but smashing."

"I don't know who I am either. I'm an ageing Nat."

"It's good of you to spare the time to be with us. Are you writing something at present?"

"No, I'm between novels. This is when I allow myself to live."

"Well, thanks so much . . ." She pulls herself to her feet. Angus is hovering near. He's been sitting and swimming with her for most of the afternoon, and I'm sure she appreciates he's well hung. But can she possibly be impressed by a pigtailed medieval historian? By this outspreading banyan, braying donkey, tuba, G and T, New Orleans, purple cravat, red-faced Apollo? Well, she flings an affectionate arm round his ample waist as she passes him, heading for the beach taverna. I have thought him possibly gay, but it appears not.

Flopping down, he wants to tell me, in his booming voice, an anecdote about Eleanor of Aquitaine he's sure I already know.

He has written almost five hundred Petrarchan sonnets, he tells me, about Heloïse and Abelard: a dialogue between them. He wishes he had brought some to Skagathos. He has had a not dissimilar relationship with a fervent Catholic lady, who is unfortunately married, for twenty years. — Though, of course, also lots of normal *"conquêtes,"* he assures me.

He leaves eventually. I have assumed he is the last; Jeanne is on my list, but she's off sick. However, she turns up, pale and shaky on her feet, but recuperative and determined to see me. I give her a lackluster consultation. I feel that she is disappointed in me.

I rub on lotion, I drowse, I swim. The wind is strong, though less strong than at the Centre, whipping up fierce billows, even in this quiet haven protected from the elements and the stares of the shockable.

* * *

The Lotus Room is a haven from the gale, next morning, as the staff gathers for its meeting. Breakfast has had to be in the house, bowls of muesli balanced on knees, and everyone crammed shoulder to shoulder. The Skagathos Centre is not equipped to deal with bad weather.

My mouth tastes foul, and I'm conscious of again having drunk too much last night. I found myself, to escape from Greek dancing, strolling with Lucy (laurel, gazelle, Ariadne, etc.) down to the beach for a skinny-dip; which led inevitably to some romantic words about her lustrous eyes, hair like moonlight, and so on, and a prolonged grope. The sniping, warm wind, blowing fine sand into our faces, seemed only to increase lust. I don't remember very clearly, but I'm sure I pulled back from going too far. I recall saying we facilitators aren't allowed very much sex. That maybe late in the fortnight it would be safe to get together, but I didn't want to create a special relationship. Which was both truth and falsehood, but it seemed to satisfy her. I was so drunk I'm not sure I could have risen to the occasion anyway.

It's odd, I reflect, that the first two I've had mild sexual contact with are called Lucinda and Lucy; and both are thin, highly strung, feminist, ambitious. Lucinda's much the more talented, Lucy the more vulnerable, I'd guess. It would be highly dangerous to proceed further with either.

All but a couple of the domestics, including the Greek widow, are present in the Lotus Room this morning. We sit in our cross-legged circle. Elke, looking unusually tired and somber, calls upon Stephanos to speak first. His bronzed and handsome face looks haggard, as if he too has had a heavy night. He says to us in his customary shy manner: "I'm sorry I missed dinner last night, and the dancing. I hear it went well. In the afternoon I went to call on those who were sick and living in the isolated units, to check if they needed anything. I saw Robin, Sheila, Gwen, David and Rhona; they were okay, recovering a little, most of them."

He pauses. Elspeth intervenes to suggest that azo dye in the local ice cream may be responsible for the severe viral problem. In her workshop yesterday three of her group realized thanks to the gastric dancing they had azo dye in their stomachs, as a result of eating the village ice cream, and all had had upsets since arriving here.

"That's important, Elspeth," says Elke; "you must announce it at *demos* tomorrow."

(*Demos*, which comes straight after breakfast, is when people belly-ache, make announcements, and praise the good earth.)

"Right."

Brenda, our Reiki expert, born and bred in Tower Hamlets yet always orientally serene, says, "How is Rollo, Elke?"

"He's very sick. I don't know if he had any ice cream. I was up almost all night with him."

D. M. Thomas

There is a murmur of sympathy all round the circle. "Would he like me to come and try some Reiki?" Brenda asks.

"I'm sure he would, Brenda. Thank you."

"Okay. After the workshop."

Elspeth, flexing her shoulders, says her back is a problem; she also would value some Reiki, if Brenda can find the time. Brenda says yes with her eyes.

"Then I went to see Lucinda, the New Zealand woman from Simon's group," Stephanos resumes in his customary quiet, shy voice. "I couldn't get an answer and had to use my key to get in. I found her in the bedroom, and I am sorry to say she is dead."

"Oh my God!" Ezekiel groans.

Everyone stares at the manager, horrified.

"She was dead for some time. She was lying fully dressed on the bed. She was wearing the clothes I saw her in three nights ago, when she ate at Fat Anna's with Simon and some others of the writing workshop. The body was already . . . well, the smell wasn't very pleasant. The light was on, so she died at night."

He pauses again as the door opens and one of the kitchen helpers enters. Sue is almost blown in by the howling wind, and has to force the door shut. She shakes rain from her tousled hair, then apologizes for being late. Elke says in her heavy voice, "We have a fatality, Sue. Lucinda. Did you know her?"

"Yes, I did." Sue sinks down on a cushion beside Ezekiel. "Stephanos has already told me. It's terrible. Terrible for her family, and also a suicide isn't good for the Centre."

"Suicide?" I exclaim.

"It's likely," says Stephanos. He had tried to get hold of Dr. Sklaniatos, the only doctor on the island, but he was away on the other side of the island at a confinement. He turned up later, but Stephanos had already asked one of the participants to take a look: Bob, from Ezekiel's group. He is a doctor."

Ezekiel says he hadn't known that.

Bob has diagnosed barbiturate poisoning; there was an empty bottle by the bed. Elspeth asks did it have to be suicide? Could it have been accidental?

No, says Stephanos; Lucinda owned a small computer. He and Pasha—who, as an ex-policeman, had been a great help in the absence of any regular police on the island—checked to see if there were any messages, and they'd found a very brief one: "Midnight, 18th. I'm sorry, can't take any more."

My heart racing, I am calculating times. We had parted just below the Centre at around eleven that evening. I tell them I was probably the last person to see her alive. How did she seem then? Elke asks. Fine, I say. Somewhat the worse for drink, and she'd shown signs of developing the bug; but her spirits seemed fine.

"Someone, from the police, would normally come over by ferry from Skiathos," Stephanos says; "but the weather is too bad. She's been removed to Lukiades', the funeral director, to await the better weather."

"This was an awful experience for you, Stephanos," says Ezekiel; and the rest of us murmur our agreement. Stephanos shrugs and smiles; it's what he's paid for; though it's the first suicide, the first death. He has phoned London, and no doubt they will already have contacted her family in New Zealand.

"But you can't shrug it off so easily," Ezekiel presses. "Do you want to share your feelings with us?"

He shakes his head. "Perhaps later."

"Okay. We're here for you. I feel very close to you."

Others say they regret they didn't really know her, didn't get to talk to her. Perhaps they could have helped. She'd written a good piece of fiction that morning, I say (and Ezekiel says he remembers me saying it); and was a promising, very ambitious writer. I was amazed she chose to do this.

"I told Elke last night," continues Stephanos; "we thought it best that Bob and Pasha didn't say anything. People were having a good time, it didn't seem the best moment to tell them, only of course we'll have to."

"Sometimes," murmurs Ezekiel, his hand to his brow, "a tragedy like this can bring a body of people together; and I hope that will happen. There's nothing we can do for Lucinda."

"We'd like you to tell your groups this morning," says Elke, "and Pasha has been asked to do some questioning, make some notes. I know his English is not good, but it's very useful that he is here, as it turns out."

She suggests that we hold hands, close our eyes, and think

prayerfully of the dead woman. I grasp the thin, warm hand of Elspeth, the gnarled hand of Brenda. I close my eyes and picture Lucinda in her white shirt and brown divided skirt and sunglasses, with her laptop before her. So efficient and enthusiastic. I think of the freshness of her kisses, just an hour before she took an overdose on top of lots of drink. Why the fuck did she decide to kill herself?

* * *

Why? Why? is the question echoed by my group, when I have told them the tragic news.

I have joined them huddled together in a small room used to store food. Bags of fruit and vegetables surround us; the scent of apples, onions. Lucy and Jeanne are dabbing their eyes with tissues.

The *meltemi,* howling all round us, seems to pick our little room up and shake us.

She'd had glandular fever, I report. That can make one feel depressed. I know of nothing else, she hadn't invited personal questions. Harold, reaching into his shirt pocket for his cigarettes, then thinking better of it because we are indoors, tells us how deeply he regrets criticizing her "Mildred" story so severely. "I called it cold and unfeeling," he murmurs; "if she was severely depressed that could have tipped her over."

"That's nonsense, my dear," Jeanne assures him, laying a sympathetic hand on his knee.

"Death is always followed by guilt on the part of the living," Lucy reflects; "even when you hardly know them, as in this case."

"She didn't seem depressed," says Caroline. "She was so positive and dynamic with her writing. She quite intimidated me with her laptop and her self-confidence. At least, that's how she struck me—but I suppose she *must* have been deeply depressed, poor girl."

"She wouldn't have liked you calling her that," says Harold with a sigh: "girl. But you're absolutely right, Caroline—poor girl."

"Did she have a co-listener?" I ask.

Lucy lifts her hand from her long loose skirt. We are all sensibly attired today. "I was her co-listener. We only met once, right after our workshop on the day she died. I didn't get much from her. She said she felt uncomfortable with one or two people here."

"Who?"

Lucy looks slightly uncomfortable herself. "You, Simon," she says. "I'm sorry."

"That's okay."

"I told her she should talk to you."

"And she did; she made a point of asking me to join her at Fat Anna's for dinner. Natasha, Eddie, and Andrea and Danny, were with us."

Andrea nods, and Natasha says, "Yes, we had nice time together. She give no sign she is unhappy."

"Elspeth's been warning us about azo dye in the ice cream," John says; "I wonder can it make you depressed?" He glances around. "No? I just wondered."

"She also felt uncomfortable with Krystal," Lucy continues. This evokes surprise; Krystal was so pleasant, so friendly. "I know, that's what I said; but Lucinda said she had a hangdog look, the way her back was hunched, as if apologizing for her existence. She said she knew it was irrational, and probably Krystal reminded her of her mother. She also thought she wasn't ambitious or serious enough about writing—only wanting to write detective stories."

"Lucinda could be quite arrogant," Andrea observes, bringing murmurs of agreement.

"Well, again I said to her she should make a point of going to Krystal and having a talk with her. And she did; she sat with her at lunch, and afterwards, when we went to the beach, she told me she was starting to feel better about her." Lucy lowers her head; strands of fine hair trail over her scrawny, white-T-shirted bosom. "I feel awful; I should have recognized she was desperate and helped her."

"You didn't have time, Lucy," I point out. "That's nonsense."

I assure them, in answer to a question from Angus, that there's no possibility of the holiday being abandoned. I feel a lightening of mood at this news, and a consequent guilt. Silence falls.

I break it to say that, of course, we had better put off the trip across to Brooke's tomb on Skyros until next week. We don't want to appear as if we're going off on some kind of group picnic. In any case there's little chance the weather would improve enough by Saturday. There are nods of agreement, and again silence falls.

Harold says he feels far too dispirited to take part in a workshop. We should go away, each by ourselves, and meditate on Lucinda, life and death, he suggests. I suspect he wants a smoke, and know how he feels. In any case, he has struck a common chord. Before we break I pluck out of my memory a lyric about the fragility of life, which begins: "Margaret, are you grieving / Over goldengrove unleaving? . . ." Natasha especially seems moved by the Hopkins lyric, and asks me to repeat it so she can take it down and try to translate it into Russian.

"Ah, Gospodin Hopkins! Simon!"

As I step out onto the terrace, and find myself almost lifted into the air by the gale, Pasha, in greatcoat and fur hat, accosts me. He is sitting in a sheltered alcove, an open notebook on a table before him. He motions to me to join him and sit down. *"Byednaya Lucinda!"* he shouts above the wailing *meltemi.* *"Uzhasno!"* Yet his face does not reflect the terrible death of poor Lucinda; I have never seen him look so animated and enthusiastic. The young woman's death has given him a purpose. "Please, just a few questions. You are, I think, the last person who see her?"

"That's right. We had a meal together, there were six of us."

"Could I have the names of the others. I must talk to them all."

"Of course." I give him the information he needs. "They left first; Lucinda had to go to the toilet; in fact I thought she was coming down with the virus that's making the rounds. She'd drunk a fair amount. I made sure she got back to her flat okay; I left her at the corner just below the Centre."

"Ah yes, I know it. And she appeared normal, mentally?"

"I don't know what was normal for Lucinda; but yes, she seemed perfectly normal."

"So nothing unusual? Did she say Cheerio, see you in the morning, something like that?"

"Something like that."

Pasha sighs. "Ah, well. Thank you. Good at disguises, hah?"

"I guess so, Pasha. There's Lucy—you should talk to her too; she was her co-listener; her *soshlushitel'*. I'll get her for you."

Picking up his camera, he says, "Wait; you mind?" And takes three or four photos of me in quick succession. "Must take everybody," he says apologetically.

Moving off, intercepting Lucy as she is about to vanish through the gate, I tell her Pasha would like a word with her about Lucinda. She says, "After you left, we all decided we should try to go on with Lucinda's story, each in her own way. It's all we can do for her. Do you agree?" She gazes at me through watery eyes, having been crying; her hair streaming out behind her in the wind, her ethnic skirt flattened against her narrow hips.

"I think that's a fine idea, Lucy."

"And we thought we should read some of it as a tribute, to the whole group, one evening. What do you think?"

"I like it. I'll mention it to the other facilitators; I'm sure they'll agree."

"Good. This must be awful for you, Simon. I wondered if . . . perhaps this evening you'd care to have dinner with me. Alone somewhere. So you could relax for a few hours."

"It's a lovely idea, Lucy; I wish I could. But it's still far too early to risk letting everyone think, or see, there's something special between us."

"I didn't mean we should have sex. There's nothing wrong with us talking on our own, surely?"

"It would still look special."

"For chrissake they don't own you!" she exclaims.

"I'm sorry."

She touches my arm. "No, *I'm* sorry. You're being very professional about it."

She turns away, searching out Pasha. I climb the steps to my room, throw myself on the bed. Guilt gnaws at me. These lightly meant flirtations so quickly become a vortex here. I remember my parting embraces with the tall and stately Lucinda. I shoved my hand down her waistband; she said no; I tried again, and this time got further, into the slightly damp and tender cleft; she said no, more harshly, and I apologized. I can't escape the knowledge that I didn't take no for an answer; it was, really, a kind of sexual assault.

I recall, with shame, putting my finger to my nose, on entering my room.

Did my slight aggression work on her depressed mind? Was it the last straw, following in the wake of other, more serious, assaults?

And I've been too cowardly to admit what I did.

I tell myself she encouraged me with French kisses; that in my youth—or indeed only ten years ago—no woman would have thought a single No should stop a man dead in his tracks. Lucinda had kissed me on the cheek, and laid her hand on my arm, before parting.

Yet these are different times, I remind myself; sex is now a continuous negotiation, and I broke the rules. She may have drunk more back in her room, feeling more and more angry with me and with life. Her sleeping pills are at hand; barbiturates are not normally prescribed now, but this bottle, Stephanos said, was prescribed in Athens, where the doctors know nothing. My act has brought whirling into her troubled mind memories from her New Zealand past . . . She taps out her brief message on her laptop . . . pours out the pills . . .

After tossing and turning on my bed for an hour or more, I decide to take a shower. It freshens me, body and mind, and I start to feel wolfishly hungry. Shock, unless it relates too closely to you, can make you hungry.

I walk down to the village and sit outside a cafe advertizing English breakfast. It's calmer, almost windless, and warm again; I feel the sun striking down at me, beautifully. The waiter brings me ham and eggs, bread and butter—real butter!—and tea. It's not quite an English breakfast but it tastes sublime. My pleasure is somewhat spoiled by seeing Lucy coming down the lane. Catching sight of me she stops in mid-stride and comes over. "Don't worry," she says, "I'm not going to embarrass you by sitting with you. I do understand. But just tell me one thing: did you mean what you said to me the other night? I don't mean the romantic flannel; all men exaggerate that stuff; but when you said you felt close to me. Is that true?"

I soak up the last of the egg yolk and bite into the crusty roll. I don't want to lie to her. She has given me a way out by using the past tense, "felt close," though she means it to cover the present too. I did feel kind of close to her, with the Metaxa and the moonlight and her beautiful eyes. Her skeptical feminist toughness had fallen away too; she had been vulnerable and tender, gazing into my eyes as the surf seethed and whispered near us. She'd been swathed in a heavy sweater. But naked in daylight, she is much too skinny; and the softness also vanishes in daylight. A relationship is unthinkable.

Dabbing my mouth with a napkin, I reply, "Yes, it's true."

Lucy smiles. "Thanks. That's all I wanted to know." She takes a deep breath and looks up, blinking at the sun. "The burning egg yolk!" She chuckles, recalling one of our images thrown up by chance. "Isn't it wonderful? How could Lucinda have preferred death to this?"

* * *

. . . "I'm sorry I rang at such an awkward time, darling."

"It wasn't particularly awkward."

"I thought it might be why you're in a frosty mood today."

"Frosty? Who's frosty? I'm not frosty," Marie snaps.

"You're not upset about something?"

"Why should I be upset?"

"I don't know; that's why I'm asking."

I hear her yawn. "I'm tired; I didn't sleep very well last night."

"So who was he?"

"Does it matter?"

"No, but I'm curious. It couldn't have been Pargeter by any chance, could it?"

Pargeter was Head of School two years ago, and is now at Sandhurst. Blond and athletic, he made no secret of his admiration for Marie, and I knew it was mutual. There was a little of the *Brooke* in Pargeter, and a little of the Masterson of Nailsea Grammar long ago. I can therefore understand Marie's attraction to him.

"It might have been," she admits.

"Ah! So! He made it at last, did he!" Or should I have said,

75

D. M. Thomas

You made it at last? There's a touch of amused admiration in the smile that's pressed to the phone.

"I haven't said it was him. So why did she take an overdose, this woman?"

"God knows! She was bright and ambitious and she could write. Neurotic as hell, of course, like everyone here, but I'd never have thought her suicidal. Still, you just can't tell."

Marie yawns again and says, "But apart from that, you're having a good time."

"Apart from that, Mrs. Kennedy, did you enjoy the drive through Dallas!"

But my jokiness finds no answering lightness in her. She just says she's sure I'm having a good time. I tell her I love her and she reminds me to send a postcard to my father. I feel disturbed at the end; not by the thought of Pargeter; she seems cool and remote, more even than usual; the toothless crone has to call me back to give me my change.

In the sheltered village the sun is hot. I stroll aimlessly around the silent, almost deserted lanes. Mangy dogs snuffle past; lean cats. Two urchins play football; the ball bounces away from them down steep steps. Roses, Michaelmas daisies, in tiny gardens, against sun-drenched white walls. Occasionally a door is open, revealing shadowy lives, humble yet houseproud; ikons, plate, photographs. Bent, bonneted, black-clothed crones stare up at me, toothlessly smiling. *"Yassou!"*

I must write postcards, or they won't reach home before me. "Felt up a student, and an hour later she topped herself."

I am between novels, anchored for a few weeks in reality.

* * *

Drifting again, after buying some postcards, charmed by shadowy well-kept mysterious interiors, I spot Angus's purple cravat and tartan Bermuda shorts. He sits at a scruffy outdoor table, a coffee before him and a notebook, at which he gazes preoccupied. He doesn't hear me approach. I lay a hand on his shoulder.

"Ah, Simon! Just the man I need! I'm stuck." He leans out of the way so I can read over his shoulder.

"What's the problem? It was good."

76

"I just don't seem to be able to follow on. May I go back and change something, old chap?"

"Afraid not! What's written is written."

"As in life. Yes, I see . . . Join me for a drink?"

"No, thanks, I just had one."

"Look at her!" he says, grabbing my arm, pointing to where a woman tourist stands poised by a table, across the street, short-sightedly reading a letter. "Isn't that just *absolutely* Vermeer! Not the *Young Woman at the Window* of the Gemäldegalerie in Dresden, but the *Woman in Blue* of the Rijkmuseum. Tell me if I'm wrong!"

"It does have a Dutch feel to it." The woman sits, still reading intently.

"Yes, but only Vermeer. Except this young woman isn't pregnant. Well, she could be, we don't know!" He starts a chuckle, curbs it. "We have no right to be cheerful." I'm moving off when he says, "Wait, I've something to show you . . ." He removes from a yellow folder a scrap of newspaper. "I found this in the revolting loo at Fat Anna's last night, and I thought I might try to weave it in somehow." It's a torn-off piece of a newspaper, which he hands to me. I pretend to read it—a piece about war-torn Bosnia; but the image I have is of Lucinda grabbing the *Herald Tribune* outside Fat Anna's to rush to the toilet.

Handing him back the scrap of unused toilet paper I say, "This is probably a relic of Lucinda." I explain. The Scot with the strangled English public school accent expressed shock, wonderment and compassion in a single loud syllable resembling a chord on a bagpipe.

Moving on, I meet Ezekiel coming out of Olympic Airways Travel. "Hi!" he says. "Howya feeling? This is a bummer."

"It's knocked us all back."

"I tell you, Simon, there are others here who could go the same way, if we're not careful. I'm trying to keep the lid on, but it's hard. And at best it's only containment. You'd better look after yourself. We're here for you if you need us."

"Thanks."

He strolls down the lane with me. "Stephanos got a fax from London. They contacted her only close relative, a sister, who doesn't seem too bothered. Apparently Lucinda made a previous suicide attempt in her teens. This sister wasn't interested in having anything to do with the funeral arrangements. She's to be interred at sea tomorrow afternoon, *meltemi* permitting. Steph is going to pin a notice up to that effect."

"Gosh, it's quick. Doesn't there have to be a post mortem?"

"Sklaniatos, the doc, got permission to dispense with it. By the way, take a look inside that church sometime." He points at a white dome down a zigzag of steps. "It's beautiful . . . On the grounds that the *meltemi* is still raging pretty well everywhere except Skagathos, so nothing can move; it's hot, and there's a refrigeration problem; the relatives don't care; it's a clear case of drug overdose; and there's a nice fat EC grant if the emergency is handled locally." He grins. "These guys don't miss a trick. I wished she'd felt able to talk to *me*. Somebody, anyway. Ah, well . . . You going to the beach?"

"No. I think I'll find a quiet shady place and reflect."

He nods. "I can resonate with that."

* * *

A quiet day. Cool church. Herodotus. A subdued meal at the Centre. Brooke. Sleep.

And walking to the low sounds of Borodin, used by Elspeth for her early-morning dance group: thoughts of death mingling with amusement at Marie sleeping with young Pargeter.

SEVEN

A Kind Baseball Cap

Despite his promise or threat to get Agnes pissed out of her tiny mind at the Prince of Wales, Nat opted out of going to the pub after supper. There was a European Cup match on TV he wanted to watch.

"He's so thrilled to see me, aren't you, Nat?" Agnes said with an ironic chuckle, scuffing his hair. He reached over his shoulder to grab her hand and kiss it. "Make it up to you later, sweetheart," he said, his eyes not leaving the screen.

Mildred used the kiosk in the village square to check up on her sons. They were staying with their father in Brighton. His cheery voice said it was pissing down there too, and the boys were fine; Kate was upstairs telling them a story. Mildred said not to disturb them, she'd see them at the end of the week. He wished her a happy holiday.

Approaching the pub they heard a loud singsong of Welsh-speaking voices. It muted as they came through the door, and a dozen squat, dark-complexioned men and women eyed them suspiciously. The singsong rose again as Agnes ordered their drinks and the sisters withdrew to a quiet corner.

79

"Cheers, Mil!" They clinked glasses.

"Here's to a good degree," Mildred said. *"You deserve it, my dear."*

"Thanks."

They sipped their drinks and were silent for a time. Mildred felt she was floating along on a tide of horror. Wishing this dead woman a good exam result. Nothing made sense any more; hadn't done, really, since she'd started sleeping with Nat. *"Kate took the boys to see* Jurassic Park,*"* she said. *"They've been agitating to go for ages."*

"As long as they're happy there. Do you ever regret divorcing George? I liked old George."

Mildred saw the rubicund, kindly face, the bald head, the mild brown doglike eyes. *"No, I don't regret it. He's a nice man, yes; but so dull! If we could have had exactly one point eight children, and made love two point three times a week, he'd have been perfectly contented—even more contented than he already was. Poor old thing. Kate's much better for him."*

Mythic sex, that's what she needed, she thought. At least, with a man; with a woman, tenderness was enough. Tender, humdrum sex with a male was just boring. God, all those fucking years with George! . . . deceiving herself that they were happy just because they were both in the Brighton Labor Party. The horror every time she had to endure his cock.

But now, if there was a wild, perverse element . . . Pasiphaë lusting for the white bull; ordering a cow on wheels to be built that could be brought close to him. Burning up for him; not caring if the carpenters and wheelwrights knew about her lust, *"A hole back there, that's it,"* the urge of her hot, itchy cunt for his giant white pizzle. Not that awful, oh God, it's Friday night, we've had a meal out and a few drinks and there's a gleam in George's mild brown eyes . . . Not like these bored middle-aged Welsh couples.

Agnes smiled rather sadly. *"I think Nat would settle with two point three screws per week with me."*

She waited for her sister to take this up, but she failed to: seeming suddenly entranced by a group of old mining photographs above the stone fireplace.

"He's in one of his sulky moods," Agnes observed.

"It's the weather, I think. He's been looking forward to this

week. He hasn't seen too much of you lately, Agnes; you having to study so hard."

"Oh, I don't think he's been looking forward to being with me!" She smiled grimly, and Mildred's heart missed a beat. "You cheer him up a lot more. I'm not blaming him; we're not very well suited; in bed, at least. Well, probably in other ways too, but certainly in bed." She gulped the last drops of vodka tonic.

"I'll get you another."

At the bar, a red-faced farmer, not unlike George in build though shorter, tried to chat Mildred up. "Here on holiday, is it? Where are you from? Pity about the weather. Me and my nephew Owen there could drive you and your friend into Cardiff, is it, and show you a good time . . ." Mildred promised to let him buy her a drink if they came in again on Friday, when he said they would hear some good singing.

"Yes, I missed out somewhere," Agnes continued, taking the offered drink, gazing out of the blank window as she had been doing for the past five minutes. "I've never been exactly passionate. I take after Mum." She swished her vodka around, her mind's eye seeing the cool, dead mother, then continued, "When I first met Nat he seemed just as cool as I. He was the first man I'd met who could be content with a cuddle and not try to rush me into bed. But of course he was shooting up then; and heroin is as demanding as a mistress. It's as good as a fantastic screw, Nat says, so you really don't need sex. Now he's off it, he's just like any other young man. He wants it, and often. I can't give it to him."

Not knowing what to say, Mildred said nothing. It was a relief to her when Agnes changed the subject, and smiled, calling her attention to the awful mauve perm and even more awful canary-yellow trouser suit in a huddle of hymn-singing men. Guide me O Thou Great Redeemer . . . "What music . . ." she recalled with a shiver, "What music do you think Agnes'll want at her funeral? . . ."

It was ridiculous; she would make sure she felt unwell in the morning, unfit for the hills. They would drive to Hay to look around the secondhand bookshops. A weight lifted from her.

Then a knifeblade burned through her as Agnes said brightly, "I know you've been sleeping with him, Mil. It's all right, I'm not blaming you. Like I said, it's mostly my fault; and he's a great

D. M. Thomas

charmer." Mildred gave a choking sound, and the younger woman seized her hands, stroked them tenderly, murmuring, "I really don't mind. Sex doesn't seem that important to me. I don't feel betrayed by either of you. I'd just like you to feel you can tell me the truth. You are sleeping with him, aren't you?"

"Yes."

Agnes stroked her sister's hands more firmly, and smiled with her thin lips and narrow, rather slanted eyes. "Thank you!" She removed her hands to take up her glass: holding it to her mouth with both hands and gazing out of the blank window. "At least you've admitted that much; that's something."

"How . . . How did you find out?"

Agnes shrugged and said, "Oh, the odd hairpin in our bed, after I'd left you and Nat together for an afternoon. Lipstick on the pillow. That kind of thing. And it did prey on my mind for a while. I wasn't quite sure *it was you, darling, so I sent you both off to this crappy village and hired a private detective. You know, the chap who called to check the meter on your first day here . . . ?"*

A roaring in her ears, Mildred felt turned to stone, like one of those stones in the hill circles which had once been maidens caught dancing on the sabbath. Bread of Heaven . . . Feed me till I want no more . . .

* * *

Agnes Redland (or "Ledrand") sat in Mr. Kagawa's hotel room, a comfortable double, on a drizzly June evening. She sipped saki and nibbled peanuts from the fridge. Mr. Kagawa, squatting on the queen-sized bed, looked at her appreciatively. She felt ill-at-ease, and no longer had her legs crossed, since Olwen's long black velvet skirt, which she had borrowed, had a slit which showed too much of Olwen's sheer black tights. Agnes sat up straight, her knees together.

Her stomach rumbled; she was hungry; Olwen, as plump as in her College "puppy fat" days, was on a diet too, and they had skipped lunch. Agnes had expected an early dinner, before the opera; but Mr. Kagawa seemed to feel there wasn't time, they would eat after; and besides, he had eaten something already ("I have snack before"). It was extremely rude, but possibly would not appear so in Japan, she thought.

82

He was very pleased with how his lecture had gone; the auditorium packed, a video made for psychology students at the university, lots of clapping and questions. He seemed, to Agnes, to be showing a childlike pleasure at his reception; it was rather touching. She asked had he always been interested in psychology, and he replied that he hadn't—not until he himself had had certain problems and spent two years in a mental ward in Tokyo. "Very bad for family," he said, "very bad," and looked sorrowful.

"But you've come through it, and now you lecture on psychology—that's really wonderful!"

His face brightened. "Yes, I well known!"

She spoke of her sister Mildred's illness; she had been in and out of mental hospitals for the past five years. She was a lot better now, but still on quite strong drugs. For schizophrenia. She nodded repetitively, after speaking the dreaded word.

"So sad . . . Sister cuddly like you?" he asked, drawing a circle with his hands. Agnes reared back in her chair. The astounding rudeness! He a psychologist! But then she broke into a chuckle; it was impossible to take offense. She could dine out on this little man for months.

"No, she's much slimmer."

"Ah! Slimmer no good! Low-calorie bad! Excuse me!" He smiled; stretched the bottle of saki towards her to refill her glass.

"My husband is a psychiatric nurse," she said; "he's with my sister now, sort of looking after her. I should be with them." She drank and felt guilty. At his last call home Nat had said she was okay, but Agnes had sensed all was not well with her.

He had been lecturing about sexual fantasy, her host remarked.

Her head felt a little muzzy; doubtless because she had eaten nothing all day. And it had been quite emotional too; they had chattered and giggled and cried. She accepted another refill from the odd little man, and relaxed a little, reclining back in the chair, easing her skirt to cross her legs. His fantasies, she thought he was saying, though his words had started to swim like his stunted frame, the bed he was sitting on, and the window behind him, had revolved around a rushus woman. Because she was white.

She asked if she could use the bathroom, and lurched against him in passing. In the bathroom of mirrors she looked at three reflections of herself at once, thinking, God, how fat I am! How

83

can Nat fancy me as he does? I really must lose some weight. I'll decline supper; after the opera I'll make an excuse and get a cab back to Olwen's flat.

She slapped water on her face; then refastened the blouse button that had come undone at her bosom. That frightening 40D. Under it, the even more frightening roll of fat where the waistband pinched. Yet her features were pleasant: expressive grey eyes, a warm mouth; and if she raised her head a bit the double chin wasn't too apparent. She reapplied some makeup and combed her curly brown hair.

Returning to the bedroom, she glanced at her watch and asked, "Should we be going?" but he ignored her. He carried on extolling his rushus friend in Paris. She was someone he had gained strength and virtue from. Being white. He leaned towards her; she thought for a moment he was going to touch her, and she moved her legs away. "Was she your first lover?" she asked.

He shook his head, saying, "I ate her, but I did not have sex with her."

Agnes choked back a giggle. "Do you mean you hate her because *you didn't have sex with her?*"

"No, I ate her, but we did not have sex. Just—" He made a gobbling movement with his small lips.

"Oh, I see! You mean you didn't screw her, you only—"

It was a gross term: to eat. It seemed more American than English. She couldn't imagine anything more revolting than to have his lips and tongue rooting in one's vulva.

"Screw," he said, with a prim shake of his head; "not a nice word."

"I'm sorry."

"Okay. Anyway, she very tasty. And she make me strong. I have agent, editor, lots of money, lots of people clapping me, all because of her! Kagawa famous, all because of white woman! Excuse please, I go bathroom."

Left on her own, Agnes wondered if she should grab Olwen's opera cloak and get the hell out. Yet she did really want to hear Jenufa. Soon she could forget him, transported into the warm Moravian world. His telephone rang. She waited to see if Mr. Kagawa would pick up the bathroom phone, but the ringing went on. She picked the phone up. "Hello," she said.

A surprised, gruff, Anglo-Welsh voice said, "Is that Mr. Kagawa's room?"

"Yes, it is. He's in the bathroom. I'll give him a shout."

"No, don't bother; would you tell him John Saunders rang? I'm supposed to be meeting him outside the Welsh National; but say I'll be held up, could he please leave my ticket at the box office and I'll join him inside?"

"Right, I'll tell him."

"Thank you so much. Goodbye."

She replaced the phone. A few moments later her host appeared, and she was startled to see him naked to the waist. He was holding before him a towel, almost ritually. She gave him the message. "Ah, so, Dr. Saunders," he said. "Head of Psychology. He go with us to opera."

"Fine. Though I thought you said you had only two tickets?"

"Only two. Yes. Is okay with you?"

* * *

Margaret spoke, over the coffee and Red Leicester, of a nightmare she'd had. Of falling, or being pushed, over a mountainside. She recalled reading such a scene in a library book she'd glanced at—the very morning they had literally bumped into each other at the supermarket.

Richard commiserated with her. It was very easy to talk. A retired diplomat, he'd set her instantly at ease. He agreed it was so hard to find decent readable books today. He'd fallen back on good old Trollope and Thackerey. She repeated their names respectfully, even though she'd never actually read either of them.

"And there's absolutely nothing *on TV these days!" he complained.*

"Absolutely nothing!"

Dabbing his mouth with his napkin: "That was a wonderful dinner: thank you!"

"It's been a treat for me, having a man to cook for again. You sure you won't have a liqueur, Richard?"

"I mustn't. But do you mind if I smoke?"

"No, please do! David used to enjoy a cigarette after his meal. I'll get you an ashtray." She brought it and said, with a smile, "I think every man should have an occupation."

He threw his head back quizzically, an unlit cigarette in his hand. "Ah! now where's that from? Don't tell me . . . Importance!"

"*Yes! I love Oscar Wilde.*"

"*So do I!*"

"*The elegance, the glamour, the innocence, are gone. Why must everything be spelled out so brutally?*"

"*I so agree! There was an innocence in our youth. Lavinia and I were engaged for five years, and never did much more than kiss! One's children would never believe it!*"

"*But I expect those kisses seemed absolutely wonderful!*"

"*They did!*" *Margaret saw his eyes dance.* "*And even the slight liberties one was granted after a certain time could be quite thrilling in those good old days when all girls wore stockings! Some variety, to console one for not reaching the end of the journey— unlike the motorway boredom of tights! I'm sorry, Margaret, am I embarrassing you!*"

"*Of course not! I'm not a prude. I so agree with you. Tights are frightfully unhealthy, and David didn't care for them. I tried them when they came in, but I never got on with them.*"

"*Oh, so you still wear . . . ?*"

"*Stockings, yes. David always said a woman should be well controlled; and I must say I agreed with him; especially if you're on the plump side, as I am. So I'd wear, I wear, a light support with, you know, suspenders . . .*"

He nodded. "*Control is very important, in a woman or in society for that matter.*"

"*It's what we lack. Control. Everything is so out of control.*"

It was so true! She felt a sudden deep yearning for tradition and discipline. Everything in the world, from floppy stomachs and sagging tights to illegitimacy, was out of control. And she had a sudden intuition that that was what her nightmare meant: she was totally out of control, in freefall, in this chaotic insane world.

"*So you never went in for bra-burning, Margaret?*"

"*Good heavens, no! David would have had something to say about that. I firmly believe the man must be head of the household. I think I'll have a small nightcap.*" *As she lifted the decanter he said he would join her. Good, she said, pouring him a generous measure. He observed her intently as he sipped.*

"*I must say,*" *he murmured, his smooth voice deepening,* "*you're very firm.*"

She glanced down. "David always said a well-fitted bra is a woman's most important item of dress. I still get fitted for my bras, and I think it pays. Uplift is very important, at my age."

"*It seems to me we have a lot in common. We're both hopeless old-fashioned romantics, Margaret.*"

"*It seems so! Marilyn, my daughter, thinks I'm a frightful square!*"

She stood up, and asked him to bring the decanter into the drawing room. They watched Sky News for a time. She had had Sky brought in so David could watch the sports when he got ill— but the news was horrid, as it always was these days—murder, rape, terrorism. She switched it off and put on a tape of Mantovani.

"*That really is a lovely dress,*" *he said; and she ran her hands over her hips and thighs, smoothing the black silk over ample but well-controlled flesh, saying it hadn't been expensive, she'd bought it in a sale, as a matter of fact; when she'd been in mourning. Mourning was out of fashion, he said, but it was important to mourn; and she agreed. Only through mourning properly could you get through the grief.*

"*I ought to go, Margaret,*" *he said, getting to his feet, stretching. She stood up, rubbing her painful hip; he took a few unsteady steps towards her. "I have a terrible impulse," he murmured, "to touch you. I don't mean—in any wrong way. Outside. I've been deprived of anything feminine. May I?"*

"*Of course.*"

Tentatively he touched her waist, then stroked the silk gently over her rounded stomach to her thigh. "A firm foundation!" he said, smiling into her grey eyes. "I like that." He removed his hand.

"*Thank you.*" *He took car keys from his pocket.*

"*Are you fit to drive?*"

"*I think so.*"

"*It's not worth the risk; there's a spare bed here.*"

"*Or I could order a taxi, I suppose.*"

* * *

D. M. Thomas

In the morning she was taking a bath. He knocked gently at the slightly open door, popped his head around and asked, "Is it all right to come in? I must leave in fifteen minutes."

"Of course. You can borrow David's toothbrush and shaving gear. I could never bear to throw them out, you see."

He sat on the side of the bath, in his jockey shorts, and stroked her wet shoulder tenderly. "It was wonderful!" he murmured.

"Yes, but I'm so embarrassed! How could I have done such a thing! . . . Did you sleep well?"

"Yes. And you?"

"The best for months."

"No nightmares of falling off cliffs?"

"No nightmares." She raised her face to meet his kiss.

That odious book. All that filthy swearing and violence. What was the world coming to? Margaret blamed a lot of it on too much black immigration.

* * *

"No more words," said Tony Fontana; "it's time for a little action, cara mia. *Pull up your skirt a little and open your legs."*

"Not here!"

"Yes, here. Nobody is looking."

Agnes wondered how many other girls Tony had entertained in this discreet alcove in a bar off the King's Road; but it did not matter; it almost made the excitement greater. He was gazing across the table into her eyes; the slight scar at the left corner of his pale lips made him look even more desirable. She raised herself from the chair to tug her slim black skirt up, allowing her to open her thighs.

"Slide forward a little," he commanded.

He bent, fiddling with his shoe. Sitting erect again, he stretched his right leg out under the table. She felt his shoe gently brush against her tights, at mid-thigh; nothing more. His smile and his gaze did not waver. He removed his foot and stooped again, untying his laces.

She didn't recognise the tape that was being played, softly; but it was sweet and violiny and sexy; relaxing.

He fumbled in his case and brought out his phone. "Here," he said, "I want you to call your husband. Tell him you can't make it *today. Tell him you've been celebrating too much to drive; you're in a restaurant with a friend. —No, don't move; stay as you are."*

As if mesmerized, she took the phone from him. She would have to move, she said, to find the number of the cottage in her bag. Okay, he said, but then slide forward again and open your legs.

She found the number, and dialed. As she heard the phone trill in distant, unknown Wales, she felt something—a toe! yes, his big toe!—press against her pussy, and she let out a gasp. She opened her legs wider and felt the stretched seam of her tights yield, rip slightly. "How—?" she began.

"A party trick," he said. "A razor blade can be very useful; and not a nick, not a drop of blood, you felt nothing—"

"Nat!" she exclaimed, waving her lover to be silent. "It's me." The toe was pressing, moving, agitating; it was crazy, wonderful; she strained her bottom forward.

"Are you on the way?" she heard Nat ask.

"Yes, yes! . . . No!" She chuckled. "No, I'm in a restaurant. With my friend Antonia. We were celebrating. I've drunk too much, darling; I don't think I can—aaargh!"

"What was that?" Nat asked, alarmed. "What the fuck is going on?"

Tony had his whole foot—well, all his toes, or so it felt—inside her; jamming her full, making her ripple with pleasure and pain all through her body. It was like all the musical notes on the tape were running about deliciously inside her. "Sorry!" she gasped. "I spilled some wine on my skirt."

"You must be bloody drunk!" he snarled.

"I'm—aaah—rather tipsy, yes!"

Tony was gazing at her, speaking very softly, mouthing the words clearly: "I love your cunt so much. I love filling it up, with anything, everything. Bellissima Agnes!"

"There's a man there," Nat said suspiciously. "I can hear him. Who is he?"

"Oh, just the waiter! You know what Italian waiters are like." And she chuckled, she couldn't help it, his foot was giving her such pleasure.

"It's so wet!" Tony was purring. "So magnificently whorish!" She was one helluva dame. She claimed she'd never been unfaith-

89

ful before; which increased his pleasure. His foot slid in even deeper and his toes danced inside her wetness.

"When are you coming?"

"Oh, now, now! . . . Sorry—no—tomorrow; I thought you said—I thought you said something else. How's Mildred?"

"Okay."

"That's wonderful!*"*

"That she's okay?" he snarled incredulously.

"Well, yes! I mean, she seemed a bit sniffly when you left; if she's okay, that's WONDERFUL!*"*

EIGHT

The Drowned Computer

Natasha, after reading her piece, to howls of merriment, shrugs self-deprecatingly and says, "It's very frivolous and pornographic; but I think when in the West do as the Westerners do."

"It's terrific," I say; "you've given us an incredible variety—all of you. So rich, so imaginative!"

Also misspelled, ungrammatical, and often linguistically impoverished—desperately in need of editing, and in some cases transfiguration; but I let that pass.

"Thank you, Simon," murmurs Harold, placing his first cigarette in his holder; "we did it for darling Lucinda. I'd like to know what you all thought of my poor offering. I know it was off the subject, but it was the best I could do, and actually I've become quite fond of my old-fashioned Margaret."

"I really liked it, Harold," says Caroline, flicking over to find the relevant photocopy; and others break into similar praise.

"I liked it too, Harold," I assure him. "Very unusual. I liked the way a short scene she'd skimmed in a library gave her a nightmare."

"I thought it was quite erotic," Andrea says. "Cool."

"So did I. Not so erotic, though, as Natasha's. Phew!" Humorously Caroline flicks mock sweat from her brow. "I have to know, Natasha—did you make it up?"

"Well, not quite. We have Mafia also in Moscow now, as you probably know. A friend of mine has Georgian Mafia boyfriend. He did this to her in restaurant while she talk to her husband on phone. Just like that!"

"Ah, it wouldn't have happened in Brezhnev's day!" says Harold.

"Don't be so sure, Harold! In Politburo, the first duty of typists in the morning was to suck off their bosses."

The donkey brays.

Someone screams loudly in Ezekiel's workshop.

"It was the cry of women, good my lord," Angus mutters.

The sun emerges from behind a dark cloud, bathing us with warmth and light.

The bray, the scream, the sunlight—perhaps too the thought of secretaries kneeling to fellate dark-suited bureaucrats—have stricken us into silence. I look around the circle.

Harold breaks the spell. "But which of them is the real Nat, the real Mildred, the real Agnes? Andrea, what do you think?"

She looks up, startled. "About what?"

"Who is the real Agnes? The real Nat? The real Mildred? We've got a Mildred who's a bisexual Socialist, only interested in kinky sex if she's with a bloke; a conservative Classics mistress; a schizophrenic who's presumably imagining the whole sex-and-murder plot with her caring brother-in-law . . . Who's the real one?"

Andrea stares into space, saying at last, "I think they're all real. They're like the Greek heroes and heroines. Take Ariadne; Is that how you pronounce it? Can I read you something?" Receiving my nod, she dips into her black sports bag and brings out a glossy-covered hardback. "I've just started reading this. *The Marriage of Cadmus and Harmony,* by Roberto Calasso. Danny bought it for me when we knew we were coming here. I've always loved the Greek myths." She flicks through the early pages. "Listen to this. I'm not very good at reading aloud, so you'll have to forgive me." She reads, stumbling a little over names, her face alive:

"Mythical figures live many lives, die many deaths, and in this they differ from the characters we find in novels, who can never go beyond the single gesture. But in each of these lives and deaths all the others are present, and we can hear their echo. Only when we become aware of a sudden consistency between incompatibles can we say we have crossed the threshold of myth. Abandoned in Naxos, Ariadne was shot dead by Artemis's arrow; Dionysus ordered the killing and stood watching, motionless. Or: Ariadne hung herself in Naxos, after being left by Theseus. Or: pregnant by Theseus and shipwrecked in Cyprus, she died there in childbirth. Or: Dionysus came to Ariadne in Naxos, together with his band of followers; they celebrated a divine marriage, after which she rose into the sky, where we still see her today amid the northern constellations. Or: Dionysus came to Ariadne in Naxos, after which she followed him around on his adventures, sharing his bed and fighting with his soldiers; when Dionysus attacked Perseus in the country near Argos, Ariadne went with him, armed to fight amid the ranks of the crazed Bacchants, until Perseus shook the deadly face of Medusa in front of her and Ariadne was turned to stone. And there she stayed, a stone in a field.

"No other woman, or goddess, had so many deaths as Ariadne. That stone in Argos, that constellation in the sky, that hanging corpse, that death by childbirth, that girl with an arrow through her breast: Ariadne was all of this."

She finishes triumphant, smiling, and snaps the book shut.

Harold exclaims gently (an oxymoron that Harold makes his speciality): "By Jove! you read that beautifully, Andrea! This isn't meant to be rude, but I don't often like to hear Americans reading, yet your New England accent actually added to it. And that's a *smashing* passage. I must get that book. I shall get the details from you later."

"Yes, I must too," several voices murmur.

"The thing is," says Andrea, ignoring the praise, "maybe everybody has many lives, many deaths. I love Danny, and I'm faithful to him. But I can quite imagine being in a situation where I'd just love to be toe-fucked in a restaurant by some rich, good-looking, arrogant guy!" She laughs. "And even be talking to my husband over the phone while it's happening. Can't *every* woman here?" she asks challengingly, looking around the circle. Grinning an apology to Emily, next to her, she says, "Guy or gal!" Emily grins back; Lucy alone has a sour face, saying, "No, I think it's disgusting."

"Well, maybe it is," Andrea continues; "but I'm perfectly capable of doing something disgusting, in the right circumstances; and sometimes enjoying it more just because it *is* disgusting. And . . . and I'd even like to know what it feels like to rape someone . . . Well, so I think, I think Agnes and the others are all these things, and I don't have any problem with that. I'll shut up. I've said too much." She glances at me with a nervous smile.

"No, you haven't, Andrea. That was most helpful."

A shout carries down from the road above us. We look up and see the stubble-faced old mayor, in his black suit and off-white shirt buttoned to the neck. He is gesticulating. Emily says, "The water's off again. Damn!"

"Efkaristo!" we shout, and he waves and disappears.

"We'd better grab coffee while we can."

"Wait, please!" says Harold. Our shorts and brown thighs settle back down on the seats. "I have something to say to you all. I have suffered pangs of remorse since dear Lucinda died, because I attacked her piece very harshly and undeservedly. I was upset by the sex and violence. But I realize now I was hiding away from the violence in myself. Coming here, being with you all, has been a revelation to me. And Andrea's words have made something click into place in my mind."

He rises to his feet and paces around within our circle, staring at the ground. "I am a great, an insufferable *poseur,* I know that. It's my way of hiding. I grew up in the East End of London. It was a pretty tough neighborhood, I can tell you. My father was killed on the beaches of Normandy; my mother was already tangled up with a very unsavory, but rather attractive, man who traded on the black market. Terry his name was. A spiv: he had an Anthony Eden mustache, snakeskin shoes, and padded shoulders. A few years after the war, when I was ten, he raped me in the old Anderson shelter we had at the bottom of our back garden. It had, of course, a strong effect on me. In my teens I often used to dress up in my mother's underwear. You will have noticed a fetishistic interest in my contribution. On one occasion Terry found me in their bedroom, duly attired in the feminine clothing. He summoned my mother, and she stood by approvingly as he buggered me again—as they said, to teach me a lesson."

A cockerel crows. He waits for him to finish his untimely call.

"My mother," he says in emotional tones, "was working class, but as correct and prim in manner as my character Margaret. Yet she allowed Terry to do that to me, and even approved."

He relights his cigarette which has gone out; draws on the holder and throws his head back. "I can understand now that it was what I had wanted; it was why I had dressed in her underwear and stockings. I hoped to attract Terry again. If we had broken for coffee I'd not have dared tell you this when we came back; it had to be now. I wanted you to know it, because you are giving me so much. I trust you all implicitly. I must begin to acknowledge my bisexuality. Emily's bisexual Mildred has helped me too. I must recognize and accept that I find Angus attractive; and even you, Simon, so charming and helpful to us in your cool, rather reserved and detached way . . . Well, that's all I have to say. Thank you for listening."

He stands fixedly, puffing on the holder. Breaks the transfixed silence with: "Coffee, I think."

"Thank you, Harold," I say, standing up.

"Yes, thank you, Harold," says Emily. "That was so giving."

All stand and stretch. Emily goes to him and gives him a hug. Caroline joins her, and all three hug, swaying. Stately, huge Angus attaches himself to them also, his arms thrown wide to embrace them.

I leave a positive rugby scrum of tight-knit bodies, taking the stony path down. I gaze out at the heat-dazed sea. It's good that it's calm today. This afternoon we—the staff—go out with Lucinda's body and consign her to the Aegean.

Pasha, in black slacks and short-sleeved blue cotton shirt, is the first to greet me on the terrace as I head for the kitchen. "Ah, Simon! Good morning!" His red face looks downcast. I ask him what's the matter and he shrugs dolefully. *"Samo-ubi-istvo,"* he says; "suicide. It was suicide."

"Well, we knew that, Pasha."

"Da, pravda, but I think for a time I have a lead. I speak with the old Greek guy who lives next door to Lucinda's apartment. Stephanos, he interpret. This old guy wake around mid-day— sorry, midnight—to have a pee. He hear, he say, two women talk in apartment. Windows are open. I think this is beeg break-through, this is *Gorky Park* of the West, huh?" He smiles bleakly. "Then I remember Lucinda have long-wave radio, and your student Lucy she tell me, yes, Lucinda listen to it a lot." He pushes his mouth out in disgust. "She listen to BBC World Service, according to Lucy. Is very confusing—Lucy, Lucinda. I call friend in Moscow militia—much expense, much drachmas; and he check program for this night. And what do you know? This midnight—wait a moment . . ." He pulls a small note-book from his trouser pocket, flicks over a page, thrusts the notebook at me. I see the names A. S. Byatt and Victoria Glen-dinning. "I think A. S. Byatt man, right?" I shake my head. "You're right. Woman. My friend he check up and tell me. AN-TONIA Byatt, writer. Interview. So . . ." Another gloomy gri-mace and gesticulation. "My lead gone. Now, boredom again. Every day like a year in Kolyma, no?"

"Well, you tried, Pasha. Excuse me, I must get a coffee." He nods; I glide away. It seems so bizarre, to take an overdose after listening to a discussion between A. S. Byatt and Victoria Glen-dinning. Other groups are emerging, milling around. I hear one of them, slim, pale, hollow-chested and solemn, in metal-framed glasses, say to someone passing, "Ted! Geoff's in a bad way. We've got to arrange some hands-on for him this afternoon. Pass the word around." And the studious-looking, bald guy he's addressed nods and replies, "Okay, Arnold. I'll tell Steve," and hurries off. Arnold, pausing only to say "Hello, Simon!" even though we have never spoken before, rushes off and collars an elderly man with a flowing white beard. Fred—that's his name. I can sense a sudden exhilaration, a spurt of unusual energy; and, in pale hollow-chested Arnold, a "leadership" streak, as if he's marshaling a small SAS team for a difficult mission. It's hands-on instead of hand grenades, but the adrenaline is flowing.

Standing in the queue for the coffee urn, I feel my arm gripped. I turn to see Elke's Sumo figure and piercing polar-circle eyes. "Simon, when you've got your coffee could you join us for a short staff meeting in the Lotus Room?"

"Okay."

I take my mug of coffee to the Lotus Room. Most of the staff have gathered, and are sprawled around, sipping their coffee or herbal tea. Elspeth slips in after me and Elke nods to her to close the door. We're all here except Brenda, says Elke, and she has the tummy bug; her students have been set work to do. Stephanos asks me about the boat trip to Skyros, to the grave, and I say Lucinda's death has thrown our plans awry; we'll leave it till near the end. He nods approval then, straight from his squat, leaps to his feet and tells us in his gentle voice that there has been a change of plans for Lucinda's funeral. It can't be this afternoon; the Skagathian boatmen refuse to commit a suicide to the waves; they say it would bring misfortune and pollute the fishing waters. A land burial is also out of the question. The only alternative, though it will sound barbarous, is to take the coffin to the Acropolis and drop it into the sea from there. This will apparently *not* cause misfortune and pollution.

"Do we know why?" asks Ezekiel, who sits, his arms round his drawn-up legs, in front of me.

Stephanos's fine, kind eyes dart around sheepishly. It must be, he says, because malefactors were once thrown from the rock in question. There is an element of punishment. But *we* don't need to subscribe to that.

"That's true," says Ezekiel; "we can and will show the same reverence. I think we should accept this alternative; we must respect the views of the local community."

Elke is nodding her assent, her eyes fixed intently on the facilitator of Orgasmic Consciousness. There are murmurs of agreement.

"Thank you," says Stephanos. "But I think it's best we do it when very few people are around, and I don't think we need to tell the students. Don't worry, it will be done with dignity." He has arranged for the coffin to leave the funeral home at five thirty tomorrow morning, arriving here a quarter of an hour later. He knows it's awfully early, but he hopes most of us can attend the funeral, proceeding with the coffin up to the Acropolis. It should be dawn just as we reach it.

"That will be good," says Ezekiel; "who could want more than to be given to the Aegean as the dawn breaks? I know I wouldn't. Unfortunately, though, I won't be able to attend. As you're aware, Elke, I'm taking the evening ferry to Skyros, then flying to Athens to meet Teresa. Her plane arrives at midnight. We've not seen each other in three months, and it's her first time in Europe; I'd like to be there to meet her."

Elke nods, and says, "You must go, Ezekiel."

* * *

I am lying on the beach, my eyes closed, in that daydreamy state so important to writing; I'm vaguely meditating a novel about Kennedy's brain, cut into thirty-one thousand slices, resting in a secret, locked cabinet of the Moscow Institute of the Brain. A westerner, based loosely on Caroline, hears about it and becomes obsessed with getting hold of his brain. I feel a scuffle of sand on my shin and a shadow over me; I open my eyes to see Ezekiel. He has put on shorts and T-shirt and carries his beach bag. "Just wanted to wish you luck for tomorrow, Simon," he says, squatting down in front of me; "for the funeral service. She was your student and you're bound to be feeling it. Hope it goes well."

"And I hope—you know, it goes well in Athens."

"Oh, I'm sure it will. You'll like Teresa. I've told her what a swell guy you are. It's been great getting to know you on the beach like this. I'm glad you've been able to find time to relax. O'Brien seemed to be working all the time, marking and seeing students. Of course he had a huge group—about eighteen, I think, and they had to disappoint as many again. His students adored him for his commitment to them, but it seemed a pity he couldn't enjoy a holiday too. It's great you seem to have a different philosophy."

With a final "Catch up with you later," and a wave, he lopes off towards the beach road, kicking up the sand as he goes.

After a refreshing swim I sit beside Caroline. She is sad, she has even thought of quitting Skagathos. I urge her not to. "Well, no, I've got over that. But I keep wondering what made her do it. Do you think it was a relationship? We women get into very destructive relationships. There were many times I thought of suicide when I was with Gavin, my two-vodka-bottles-a-day painter. But I kept hoping I could help him over it. And I'd left a good guy for him. Shit!"

I offer to rub lotion on her back. She turns over on her beach towel; I rub the lotion slowly and enjoyably into her plump back. Running my hand down to the divide of her buttocks; she has flung her legs wide apart.

"How about you?" she asks dreamily, her eyes closed.

"How about what?"

"Your boundaries seem somewhat blurred. As a tutor, that is."

"You think I should keep my distance?"

She heaves her heavy shoulders in a shrug.

"I'm not teaching Geography, or Economics, I'm teaching how to fucking write," I snarl.

* * *

At night, some singing in the village as we try to mitigate the gloom. Angus and Caroline sing a duet: *Ye banks and braes of bonny Doon.* Emily and I talk about the stone maidens in her continuation of Lucinda's story. There is a circle of stones near Emily's cottage in North Wales. They were girls unwise enough to hold a disco on the sabbath day. "But I think the true story," she says, "is that they're on their way to *becoming* women. Or men. I've felt their dream energy. The last time I was here I took a Dream Stone Workshop with Eddie Woodcock. Have you heard of him, Simon?" I shake my head. "He's a potter, and also runs a self-help male-feminist group in Glastonbury. He believes everything, including stones, are dreaming, on their way to becoming conscious. The dreams of stones are very misty, he says, but they exist; and he showed us how to get in touch with them. He's fantastic."

Later, towards lights out, the talk round the table turns back to Lucinda and her despair. They don't know she's to be dropped from a great height into the sea at dawn, only that the arrangement for a sea burial, hurriedly announced, was as hurriedly canceled following a request from the bereaved family. I feel guilty at hiding the truth from them. At midnight I make excuses and leave them still drinking and talking gloomily. Before lying down on my ever-less-comfortable single bed I set my traveling alarm for five. I sleep like a stone.

* * *

It is cold in the pre-dawn murk on the Acropolis; I wrap my windbreaker about me; we wait for the dawn; out of the intense stillness, the funeral home's donkey brays; and at that moment the first rays of the sun shoot up from the horizon, Homer's "wine-dark sea."

As the flaming light spreads, we see etched in a deepening orange glow the mangy donkey, the cart he has pulled with immense difficulty up the steep track to the top; the cart with its coffin, weighted so it will stay at the bottom of the sea beneath us; four Greeks in black suits. They are poised on a bluff, known as the Atropien Rock. We the mourners—Stephanos, Elke, Elspeth and I—stand some way off to the right, at the suggestion of the funeral director, Mr. Lukiades. From here, he has pointed out via Stephanos, we can watch the coffin fall into the bay. The overhanging Atropien Rock falls away sheerly, to a dizzyingly distant dark swirl of foam.

It adds to my chill to think of all the malefactors who have been pushed off this bluff.

The sun is a scarlet ball resting on the sea; already a gold band stretches across the sea towards us. Ezekiel was right: it's a wonderful setting. The men, at a signal from their director, are hauling the heavy coffin on ropes from the cart, the struggle causing the donkey to edge forward, away from the clifftop. They rest the coffin on the ground, at the very edge. Stephanos says to me, "Okay, Simon."

I recite: *"Death, be not proud; though some have callèd thee / Mighty and dreadful; for thou art not so . . ."* Then, in a flowing skirt, her fine fair hair shimmering, slender Elspeth sings a gentle French lullaby, hands pressed together as in prayer.

As the song trembles into silence, Stephanos calls another signal to the Greeks. Stooping, they maneuver the light-colored casket until it projects over the edge. A muttered command, and the casket topples. It plummets for about thirty meters,

100

then crunches against a small projection and bursts apart. We see, with horror, Lucinda appear, tumbling, her familiar brown divided skirt keeping her decent, a white polo-necked sweater we hadn't seen, and falling—limbs flailing like a rag doll's, along with stones, the broken pieces of coffin, a radio, a laptop computer (her sister has requested that those precious objects be with her)—falling, falling, and at last vanishing beneath the swirling foam.

"My God!" cries Elke, and Elspeth screams and bursts into tears. Elke and I put our arms round her. Stephanos strides over to the funeral party; returning, he says, "They're sorry. It's never happened before, in their experience. Probably there has been rock fall, so it's not quite a clear drop any more."

II

ONE

A Saintly Arrival

This morning, following our secret, botched committal of Lucinda, *demos* is led by an excitable young man, Geoff. He has black hair standing stiffly up, jug ears, and hectic eyes ringed by red as if he has spent much of the past week in tears. I guess, rightly as it happens, he is the Geoff whom Arnold and his holistic rescue team described yesterday as being in a bad way and in need of hands-on. He speaks, in a high-pitched strained voice, of the healing powers of Skagathos; offers exalted praise of Brenda, his Reiki tutor (his eyes seek her out, but she is still down with the stomach bug); Ezekiel (seeking him out too, but he has beat it to Athens); Harriet his co-listener (who, though a professional carer in England, is being driven mad by him, according to her friend Emily); Peter, Sue and Tamsin for the wonderful vegetarian food; and indeed everybody. As he sits down he receives a big clap.

Stephanos, wearing his usual shy and courteous smile, stands up. He reminds everyone that as this is the weekend there will be no formal workshops. Everyone's been working very hard, it's time to relax a little. "It's not been an easy week. But now, well, it's a beautiful day. Enjoy your weekend. There's bread, cheese and fruit in the kitchens, if you want to pack a lunch; there'll be no lunch or dinner at the Centre today, but dinner tomorrow night before the celebration of Lucinda. Don't forget that, by the way. Any questions?"

Lucy stands to ask him about arrangements for Lucinda's funeral. Following yesterday's postponement of the sea burial, what's going to happen? Stephanos says the funeral arrangements are in the hands of Lucinda's family; in any case he's pretty sure the funeral will be private. Lucy says surely a few people should represent the Centre, and Elke raises her bulk to say we should regard tomorrow's celebration as our way of saying farewell to Lucinda. Arnold, the hollow-chested SAS captain, asks if anyone has a photo of her, since a lot of people don't know who she was. He draws a blank.

Someone murmurs a question about the water. Stephanos can't say when it will be back on, but it should be today sometime. Priscilla, a tall, thin, middle-aged woman with a cultured American accent and a querulous expression, demands to know why the Centre doesn't provide mineral water. She's holidayed at the Skyros Centre twice, and only once was the water turned off, and then the Centre provided lots of free mineral water. Stephanos says he can't talk about the Skyros Centre, but of course its holidays are more expensive, and the shops here in the village are full of mineral water.

Silence follows. "Well, if that's all? Thank you, Geoff; thanks, everyone. Have a nice day!" Oh yes, one more thing: he has offered to lead a midnight walk to the holy well of Daphne. It's a very nice walk; how many would like to come? Seven or eight raise their hands. He tells them to meet him here at eleven thirty tonight. "Now enjoy and explore this island called by Homer the whitest pearl of Greece . . ."

* * *

The morning clouds over and becomes cooler; finding me in the village, Andrea and her husband persuade me to cycle with them to a "sacred grove." We set off on hired bikes into the island's flat and rather barren interior. After about three miles we reach a small, sad clump of pines, near the road. Here, according to Skagathos's only guide book, the god Dionysus "ravaged a lymph," Aura, in her wine-drugged sleep. We rest and drink Cokes. Andrea and Danny start nuzzling each other, and I wander off.

I sit with my back against a pine, gazing up at the spangles of bright light penetrating the foliage. This should have been the day for Brooke's grave. I have a yearning for that other, English myth—and for everything that lay *before*—before my birth, before the destruction of England's flower—and indeed flowers; before the motorways and council estates and TV aerials and mass culture ravaged our fair land. To read, with my picnic of tomatoes and cheese, I have brought Hassall's biography of the poet. Or reread—for I know parts of it almost by heart. I turn at once to the fine description of the burial. With infinite slowness the bearers, mostly Australian petty officers from the *Hood,* carried the coffin from the shore, up the dry water course, to the olive grove that Brooke had liked so much, and which fellow officers had picked out for his resting place. "Shortly before eleven o'clock, Lister and Asquith saw a man with a lantern coming slowly up the gorge. Behind him walked Platoon Sergeant Saunders, holding aloft a big, roughly put-together cross painted white, and along the cross beam, painted in black, the name of the man they were burying; then came Shaw-Stewart with drawn sword, leading the firing party, then the bearers with the coffin, and General Paris walking behind it."

It's hot as I read. The sun, even through the pine tops, burns me; rapes me almost. How different was Brooke's funeral, I reflect, from Lucinda's botched interment.

"When Asquith saw the coffin, he asked for a spade and jumped into the grave and lengthened it a little, and he found it all lined with sprigs of olive and flowering sage. When all was ready and the men assembled, Quilter threw in a wreath of olive. The moon remained clouded, and a slight breeze got up, stirring the foliage, as the chaplain read the burial service of the Church of England. Brooke, surely, would not have scorned to receive the same obsequies as Swinburne. 'The scent of wild sage,' Kelly remarked in his journal, 'gave a strongly classical tone, which was so in harmony with the poet we were burying that to some of us the Christian ceremony seemed out of keeping.' Three volleys were fired into the air, Shaw-Stewart presented arms. The hills reverberated, and startled goats were heard jingling away. 'One was transported back a couple of thousand years,' wrote Kelly, 'and one felt the old Greek divinities stirring from their long sleep.' Then the Last Post."

They were aware they were helping to create a myth. As they walked away, back to their ship, one of them said, "He has it all to himself, except for a few shepherds." Four hours later the mourners were heading for Gallipoli. Of five friends and officers who heaped the cairn with pink and white marble stones, only two would live to see the armistice. As Brooke himself had observed, "half the youth of Europe, blown through pain to nothingness."

After Brooke, I get a longing for English summery coolness; and it seems characterized most perfectly by the little patch of tall nettles that Edward Thomas celebrated, the tall nettles in the corner of a garden; imperfect, and therefore especially English, especially lovely. Or was it "cool nettles"? Another casualty of that devilish war.

Tall, cool nettles, and winding country roads with haywains trundling along them; beautiful whitewashed, rose-wound cottages; calm, cool pipe-smoking young Englishmen playing croquet, or in white flannels on the village green, cricket.

Yes, a deep yearning for that quietness and peace of England overcomes me. Unawares I drowse off, and see again my mother, young enough to be my daughter, smiling at me through her tears, in a patch of nettles and violets. She holds out her arms, calling me. But I ride off on my bike. Just as I did when Dad came home from the hospital and told me she was dead. I didn't want to know.

Yet, screw it, I go on searching for her.

As, I think, my father goes on searching for his father, Corporal Frank Hopkins, shot through the head after two strides into No Man's Land on the first morning of the Somme. One of twenty thousand killed on the first day, when they were led to expect a walkover.

And staff officers watched it through binoculars, as if it was Ascot.

I'm silent on the bicycle ride back. Danny and Andrea are quiet too. They ride close, slowly, hands clasped. I guess they have been emulating Dionysus and Aura.

Late in the afternoon I take part, with a few others, in some impromptu Gastric Dancing led by Elspeth. And after I have tried, in vain, to identify and love the foods that are in my stomach, we break open a bottle of retsina. Elspeth is worried about her father, a sub dean of Salisbury Cathedral who has stomach cancer. She has tried so hard to get him to try Gastric Dancing, but so far without success.

* * *

Angus, leaning back from his cleared plate, observing with relish the lively lit-up village square: "How wonderfully jolly! Emily, this must remind you of that classic poem by Giacomo Leopardi, 'Saturday Night in the Village.' "

"You're right, Angus, it does."

"It's an amazing poem, isn't it! Don't you just love that Leopardian image of the girl leaping from crevice to crevice like a goat—holding violets and roses she'll wear tomorrow at the boring Mass, doubtless to try and attract a lover!"

Skagathos,
Grease.

My dear Carla,

It's midnight; a Greek island; a bedroom with a hard single bed and a single hard chair; a bottle of Metaxa. Skagathos is a poor relation of the Skyros holistic center we talked about once. I tried Skyros but they didn't want me. Unfortunately Skagathos did. Today began at 5.30 a.m. with our hurling a dead student over a cliff (true: more of that later), and has ended for me with an awful chicken and rice dish in the village, a place called Fat Anna's. Anna is grossly fat, and so is her food. The food at the

D. M. Thomas

Centre is veggie rubbish; a lot of the time there's no water, so
the loos and the shitpaper buckets overflow. Not surprisingly, a
third of us at any one time are down with dysentery. Wish you
were here!

This is by way of thanking you for the Christmas card—
somewhat belatedly! By the time I got round to buying cards it
was Christmas Eve, so nobody got any from me last year. I've
no excuse for not being in touch, except that I've done the usual
opting out of living to write a novel. Are you still writing yours?
It sounded very promising. I read your piece about AIDS'n Literature in the—was it *European?*—a few weeks ago and enjoyed
it very much. It reminded me how well you write; you should
have a regular column somewhere. It will come.

You've never been far from my thoughts; and this evening,
eating and drinking in Fat Anna's, on the verge of sleep, I
started to "feel" you very strongly. And wanted to feel you literally . . . The women here have no style, no glamour—well,
you can imagine. I've found my sexual desire withering almost
to nothing—not at all what one would expect from sea and sun
and swimming *au naturel.* I think New Age is the original Isle of
the Lotus Eaters.

There are about fifty students here altogether, but two-thirds
of them I haven't even spoken to yet and probably never will.
Some of them have gone tramping up a mountain tonight to
look at "holy well of Daphne". . . . Today I cycled with a young
Americans-in-Paris couple, ridiculously in love after six years of
marriage, to a pine wood where Dionysus fucked a nymph. (Local guidebook: "lymph.") Actually it was quite atmospheric.
There are only a couple of couples here; most are divorced, and
desperately hunting. For a partner, but also for some meaning
to life in this post-Christian, post-Communist, post-Socialist,
post-Fascist, Postman Pat, Washington Post, Post Early for
Christmas, world of ours.

So we "facilitators" are supposed to provide it for them. Our
leader or Leda is Elke, a Sumo wrestler from Iceland. At the
other end of the size scale is Ezekiel Morgenstein . . . I almost
need say no more. He teaches Orgasmic Consciousness . . .
Four-foot-tall Canadian Jewish. He's to be joined by his "assistant and lover," by the name of Teresa Bombassoni. He went

110

off to Athens to meet her last night and, after a luxurious and lustful twenty-four hours in a 5-star hotel, was due back here tonight.

Soon after my arrival here I jotted down some descriptive phrases about my fiction students as an *aide memoire* in my notebook, then left it lying around! Odd comments like "boring little fart," "tits like marrows," "Pussy Galore" . . . —not the sort of thing you want them to read! I expected to be lynched, but so far no one's mentioned it. I started with eleven students, but am now down to eight; and hopefully by the end of the fortnight I'll have none. First to drop out was a dimmity widow from the U.S. who quickly decided she'd prefer R. Rendell on Skyros. Very wise decision, I said. Then a youngish woman from New Zealand decided Skagathos was a good place to take an overdose. Everyone thought she was just another bug victim when she didn't turn up for two days . . . It's the first time I've lost a student through suicide. The Greeks aren't interested in neurotic ladies who top themselves on remote islands, and her own family didn't seem terribly interested either, so Skagathos Holidays have been responsible for the funeral arrangements. The local fishermen refused to have a suicide tipped overboard in their waters, as it would bring on a curse; so, this morning, before dawn, we escorted her body to the Acropolis, where the coffin was pitched over. Unfortunately it hit something on the way down and she tumbled out . . . It's all in a day's work at Skagathos. Black humor apart, it's been upsetting, as you can imagine.

My third dropout (pardon the grisly pun), just this evening, has been rather an anticlimax—a Frenchwoman who thought she'd found her truelove but has been sadly disillusioned. I still have one-half of a modern *Anna Karenina,* Natasha from Magnitogorsk, who teaches striptease, and has found a toyboy, Eddie. Eddie and Natasha! Eddie's stripping Russian is the only member of my group who doesn't bathe on the nudist beach!! She's also very bright and well read, and comes out with the occasional theoretical remark quite beyond the others. E.g., we were discussing how one might write about this Lotus island (God forbid!) and she suggested you would use the present tense, in which everything, whether a neck massage or a death, can be related in the same smooth flow. Or words to that effect.

How many of Paul Raymond's bimbos, teaching new girls how to wiggle their asses as they remove their g-strings, would be capable of that! Her Soviet High School taught her well.

Whereas Welsh Emily, bless her heart, didn't learn much in her encounter with Bangor Comprehensive. She greets me with *"Allo!"* like a parrot. She's struck up what may be a platonic friendship with a fellow dyke called Harriet. Harriet was in great distress tonight since she's being plagued by her "co-listener," a mad young guy called Geoff, who follows her even into the loo. I did my good deed by seeing Elke and getting her to do a switch.

Red-faced Angus wears purple cravats and says, "Emily, you must know that delicious aphorism in Gerald de Cambriensis . . ." Making a play for a large and lolloping Luton lass, Caroline, who thought I should maintain firmer boundaries while sticking her sandy asshole in my face. Then there's Harold, a poseur from Hemel Hempstead who's taken to wearing Caroline's elastic-waisted skirt, with brogues and socks. It was when he appeared thus tv'd that Jeanne, his French bird, told me she'd like to quit our workshop . . .

I can hear a few voices. They must be back from their visit to Daph. My room is "above the shop." Everyone's saying "Goodnight," "Goodnight," they're not hanging around. I guess I should go to bed too. You should come here next year and write a piece about it; it would be sensational. Everyone is crazy; even the Greek manager wears *pince-nez,* a gift from an English lord, he says, when he was a steward on a cruise ship. The retsina he serves at meals is watered down, for fear some nut might start killing all the natives. I hope I've compensated, somewhat, for the long silence. It would be good to meet again. I don't forget the delicious fragrance of your skin next to me in bed. I'll give you a ring soon, Carla. Are you still knocking around with that estate agent? Do you still wear that marvelously sexy leather skirt? I couldn't believe you'd picked it up at Oxfam. I can picture it now, the way it clings to your thighs and hips and delightful butt!

Much love,
Simon

Skagathos,
Sporades.

Dear Crystal,

It's three o' the night, in the Sporades, I can't sleep (either because I've drunk too much retsina and Metaxa or because I'm coming down with dysentery), so I've decided to write you one of my sporadic letters. I'm here on a sort of working holiday, teaching New Age people to write fiction. That's to say, teaching them how to unleash their bile on ex-partners and parents, etc., in complete freedom. It's a lovely, peaceful island. While everyone else worships the nymphs Reflexologia and Aromatherapoia, I gaze out to the sea over which Agamemnon's ships sailed to rescue Helen.

Myth has it they collected Achilles from Skyros, then hit a storm the next day, so many of the ships sought a haven in the Bay of Skagathos. Whether that's true or not, it's a very poetic island. Tonight is mild and balmy, and the stars are brilliant. I have my french windows open to the balcony. I think of Thomas Nashe's lines: "Brightness falls from the air, / Queens have died young and fair, / Dust hath closed Helen's eye . . ." And I think too of that wretched scholar who argued (probably correctly, damn him) that it should read "Brightness falls from the hair . . ." Which led me naturally to think of the woman with the most beautiful hair I've ever seen or touched . . . "The downward-burning flame of her rich hair . . ." Know who wrote that? You probably do; I've never met a woman who knows so much poetry by heart as you; and I remember that evening at L'Escargot when we traded quotes for hours. That was truly a magical evening; there couldn't have been a nicer launch.

Talking of *Transplanted Hearts,* one of my students here took me aback by saying he'd bought a remaindered copy of it. Is this true? Surely I would have been told if you planned to remainder it? It seems very soon to be doing that. I'd be disappointed, I must admit.

But enough talk about shop. That's not why I'm writing. I'm writing because—well, you are very much in my thoughts. I'm sorry I've been out of touch, but it's only been for a reason I hope you'll approve: a new novel. How does *Remembering the*

113

Forest strike you as a title? I'm not sure about the title; but at least I think the *novel's* finished. I've sent it to Jim, and will be talking to him about it on my return, next week. So with luck you'll be seeing it soon. Hope you'll like it.

Are you busy? Stupid question! I'm sure you have your fingers crossed your author will win the Booker. I've brought it with me (book not Booker), started reading it on the plane, and was quite enjoying it, but have been lured away by Herodotus. Who is said to have lived on Skagathos briefly. Wonderful stuff, the Histories; they may not have won a big prize, nor even been nominated for one, but they've been around for 2,500 years, so that can't be bad! In any case, the students are very demanding of one's time.

You came into my mind as soon as I met my group, since one of them was called Krystal. A little hunched dry American lady, as different from you as it's possible to be. But I saw your tall, Amazonian form and lustrous hair behind her, like a phantom. And *you* remain, Crystal, whereas Krystal has buggered off to Skyros and Barbara Vine alias Ruth Rendell. Can't blame her.

Will you have lunch with me soon? Better still, dinner? I don't want to have to wait until *Remembering the Forest* is launched! That is, assuming you like it enough to persuade your fellows to make Jim a decent offer for it! Confidentially, Jim has been trying to persuade me I'd get a better deal from another publisher—who shall be nameless; but I've said firmly I'd prefer to stay with you.

Well, I must try to snatch some sleep, as it won't be long before it's dawn. Yesterday I saw the sun rise from the Acropolis; it was stunningly beautiful. Could do with a nap today, but there's a staff meeting in a couple of hours, sod it. You'd think we could be spared staff meetings on a Sunday, wouldn't you?

Reading this through, it's not terribly professional. That's the problem of writing in the middle of the night. I think I'd better fax it to your home!

Love,
Simon

My head bangs, my eyes will scarcely unglue. I listen to, rather than see, white-bearded Fred, old as Chronos, give the *demos* prayers to the New Age gods. A spear carrier once in a local rep performance of *Trojan Women,* he talks about the Greek tragedians, Aeschylus, Sophocles, Euripides. Though their ideas were primitive, in some respects they did anticipate the holistic philosophy. Naturism, for example. He is given a warm clap.

I stumble off to the Lotus Room. Most are here before me, the circle two-thirds complete. Elke bows to me from her yoga position. As I subside to the floor her eyes glance around the circle yet home in again on me: "Simon, you look pale and tired. I hope you're not coming down with this terrible bug."

"I don't feel great. I haven't slept much. Fat Anna's didn't agree with me last night."

A fleeting, sympathetic Icelandic smile. "Take it easy today. You must not carry everyone's burden; but thank you for telling me about Harriet's problem." She explains for the others who Harriet is, and how she was being plagued by Geoff. So she's done some general switching round, to avoid hurting Geoff, who was already in a bad enough mental state. She's put Geoff with Eddie, one of her Art students, who's very pleasant and well balanced—and besides, she's noticed that Eddie and Natasha are attracted to each other, which is not good for co-listening.

She explains, for three or four, who Eddie is. A real hunk. Looks like Superman. Elke's eyes are alight. She has placed Natasha, she says, with Priscilla, the high-powered professor of English from some American university. Priscilla, whom everyone knows because she is constantly complaining at the *demos,* was with Krystal but lost her; Elke had tried to give her Fred —Fred the expert on the primitive Greek dramatists, such a delightful old man—but Priscilla refused to co-listen with a male.

"Well," says Elke, "now she can't complain; she has a very glamorous Russian woman. End of Cold War."

She asks me how Natasha is managing in the Fiction Workshop. I say she's doing wonderfully; writes vividly even in English. She's not a problem like Pasha then, says Elke; no one knows what to do with Pasha. He comes momentarily alive at night, when he brings out his violin; but his sad tunes, often interrupting something merry, make everyone depressed.

115

The door opens, and Ezekiel enters, followed by a nervously smiling shaven-headed woman in a lacy white blouse and a colorful swirling skirt. "We're sorry we're late," Ezekiel says. "I'm afraid we slept in. The plane from Athens to Skyros was delayed and we had to hire a private boat to bring us across. This is Teresa."

We murmur and smile our welcome. The couple sink onto a mat near the door. Elke introduces us one by one, and says how glad she is to have her with us.

"I'm very pleased to be here," she says quietly, melodiously. "It's my first time in Greece, or even in Europe, and I'm very excited. I'll try to do my best."

She continues to smile. Her teeth so ice-white, her cheeks are rosy, her eyes a brilliant blue. I'm somewhat taken aback by her pleasantness, even more than by her bald head. She has spoken unaffectedly. I had expected a monster of egotism—perhaps partly because of the closeness of Bombassoni to bombastic—but she seems, in her freshness, very solid and real.

I'm not sure if she's plain or attractive.

While I'm debating this, Elke is filling Ezekiel in on the switches in the co-listening program. Ezekiel resonates with all the changes. Elke asks Teresa if she knows about co-listening, and if she'd like to join in. Yes, says Teresa: very much. "I've told her," says Ezekiel, "how much I've gained from having Brenda as a co-listener. As you know, I've had problems. I don't think I'd have coped if it weren't for all of you; and particularly Brenda. I'm looking forward to going on with it when hopefully she's feeling better."

"Yes, poor Brenda is not at all well . . . We'll have to find you someone, Teresa," Elke says. "Is there anyone . . . ?"

I keep my head down. They're aware I'm the only facilitator without a co-listener. I still don't like the idea of such naked contact; yet this woman seems very sweet, very shy, and I get the feeling she'd rather like me to volunteer. I raise my head and say, "I don't think I'd be very good at exposing myself, but . . ."

Ezekiel says in a croaky voice, "I'd take that as a yes, Teresa, if I were you."

"Would you, Simon?"

"I'm willing to give it a try."

"Thank you! I appreciate it."

Elke moves us on to domestic matters. Peter and Sue and Tamsin are thanked for managing so well during the water shut off; and Maria for her work. I look at the squatting Greek woman, who seems as exhausted as I. What an existence! All that shit! Stephanos, standing by the door, thanks us all for dealing with the Lucinda problem so professionally. He is going to send photographs of the Skagathos Centre and the Acropolis to Lucinda's sister in Dunedin. Elke thanks him for handling it so well, despite the unfortunate occurrence at the end. It was not his fault, we all agree.

"Thank you. One other thing; Dr. Sklaniatos has found she died by natural causes. A heart attack." His eyes shift away from looking at us. "It's good because—well, it makes it less bureaucratic than if it is suicide. You understand, I hope."

"We understand," Elke says, glancing round at us. "It's best. What does it matter?"

"Thank you."

There remains this evening's memorial to discuss. Elspeth, who also looks rather grey and tired this morning, having risen before dawn again to go to church, says she would like to sing a Polynesian rebirth chant, if we approve. I tell them my group has prepared a reading of work inspired by, and in fact begun by, Lucinda.

"And Teresa has some ritual shamanic bereavement work that should help," murmurs Ezekiel, glancing aside at his assistant and lover. "We used it with a grieving family in Vermont this spring; they'd lost their two sons in a fire; it went well."

"It seemed to help them a lot," Teresa confirms, glancing round, seeking personal eye contact with everyone—and perhaps especially with me, her co-listener—wishing to reassure.

"And the *oekos* groups are helpful too," Stephanos says. "They seem to be going well?" He glances round for confirmation, and receives it through nods and murmurs. The *oekos* groups take place mostly during our staff meetings and after lunch; they are family groupings, huddles of five or six people of different ages, who sort themselves out into father, mother, grandfather, son, daughter, etc. I have seen them at work only briefly, but they have looked very intense, very solemn, sitting or squatting in a ring, talking, talking, talking. Crying sometimes. Shouting sometimes. I have seen Angus shouting abuse at a frightened young nurse, his temporary mother. Then hugging, rocking, weeping.

"So—I think that's all." Elke slowly straightens her back and arches her spine, at the same time pushing out her vast stomach and pendulous bosom. "And tomorrow we start our workshops again. I'm looking forward to it. I hope we can put all this week's problems behind us, and not have any more disasters." Her round, sleek face swings slowly around the circle and back. "Now it's time for a little gossip . . . Who is fucking who?"

TWO

An Offensive
John

A yearning to go again into the flat interior, to the wood of Aura; I hire a bike and go alone. Beyond the central plain, on the horizon, the arid mountain peak, up to which my predecessor led his group, including seventy-year-old old ladies. I rest in stillness, my back against a pine, drinking Coke.

Thinking that if Brooke hadn't died of blood poisoning, perhaps the whole course of history might have shifted. Locally, at least. His regiment might have been ordered to stay in the Sporades, guarding it from the Turks. They might have turned Skyros and Skagathos into another, hotter England.

Here, on this plain, they could have planted grass and made a cricket pitch. I can see a Greek batsman hitting out rustically, and Brooke, his golden hair flying, speeding like the wind around the boundary, gathering in the ball, sending it winging into the gloves of Colonel Quilter, the wicket keeper. "Howzat!" The umpire's finger goes up. Out! The dark-eyed, bewitching Greek maidens clap their handsome English hero, Brooke.

D. M. Thomas

And with Shaw-Stewart, Brooke carves an innings of polished perfection, just thirty or forty, nothing so vulgar as a long innings; a jeweled cameo to win the game. Sergeant Saunders, the good yeoman, was with him at the death. Ten to make and the last man in. "Well played, Brooke!"

Afterwards to the country pub. Good foaming ale, and a singsong around the piano, Asquith playing. The good old-fashioned, sentimental, moral songs—"The Holy City," "The Lost Chord," "Pale hands I loved . . ."

I can hear and see Quilter and Shaw-Stewart, tenor and baritone, each with an arm round the shoulders of a smiling Greek island maiden, singing the plangent refrain of "Pale hands I loved Beside the Shalimar," and suddenly an intense grief wells up in me. I weep, I sob, here in the fierce midday light, the Greek stillness; tears run down my cheeks and I see one splash close to a tiny green lizard flickering its tongue near my shoe. I'm thinking of "half the youth of Europe" wiped out; particularly those of my own race, those brave, intelligent young men who could have provided us with leadership and good sense, and fathered children of the same bright intelligence. And I seem to be grieving for every single one; each one had his wife or sweetheart, or the possibility of such, "beside the Shalimar," even if the Shalimar was a shallow, quiet English stream.

All civilization, harmony, culture, sense, reason, hurled into the abyss, like a rag doll falling, falling, into the sea. Damn them, the politicians, monarchs, generals! I go on weeping, more gently.

* * *

Teresa and I are sitting on the Calypso terrace, in the late afternoon. It's cooler; a faint, pleasant breeze blows, ruffling the washing on the line. We sit facing each other; she has taken my hands in hers.

"There's no need to be nervous, Simon."

"How do we do this? How long do we each speak for? I know we're not supposed to interrupt each other."

"I guess we speak for as long as we want. Just relax." She gives my hands a slight squeeze. Her incredibly blue and dancing eyes are kind.

120

"You start, Teresa."

"Okay." She sighs, not in sadness but in pleasure, it seems. "I feel very happy. Very good about myself. And it's the first time in my life, perhaps, I can say that. I grew up in Mississauga Ontario, a sprawling industrial suburb of Toronto; my family are decent working-class people. I tried always to be good. To be a good girl, you know? Then I got married and tried to be a good wife. I had a little girl, and tried to be a good mother. Well, I *was*, I am, a good mother." She nods, and I nod and smile back. "But it was really just a sham, I was a shell, and five years ago I had the courage to leave my husband. It was very, very painful, of course. I started to do this work, and I found I could be good at it and help people. I set up a shamanic center in Taos. That's how I met Ezekiel—he came to do his orgasmic workshop. Well, just over a year ago I found I had cancer." She lowers her shorn head, almost in shame. "I thought I was going to die. But I had an operation followed by chemotherapy, and now it's gone. I'm completely cured. I'm sure of it." She looks me defiantly in the eyes, and I squeeze her hands again and smile.

"And now I have so much energy, Simon! You can't imagine how much energy! I feel myself exploding with it! I'm very happy to be on a Greek island, and to be meeting you and the others; and I'm really looking forward to the workshop. I think I have a lot to give. Sex is such a wonderful gift, and I never knew it until recently! The sex with Ezekiel is very good; very very good; but it's like a stone dropped in a pond, it spreads ripple after ripple after ripple outwards? You know?" I nod.

"It feels real good to see him again. He's worried about his children in Vancouver. I've made it clear I don't want him to leave his wife because of me. If he wants to leave her, that's fine, but not for me. And I've told him I'm not sure I want to enter a restrictive relationship again so quickly after my divorce. I'd rather we meet as we do, and see how things go. Take things easy; enjoy each other." Her eyes, in which I can see innumerable shades of blue, hold on mine. "Well, that's all I have to say. I'm just very happy to be here, to feel so alive, to have so much love to give—even to the stones under my feet. I'm happy to help in Ezekiel's workshop, even though it's not my specialty;

maybe I can do some shamanism as an extra? Do you think they'd like that?"

Our hands part; she leans back, relaxes, closes her eyes, feeling the sun on her face.

"Now it's your turn," she says, leaning forward and taking my hands.

"Well, Teresa," I start, speaking slowly and uncertainly, "I'm fairly happy too. I'm certainly happy to be here with you. I've—well, I've messed up a lot of things. Couple of marriages went down the drain. My children are scattered, I don't see them much. Alison, the eldest, I haven't seen for five years; she lives in Hong Kong with her husband, who's Chinese. Alison's tall, blonde and cool, like her mother. The other two, Sonia and Niamh, never quite forgave me for hurting their mum. They're more Irish than English, very republican, and that's caused rows too. So we're not as close as I'd like."

Niamh's lilting voice, reciting Yeats at her comprehensive speech day, invades my mind . . . "And no more turn aside and brood / Upon love's bitter mystery . . ." I feel my fingers tremble. She squeezes them, and smiles sympathetically.

"My present marriage is . . . okay; more than okay. I love Marie. She's South African, quite a bit younger than me. She was working in accounts at the BBC when I was there, and she was living with my department boss. It caused rather a scandal when she left him for me. She was given the push, and took an admin job at Marlborough School—which is very public school. It was all she could get and we needed the money. Later I managed to get a part-time job there teaching English; which is a bloody nuisance as far as my writing is concerned, but we couldn't get by without it. And they're quite decent about time off. I brought my father to live near us, and he's quite ill, so we're rather stuck. It's terribly quiet. I get away more than my wife does. And she also regrets never having been able to have a child. I'm quite glad she can't—which of course makes me feel guilty."

I stop; look out at the vague, hazy sea, the sun declining. Helen, Menelaus, Agamemnon. " 'And see the great Achilles, whom we knew . . .' "

"I'm glad to be here. My student's suicide has cast a big

shadow; however, Skagathos is beautiful, and I've got a nice group. They moan a lot, but . . . They write pretty well, as I think you'll hear tonight. So—yes, I'm pretty happy."

I release her, and straighten on my chair. She says, "Thank you!"

"I didn't say much." And yet more than I intended.

"It was fine. We have all week. I'm so glad there's a writer here. I'd love to be able to write. I wish I could be in your workshop."

"And I'd like to be in the Orgasmic Consciousness workshop."

"It's a shame we couldn't put our groups together."

We stand and move into a hug. I touch her skull, its downy veil of hair. "It's starting to grow back," she says.

We walk down the path together. She spots Ezekiel sitting with a student, and we smile goodbye. I evade the stalking ex-cop from Moscow and head for the kitchen, where Stephanos, a mug in his hands, steps up to me. "A fax came for you, Simon. I'll get it."

As the kettle begins to boil he returns and holds out the fax. I recognize Carla's smudgy type. It's only six hours since I faxed her my drunken midnight letter. "Jesus!" I exclaim. "This was quick! This is the speed of the gods, Stephanos!"

"Yes—if Odysseus had had a fax machine he'd have had no problem with Penelope!"

* * *

I take the mug of coffee and the fax up to my room, sprawl on the bed, and read:

Herne Hill,
London.
September 16

My dear Simon,

What a lovely surprise! I was just wondering whether I could be bothered to go out in the rain to get my *Sunday Times* (and I'm hungover too) when your missive came clunking through. Am green with envy at your luck—but just in case you really are as pissed off as you sound I thought I'd lose no time in replying.

Not that you deserve it, you miserable sod! You might at least have sent me a birthday card!

I've done almost no work on the novel this past year, have had too many things on my mind. It's moldering in a drawer. I'm glad you liked the AIDS piece—*Indy* not *European,* by the way, but paying just as badly—I was pleased with it because it made me feel I could still write a bit. The only other thing I've had published was a small travel piece I managed to get taken by the *Ham & High.* I think the editor, who I know slightly, took pity on me because of my Oxfam clothes!

Not my leather skirt, I couldn't get into it at the time. Still can't, actually, though I might be able to in a few weeks. I found out just before last Christmas I was pregnant. Not a nice surprise . . . I thought you might've twigged from the Nativity and my somewhat ironic comment; tho', thinking about it, I probably made it too subtle in case your wife looked at it. Anyway, panic, suicidal despair—no, not quite, it was more my mum who came closer to being chucked off a cliff (that was amazing! Still can't quite believe you!). I wouldn't tell Mum and Dad who the father was, and they wanted me to have an abortion, but I wouldn't. I figured, what the hell, I'm 32, don't look like "settling down" with someone, so why not?

My estate agent did a quick disappearing act when he found out I was pregnant. I could have pretended it was his, and I'm sure he'd have done the honorable thing; but I knew it wasn't his, there was no chance of that. Besides, I couldn't imagine *living* with Adrian.

Nadine Anne was born three months ago, 6lb, and she's adorable. I really love having her, but of course everything else in one's life goes to pot. Fortunately Jan, my sister, is sharing the flat with me; which helps financially, and suits her while she's waiting for her divorce settlement; she's very good with Nadine. Think you met her at that Groucho do, didn't you? She never knew about us, so I'm glad she was staying over at her boyfriend's last night. She'd have started to smell a rat if she'd read your letter. It's not her business. It never even crossed my mind to want to involve you, Simon. You have your own life and having Nadine was my decision. Could've made you wear a condom, that last visit, but I hate the damn things and we were

124

both pretty pissed, so there it is. It would be the last thing I'd want, to involve you, and I'd never willingly do it.

Shit! she's woken up and is bawling. Here we go again! A change of mouths wouldn't be bad! Actually I think she's quite like you around the mouth and chin. Sorry! It would be lovely to meet—if you still want to, that is. I wouldn't blame you if you didn't. But if you do, please give me a ring. You never know, I might even be able to struggle into my leather skirt by the time we next meet—tho' can't see myself ever again getting into the red basque! Think I'd better take it to Oxfam!

Much love,
Carla
xxx

Carla's fax has blurred a shade after six Metaxas. London is a long way away. Compared with death, a child's birth is not so bad. And Carla doesn't appear to want to involve me. Well, she's proved that already. Gradually I've come back to life, like an arm one has slept on all night.

Softglowing lanterns in wall niches and spotlights above the trees blot out the stars and cast a quasi-romantic glow on the diners. Despite, or maybe because of, a somber event being imminent, there is an unusually cheerful buzz of conversation, and even the occasional laugh—notably Angus's. Normally the mood in the evening is sober and tranquilized; if the Skagathos students had been the oarsmen of Odysseus, he would not have needed to make them stuff their ears with wax, passing the island of the Sirens. With some obvious exceptions their libidos generally seem low; our response to Elke's laconic inquiry "Who's fucking who?" was "We don't think many are."

But this evening it's a shade more lively. Even Pasha's eyes are sparkling as he attempts to converse with Caroline. Fewer people seem to be absent, suffering from the bug (I notice Brenda, though she looks pale and haggard); the retsina seems stronger than usual; also a lot of people have made some minimal effort with their appearance. A few smudges of lipstick have appeared. And so people are looking at others sitting at their table with a new interest, and feel more attractive themselves.

125

The food is a little better too. Squeals of delight greet Peter's carrot cake, being sliced up by Sue on the serving table, since usually there is only one course. There is even some meat for the dozen or so carnivores: admittedly an indeterminate meat, white, fairly tasteless. John, by whom I'm sitting, making an effort to talk to him, startles us by saying, out of the blue, "Are we eating Lucinda, d'ye think?" Emily squeaks, "John! That's *awful!*" but most of us laugh. The old boy immediately apologizes; but Harold points out that it's an understandable question, since poor Lucinda appears to have simply vanished.

Most of my writing group are sitting near me, since they wish to consult me on what they're going to be reading later at the "celebration." It would take hours to read all the Nat-Mildred-Agnes material, so they've had to select. Harold has chosen just a single paragraph, which he refers to as a "Nat-byte;" but is easily persuaded to make it three pages.

After we have doused our plates in the three washing-up bowls, the relative animation dies down. Noting the more muted atmosphere Stephanos rises, claps for silence, and introduces Teresa. She stands up to identify herself. She looks flushed—even allowing for the colored lights—and radiant. In turning round to smile at everyone, she catches my eye, and I glimpse, or imagine, a special greeting, an acknowledgment of closeness. We are co-listeners.

However, I notice that Ezekiel, beside her, is unsmiling and indeed looks decidedly morose.

He's not up to her, of course, and doesn't deserve her.

* * *

Candlelight and incense. Forty or fifty people crowded into the Lotus Room, sitting in yoga posture on the mats around a central space. Elspeth has begun our celebration of Lucinda with some moonlighty music on tape and a waft of fluttery dance. When the music finishes she asks us to turn to face our neighbor. I'm face to face with a brown-haired, scrawny woman in a white vest and blue shorts. "If you have never spoken to each other," Elspeth gently orders, "introduce yourselves."

"I'm Simon."

"I'm Rhona."

Elspeth asks us to lean towards each other till our foreheads are touching; close our eyes; draw strength from each other, and let that strength and love flow towards the dead woman.

I feel the scrawny woman's warm breath. I think of Lucinda, straight-backed, tapping on her laptop, then, of her tumbling out of the breaking coffin. We hear Elspeth's sweet voice sing what I presume is the promised Polynesian rebirth chant.

"Okay," she murmurs, after the song has died away; "lean back from each other, turn to face the center again, but don't open your eyes. I'm handing over to Ezekiel."

I hear Ezekiel say, equally gently, "Go on concentrating; feel more and more love for Lucinda well up in you. It's a very beautiful feeling."

My eyes flutter open and glance round. Everyone is loving Lucinda. Angus's red face is tilted back, seraphic, his mouth open. "She trusted us," Ezekiel continues, "she chose this group to share in her death. That must be the greatest tribute anyone can give to others. Focus your thoughts deeply on her . . ." I close my eyes again. "Feel yourself to be her. You are she, you are Lucinda . . . Open your eyes now. Smile; feel joy for Lucinda!"

We open our eyes, stretch, smile, are joyful.

"Weep now for the people she has had to leave behind."

An unknown woman gives a sob behind me.

"Now Teresa will take over."

Teresa rises, girlish in a short white cotton dress, willowy and graceful as a flame, from where she has been hidden in the crowd, and steps carefully through to the central space. She lowers herself beside Ezekiel; smiles around at everyone. She asks for people at the back, near the candles, to blow out all but one of them. As the room is plunged into shadows, she takes the small tape recorder from Elspeth and pushes in a tape. We hear the softly droning OM of a chanted mantra.

Ezekiel glances aside at her; she nods. He pulls off his T-shirt, slides down his shorts and removes them; he squats again, naked. His arms are folded.

Teresa addresses us above the droning OM: "We are going to help Lucinda into the next stage of existence. Nature is always balanced; just as we are born out of the mother we have to die

into the father. An ethnic American from New Mexico, my shaman guide, taught me that. There's only one hole, correspond-
ing to a woman's vagina, that we can vanish into. The anus, the
butt hole, asshole, heini, tush, twinkie, can, Hershey Highway,
poop shoot, chocolate alley." I attend entranced, as does everyone in sight of me. Never have I heard such vulgar words spoken with such pure spiritual sweetness. They might be from St.
John's Gospel. And she goes on, as if recalling some she forgot:
"Bung, bung-hole, fanny-hole, rump-hole, back door, shitter.
We have so many terms, often crude ones, for the anus because
we see it as something shameful. Like death. Okay, Ezekiel."

He turns into a kneeling position, his bottom raised—presented, as it were. Somewhat to my relief, he is facing me. The
faces of those his ass faces are expressionless masks. He rotates
his buttocks rhythmically. At this crucial moment I hear a voice
over my shoulder saying, *"Pozhal'sto"*—"Please," with an almost simultaneous camera flash. There are murmurs of distaste,
and Teresa herself looks horrified. It's hard to tell what Ezekiel
is feeling, since only his ass is exposed to me; and indeed to
Pasha. I say, addressing Teresa, "He doesn't fully understand;
photography is all he's able to do here, basically; he thought he
was coming to a luxury hotel."

"Okay, but no more."

"Dostatochno—enough!" I say to Pasha, and he nods.
"Spasibo!"

Gathering concentration again, Teresa takes a deep breath
and goes on: "We must help Lucinda through into the world we
call death, which is only life turned inside-out. Will her to pass
through that narrow channel which Ezekiel is symbolising. Talk
to her! Tell her to go through. As vulgarly as you like—only
funeral homes are genteel."

We start to gabble. "Go through, Lucinda!" "You can do it,
Lucinda!" "Through his butt hole!" and similar urgings. I'm
aware of absurdity, yet Teresa's passion and beauty seem somehow to overcome that, turn it into a genuine ritual. Her own
legs are open, she strains back, eyes closed; her shortie dress
has ridden up so that the gusset of thin white panties is visible.
"Louder!" she commands us. Ezekiel, writhing, starts to moan.
Our voices rise to a shriek, while the mantra continues with its

undertone. We're off our haunches, shouting at the spirit trying (it's obvious from Ezckiel's screaming) to get through, get inside.

Ezekiel springs up, and flings his arms about, screaming, "She's through! She's through!" He collapses groaning onto the parquet.

"Stop! Relax!" orders Teresa, signaling with her arms for us to subside. She fades the music to silence. Ezekiel turns his body over and squats normally, breathing heavily. Stillness takes over the Lotus Room completely.

After that long silence Ezekiel glances in my direction and says, "Simon, I think we're ready for your group."

I glance around at my people. They are all shaking their heads. Caroline says, "That was so powerful; I don't feel we should change the mood."

"I agree," says Angus.

"Let's call a halt there," I confirm. "She's through; she's at peace."

"Yes, she sure is," Ezekiel exclaims.

He looks exhausted. Teresa lays a hand on his thigh. "Are you okay?"

"I guess."

THREE

A Dark Liberal

At *demos,* on another glorious morning, everyone is full of praise for Teresa, Ezekiel and Elspeth; voice after voice praises them for their lifting of the gloomy mood.

Priscilla, the American academic, unexpectedly sours the atmosphere, It has come to her attention, she says, that John made a joke at dinner about our eating Lucinda. She thinks it was an unspeakable lapse of taste. Two or three others support her. It's such a shock that John is left gobbling, unable to say a word in his defense; nor, to our shame, do we who heard him say it, and who know it was a—most unexpected and somewhat tasteless—joke. The harsh attack reduces all of us to silence.

Skagathos,

My dear Carla,

You could knock me down with a nursing bra! I was surprised of course—and also moved—to hear about Nadine Ann. I'm sure you'll make a wonderful mother. I always knew you were tremendously brave. If she grows up to be anything like her mother, she will be a star.

I can't remember, Carla, if I asked you to keep the Lucinda business to yourself. The point is, she officially died of natural causes . . . I know I can trust you absolutely not to tell any-one.

It's fearfully hot. Must go and cool off in the Aegean. Look after yourself, Carla. I'll see you.

Love,
Simon

Before taking it to the office for Stephanos to fax it, I scan it three or four times. Carla will know, from the word "moved," what I really intend to say; and that the jokiness of the opening sentence is a smokescreen in case Jan, her sister, gets to the incoming fax first. Tricky though the situation is, my needing to be discreet—and her knowing it—is a boon.

"We've both had lovers," I say to Teresa, as we sit on a wooden bench on the sea front. She is wearing a beach robe and sun hat; I can't imagine any Nereid sparkling more freshly than she does after swimming. She holds my hand, her lips are parted in a permanent smile and her eyes don't leave mine for a moment. I feel her concern and love pouring into me more intensely than the late-afternoon sun.

"We've always agreed we wouldn't necessarily be totally faith-ful. When I rang the other afternoon, I suddenly heard the click of a lighter—and Marie doesn't smoke! She had some young chap there and they were in bed. Well, it didn't matter. Though earlier this summer she was seeing a very close friend of ours, Alan, who's a fellow teacher; and that rather hurt me. I like him, he's not stuffy like most of the staff. We go to football matches together and have a pint after. He's divorced; his two kids live with his ex-wife in Italy. I knew Marie liked him, and that they flirted a bit, but I never thought they were having an affair."

Her hand tightens, she nods slightly, her smile unchanging. I look away, towards the beach and the sea. Ezekiel and Brenda, nude, squat, facing each other not far away; Ezekiel is talking earnestly. He became ill last night from a slight recurrence of the dysentery. Not surprising, in view of his anal exhibitionism. Brenda, her aged breasts drooping, looks better for her after-noon in the sun. A little farther off Natasha's leonine form (she and her toyboy Eddie appeared on this beach for the first time yesterday) is partly hidden from view by the thin, spiny back of Priscilla. The severe American academic is speaking, her head jerking forward to emphasize a point, and the feisty and beautiful Russian quiz-show winner nods. Eddie is listening to mad, spiky-haired Geoff; and Elke to Elspeth. Meager, floaty-haired Elspeth looks as if she could be engulfed at any moment by the woman-mammoth.

I look back into the dazzling blue eyes, pure as the Greek sky and sea. "Well, she finished with him; he was getting too serious. She's very honest—she told me, even though there was no need to. I've felt embarrassed to meet him, though. I backed out of the first couple of football matches of the autumn. But I'll have to put that behind me when I get back. It's stupid. He's had her, he knows her body intimately—well, so what?"

I picture Alan, taller than I; sports jacket, white shirt and MCC tie; quizzical smile. "In fact I think I might ring him from here. Just to say, Look I know about it and it doesn't make any difference. Yes, I think I will."

The intense blue gaze, the glimpse of dazzling transatlantic dentistry, the squeeze of the hands.

"I had another shock just a couple of days ago. I sent a fax to an old flame of mine called Carla, and she replied at once telling me she had my baby. Carla's early thirties, unmarried, a would-be writer; gets by with occasional journalism. She's very nice. Sort of beehive for hair—black and frizzy—wide, generous mouth, and a good figure. We'd see each other about every two or three months, for dinner and sex; she had other relationships. A lighthearted, sexy friendship; then suddenly you hear—you gave her a baby."

Brenda has started to neckmassage Ezekiel, her scrawny breasts swinging over him. It was crass of me—sheer nerves—to start my letter to Carla with "You could knock me down with a nursing bra!" And *will* she realise why I sound so unfeeling? Shouldn't have given it to Stephanos to send off so quickly. I'd be hopping mad if I were her, reading that. No one is swimming anymore.

"I don't know whether I should see her, Teresa. Them. I think Carla does like me quite a lot. She hadn't made any attempt to contact me; even though she's not at all well off." I sigh. "And that's another thing: nowadays if you're a single mother on welfare you have to name the father. I could have a letter falling through our letterbox, any time. Saying, Pay up! The CSA— Child Support Agency—keep screwing up and demanding impossible sums from men. Some have even been driven to suicide. So that's a worry. My books don't make a lot of money, and between the two of us, both working part-time, we earn just one half-decent salary."

Not far from us Pasha, in his blue short-sleeved shirt and flapping grey trousers, his face red and peeling, plows through the thick sand with his camera. He has been photographing bathers while pretending to focus on a distant cliff. He stumbles, almost falls, and utters a Russian curse.

"Life is not so easy as to cross a beach," I say to Teresa, misquoting a Russian proverb. "I started to think, just now, while I was swimming, Marie would probably love to take over that baby if she knew about it. I think I told you, she can't have children of her own. She thinks it's my fault, but I've never had any trouble making women pregnant. Quite the reverse!"

Elke has straddled Elspeth, as if for coition; but it's to massage her back.

"I've never talked to anyone as openly, Teresa."

"That's good!"

"I do feel I can talk to you. I've always thought psychotherapy was crap; but I know I can trust you."

"I feel the same." She squeezes my hand.

"I need to get something off my chest. I don't know how to say it. I may have been responsible for Lucinda's suicide." Her smile flickers like a torch whose battery's fading. "Or at least been the last straw for her. I was the last person to see her alive. We'd had a meal in the village; I tried to—grope her, but she fobbed me off. Unfortunately I tried again, and she got angry. I didn't even particularly *want* to take it further; but sometimes you do it because you think they'd like you to. Anyway, I shouldn't have done it. It's hardly rape, but she'd made it clear she didn't want to be touched and I ignored that. She left a short message on her laptop computer, 'I can't take any more.'

Maybe she'd been abused, and she thought she could trust her writing tutor, her *facilitator*. I haven't had the courage to tell anyone about it, Teresa. No one knows we kissed, or anything. Isn't that awful?"

Her smile is firm again, the eyes gently compassionate. She shakes her shorn head.

"Well, I feel better for telling you."

* * *

"Yesterday," she says, when I am holding *her* hand reassuringly and smiling into *her* eyes, "I felt nervous and shy. I was worried about how last night would go; although I've done the anal rebirth ritual with Baptists and Mormons, and they've reacted positively, I couldn't be sure everyone here would understand what I was doing. You know, it could look kind of dirty. And I was worried about fitting in with Ezekiel in the workshop. But today—I feel *great!*" Her eyes, which already seemed large and brilliant, widen and radiate blue light even more spectacularly. Nodding, smiling, squeezing her hand, I find my whole self being drawn into those pure and joyous pupils.

"The people last night were just terrific, they saw it was something good and pure and needful. And this morning we had a wonderful workshop. I really like the participants; and I think they valued having someone new, with perhaps a slightly different approach. Ezekiel's a great therapist, but he admits he wasn't in top form last week, because of his sickness and his worry. I was able to *give* them something, Simon. Do you know Danny?" I nod. "He's splendid. He was so grateful. He had his first *real* orgasm this morning! In his whole life! Because, you know, he's orgasmed superficially, not from the root." She presses her hand into her groin illustratively. "It has to come from there, for a man, and it so seldom does. And it did for him this morning. Not from actual sex, of course, nor from touching, just from the music and the right breathing. And the sense deprivation.

"It's quite frightening for them. And sometimes they have a bowel movement, which is kind of embarrassing for them at first, though later they realize it's a great liberation to have done it in public. It took Danny three hours before he orgasmed. That's why you get the screaming sometimes—I hope we didn't disturb anybody. Now I've got to teach him to use it in actual sex with his wife; and I can do that."

She looks aside, gazing at Ezekiel and Brenda, then at the dimming sea beyond. I keep my gaze steady on her. She faces me again, radiant, and exclaims: "But for myself, I don't feel I need to orgasm, Simon! I feel I'm having one all the time. Just from looking at the sea, feeling the ground warm under my feet . . . And from feeling free! For the first time in my life; feeling I can go anywhere, do anything."

This time I follow her straying gaze; and see that Ezekiel and Brenda, and Elke and Elspeth, have ended their co-listening. They have stood up; the two couples drift towards each other. Ezekiel's pubic hair is, by the way, in contrast to the rest of his hair, almost black. Also by the way—it seems appropriate to say it now, since Teresa's beach robe has parted at the top and one of her breasts is visible—her breasts are deep and firm but too narrow. I could imagine my hand being almost able to surround one of her breasts. A slight imperfection.

We are facing each other again, and her smile has dimmed. "I just wish Ezekiel shared my feeling of freedom. Of course I can understand his anguish over leaving his wife and children. And he has a very Jewish conscience. He got sick here because of his conscience, not a virus. We create our own illnesses. But I'm trying to teach him to loosen up. It's very hard for him to do that. Apparently his mother, who was—what do they call it, a Gentile—Polish—was more fun; but she died when Ezekiel was just a boy. I've seen photos of her, he gets his blond hair from her, I think maybe he's looking for her again in me. He's all screwed up, tight as a knot, I hope I can find a way to help him."

Her smile comes back. "But, like I say, I feel great! And it's wonderful being able to talk to you like this. I feel a lot of concern, a lot of goodness, a lot of power, flowing from you."

"And I from you, Teresa."

"Thank you."

I release her hand, and we move into a hug. I feel the shape of her skull against my cheek. We let go. Elke and Ezekiel are walking up the beach towards us. Teresa, standing up, moves into a hug with her lover. Elke, with a seismic vibration of breasts, flops onto the bench beside me. She tells me she's bothered about my student John. He was obviously very upset at the *demos.* I say yes, he was. Elke says we need to explain to him better, make him see no one was getting at him personally. Priscilla has suggested we form a small group to talk with him, and she, Elspeth, Brenda and Ezekiel, think it's a good idea. Ezekiel nods and says, "Clear the air, share our thoughts with each other."

"It's fine by me. As long as John's agreeable."

"Of course," says Elke. "He went to the taverna; I'll go and talk to him. We could have it later, about six. I've invited Priscilla and Arnold, to represent those who were angry and concerned this morning; and perhaps you, I and Ezekiel could represent the staff."

"Fine."

"He's a very nice old man and I hate to think of him being so upset through misunderstanding the comments this morning."

"He's a grand old guy," Ezekiel echoes. "Tough. Fought in Burma, he told me, in the war. Yorkshireman; my dad was a pilot stationed in Yorkshire." He strokes his handlebar mustache reflectively. "I wouldn't want John upset; just a friendly chat."

* * *

On my bed in the late afternoon, thinking of Carla, then of Marie. How she broke the news to me about Alan. The scene is recorded in my black notebook. We'd driven home from a wedding in London one Saturday in July. An ex-colleague of mine at the BBC had married his fourth wife, his second young secretary-bride.

We made love, inspired by the romantic occasion perhaps. We hadn't for a while. Partly because I write late into the night. Anyway, after twelve years, and in one's fifties . . . Though she's still terribly attractive. Keeps herself in shape by jogging and working out in the College gym (Ladies' hour, 7–8 on Fridays . . .) She thinks she's a wrinkled old has-been, of course.

Wants to cut her long golden hair off, though I've persuaded her not to.

I stroked that hair when I came back from taking a shower. She had picked up a book and was reading it, a biography of Alan Paton, the South African novelist. Marie herself got into trouble not long after she'd been crowned Miss Natal: took a black lover. Would probably have been jailed if she'd not been so well known. They let her take a plane out to England.

"This book is disturbing," she said, accepting a joint that I'd rolled. "Paton liked thrashing school kids. He looked so kindly and gentle when he came to our school prize-giving day." She closed the book decisively. "I don't want to read anymore."

"A great liberal is bound to have an area of darkness," I said rather pompously. She drew in the joint, her eyes closed, and handed it back. I said, *"Cry, the Beloved Country* was a good title. Memorable. I'm torn, at the moment, between *Infidelity* and *Remembering the Forest."*

"I've finished with Alan," she said, her eyes still closed.

I absorbed that for a few moments. Somehow, just by the way she uttered the name, I knew she meant our friend, not Paton. It took me a shade longer to work out the implications of *finished with.* "I didn't know there was anything to finish."

"I thought it would have been obvious, since I'm hopeless at lying."

"Well, it wasn't."

"I thought I was dropping clues all over the place."

"Not that I noticed."

"You don't notice anything." Tartly. "It doesn't matter now; it's over."

"How long did it go on for?"

"A few months. Not long."

"Is he a good lover?"

"Not bad."

"Why did you finish?"

Marie shrugged. "He was getting too serious. And he was drawing me in too deep as well. It was getting dangerous."

"Then I'm glad it's over, darling." I stroked her soft and slender arm, and wound a strand of hair around her breast. We don't, as I said to Teresa, make a fetish of fidelity. Indeed, when she drove me to the station for this trip, she asked if I'd packed condoms. No, I said, of course I wouldn't need any; but she made me promise to buy some, saying, quite rightly, "You never know."

I drowse for a while. When I wake I can hear the faint voices of Elke and Ezekiel, out on the terrace. I remember we have to reassure old John.

* * *

"It wor nobbut a bit of fun." The old Burma warrior removes his glasses to rub his eyes.

Elke has provided a bottle of retsina to ease the tension. In the background, from a natural amphitheater grazed by donkeys and goats, behind the house, a faint drumming and chanting are audible—Teresa is starting her voluntary shamanic group.

Priscilla too removes her glasses, to bite on one of its ear pieces. She sits at the table end, very erect. She has the air of being in her element. "No one's getting at you personally, John," she says, in her slight New England drawl. "But there are some extremely sensitive and vulnerable people at this Centre. You may have thought it was just a joke for the guys near you; but jokes get passed around, exaggerated, distorted. When I heard it I was very angry. I felt I had to express my anger this morning. I'm sorry if it upset you."

"You were sharing with us where you were at, Priscilla," says Ezekiel.

"Well, yes, I guess I was. I just felt John's remark was gross."

"I meant no disrespect to Lucinda," John says quietly, his head bowed.

"Well, it sure *sounded* disrespectful. 'Are we eating Lucinda?' I can't imagine a more disrespectful remark!" She barks a laugh. "The dead can't defend themselves."

"What did she have to defend herself from?" I ask her.

No one is drinking the retsina. John is clenching and unclenching his liver-spotted hands.

Priscilla replies to me when I have almost forgotten my question: "If you were a woman, gay or lesbian, or from an ethnic minority, you wouldn't have to ask that."

While I am struggling to see any logic in her answer, Arnold, New Age SAS Arnold, intervenes. "What perhaps you didn't realize, John—and if so I can understand it and I'm not criticizing you—was that your joke could be seen as homophobic."

John looks up, startled. "Hey? How?"

"Well, let me explain. Your remark, I take it, was an implied criticism of the meal: right?"

"No, it wor—"

"—Exactly, there was nothing wrong with the meal. I didn't have the lamb myself—"

"—Chicken," corrects Elke.

"—Chicken; I'm vegeterian. But the Russian chap—" He clicks his fingers.

"—Pasha."

"—Pasha, right: he went into ecstasies over it. He actually took a flash photo of his meal! We know Peter cooks superbly, on a very modest budget. So . . ." He leans his elbows on the table and touches his nose with his joined fingertips, thoughtfully: "So, since the *meal* wasn't being criticized, Peter could have seen your comment, John, as a personal criticism. Or prejudice. Regarding his sexuality. Now, please don't get me wrong; I don't think for one moment that was in your mind . . ."

"It worn't! I don't bloody understand."

There is a brief lull, then Ezekiel says, "This is very good, this is opening up difficult areas . . ." and Priscilla, "We are dealing with very sensitive feelings here . . ." more or less at the same time.

Elke: "Yes, there are sensitive feelings and issues. We have to be very careful, John. I think that's all Priscilla and Arnold are saying."

"I know that, I know that. I didn't mean to . . ."

"We know you didn't."

Priscilla suddenly looks watery-eyed and unhappy; she lays a hand on John's arm. "I wish this hadn't involved you, John; because after all you are my mother, and—well, I know, I feel, you care for me a little."

John makes an inarticulate noise in his throat and I cut in with: "How do you mean? Your mother?"

D. M. Thomas

Arnold lifts his spectacles to adjust them for comfort while answering for Priscilla. "She means in our *oekos* group. We decided John was very maternal and he's become our mother. Priscilla's right—it's more painful when it's one's mother."

Ezekiel, sliding an empty glass around in front of him, says, "I'm sure John knows it's hard for you, but this has to be brought out. You see, John, I think most people here are aware that Peter and Stephanos live together . . ."

"I didn't," says John.

"Nor I," I say.

Elke nods. "Peter moved in with Stephanos a couple of months ago. And it's fine. But Stephanos gets embarrassed if it's talked about openly. So everyone keeps up a kind of fiction"—she gestures towards me, since fiction is my line—"that they are not lovers."

"So any homophobic remark," intervenes Priscilla, "or possibly homophobic remark, is to be avoided. Also as I understand it Lucinda was a lesbian."

"I don't—" I begin, then stop; ending lamely, "know what that has to do with anything."

"No, I'm sure you don't. Have we finished? I'd like to join the shamans." ("Me too," says Arnold). She starts to rise. "There's also an unpleasant sexual connotation about *eating* a woman, but there's no point taking it on further."

"Yes, I think we've finished," says Elke.

Arnold: *"I* think so. John? Okay, old chap?" John nods. "Good!"

Ezekiel: "This has been valuable; it's cleared the air."

"Would anyone object if I talked about this at tomorrow's *demos?"* Arnold asks. "I think we should share it."

Ezekiel: "Personally I'd be very open to that."

"Thank you."

Elke, rising: "John, let me give you a hug!"

The elderly Northerner struggles to his feet and is engulfed. Ezekiel and Arnold get up, move to them, and pat John's back. It's like a big family, Ezekiel says: you have a problem or a row, you talk it through, you don't let it simmer beneath the surface.

* * *

I've found a tiny, scruffy restaurant in one of the back lanes of the village. In the early evening I'm the only diner. I can be silent, dream a little over the calamari.

In particular I can escape from Lucy, the latest person to opt out of my workshop. She came up to me after our meeting with John, and asked if I was going to eat. She said, "I want you to know the real reason why I've changed to Elke's workshop. I've just felt it was too much of a strain on us both, having to disguise how we felt about each other."

I was grateful, I said; but I'd promised to eat at the hotel with my editor, Crystal Heseltine, who had come over from the mainland to see me.

"Then why not come round to my room later; have some Metaxa?"

"Lucy," I said, "I'm fucking exhausted. You people don't realize how exhausting it is, emotionally, to carry a group for two weeks. I'm shattered. I need a couple of early nights. I can't *think* of sex at the moment. I'm sorry. Maybe we can have dinner together on our last night, in Athens. That would be nice— under the glow of the Parthenon."

She wasn't pleased. And it wasn't altogether the truth; but close to it.

Between mouthfuls I turn over the pages of *The Marriage of Cadmus and Harmony,* which Andrea has lent me. Myths I haven't thought about since old "Suetonius" Smith stuttered and blushed his way through Ovid with us in the Sixth Form Latin set at Nailsea Grammar. How complicated they are; I find it impossible to eat calamari and read at the same time. But occasionally a passage makes me stop chewing and concentrate. This, for instance:

"Myths are made up of actions that include their opposites within themselves. The hero kills the monster, but even as he does so we perceive that the opposite is also true: the monster kills the hero. The hero carries off the princess, yet even as he does we perceive that the opposite is also true: the hero deserts the princess. How can we be sure? The variants tell us. They keep the mythical blood in circulation. But let's imagine that all the variants of a certain myth have been lost, erased by some invisible hand. Would the myth still be the same? Here one

141

arrives at the hairline distinction between myth and every other kind of narrative. Even without its variants, the myth includes its opposite. How do we know? The knowledge intrinsic in the novel tells us so. The novel, a narrative deprived of variants, attempts to recover them by making the single text to which it is entrusted more dense, more detailed. Thus the action of the novel tends, as though towards its paradise, to the inclusion of its opposite, something the myth possesses as of right."

Chewing rubberily again, I reflect on this. I think of *Anna Karenina*. When Vronsky seduces Anna, when he has had his cock up her as he's dreamed of doing every moment for weeks, he has also murdered her like a mad axeman. If *Anna* were a myth, these would be variants. In one version the hero would have fucked the woman, in another he'd have killed her. And what about the hissing sound made by Emma Bovary's corset as she takes it off? In one version of the myth, she strips to fuck her lover, in another she unleashes poisonous serpents at him. This Roberto—I glance back at the cover—Calasso is right.

"Allo!" A parrot squalk cuts through my meditation. I look up and see Emily, grinning.

"Allo, Emily!"

Immune to my friendly irony, she pulls out a chair and perches on it sideways. Through the door also come her friend Harriet and Harold. He is again in Caroline's loose-waisted skirt, worn with his everyday lace-up shoes. "Hello, old bean!" he exclaims, slapping me on the back. They're not staying, they say, as they've arranged to meet others at Fat Anna's. All three are sweating and beaming and jolly. "We've been for a lovely long walk!" Harold says, draping his arms around the girls. "Do you know what? I've discovered my true sexuality at last! I'm a lesbian!" He roars with laughter. Emily, pressing her head against his waist, says, "You smell lovely, Harold! All sweaty and seamy! What knickers've you got on?" If she plays her cards right, he replies archly, she may find out. Harriet explains that they've stopped for a few drinks on the way.

Harold suddenly sobers, his face becoming grave. "Have you heard the bad news?"

"What bad news?"

"John has gone." He glances at his watch. "He'll be on the

ferry by now. He was upset by those bastards this morning. I tried to persuade him to stay but he'd made his mind up. He's going to tour around the mainland for the rest of the time."

I shake my head sorrowfully.

"We feel very angry," Emily says. "So we decided to get really pissed."

"Good idea."

Harold lights up. I notice he's thrown away his holder. "We're down to six. It's a bit worrying. Who's next for the black spot? Anyway, old bean, we mustn't interrupt your meal. Come and join us later for a Metaxa if you feel like it."

"I will."

They leave. I'm alone in the restaurant. My mind is a jumble of vague thoughts as I wait for the black-mustached waiter to bring back my credit card. Poor old John. Marie. The sixth form set I'm taking for Shakespeare this year. Alan, cuckolding Alan. Carla. You could have knocked me down with a nursing bra . . . Jesus Christ! How crass of me!

Walking through dimly lit lanes, I can hear the revelry, the clatter of dishes, raised voices in conversation and laughter, from a quarter-mile away. As I approach I see that the little village square is crammed; the occupied tables of Fat Anna's on one side spill out until they almost meet the occupied tables of Demetrios's on the other. All the uproar is coming from Fat Anna's, where Harold and Angus, Andrea and Emily, wave their arms at me, signaling me to join them. I crush into a table, meant for six, holding a dozen of us. Harold waves to a frantic waiter and shouts for more Metaxa and another glass.

Natasha, on my left, lolls against her boyfriend and ex-co-listener Eddie; Emily against Harriet; Andrea against Danny. Pasha has his arm draped around Caroline's chair, but she is half-turned away from him, listening to mad Geoff. She must be desperate, I reflect, to want to listen to Geoff. No one wants to listen to him. Warmed by all the good humor, and feeling charitable, I lean across to him, during a lull in his monologue, and say, "I thought you handled the *demos* very well the other day, Geoff."

He blushes to the roots of his stiff hair. "Did you? Oh, thank you, Simon!"

I feel further warmed by the newly arrived Metaxa and by the pleasure my remark has given.

Natasha turns towards me. "You hear about John? It's terrible. KGB!"

"Yes, I've heard."

Her shoulder nudges mine; her eyes are pouring their melancholy power straight into my eyes. "Is strange, Simon. In my youth, I hide my feelings so much. I hide my love for pre-Revolutionary poets. Now I hide again—here; I hide my feelings from that Priscilla. She try to tell me always what to feel, who to like. Who not to like. I must not like Hemingway." She shrugs. "Well, I like Hemingway. *For Whom Tolls the Bell.* Ah, she knows I talk of her."

She nods her head at the tables across the lane. I see Priscilla's lean mahogany-brown face and short fluffy black hair, among a well-behaved crowd of mostly Skagathos Centre people. They include Lucy, Peter—his shaven head unmistakable—Stephanos, Elke, Sue and Tamsin the domestic helpers, Arnold. There are many, on both sides of the lane, I still can't give a name to. Priscilla smiles: the first time I have seen this happen.

"She likes you," I say.

"Akh! Maybe . . . They all like all of us over here, as the KGB likes its prisoners. Over there, *nomenklatura*. The greysuits. But also we have *stool pigeon.*" I follow her eyes down the table to the gloomy-again Pasha, gazing at Caroline's ample back. "Mark my words."

I relate, raising my voice so that Harold and others, who are straining to hear, can do so, the afternoon meeting. "The fucking bastards," says Harold after I've finished. I've noticed how earthy his language has become; he is no longer the "wistful" Harold of early days. "Fucking bastards." He rises to his feet, lifts his glass, and says in a loud voice: "To Nat and Mildred; God bless them!" Having drunk, he collapses into his chair, almost toppling over backwards. "Cheer us up, Emily darling," he says, grasping her arm. "Give us a song!"

Emily unwinds from Harriet, gathers herself together, and launches into "Moon River"—singing in a firm, startlingly pure and beautiful mezzo. I am stunned. Where is the parrot squalk? Angus, at the next table, takes it up in his baritone that's rough but able to harmonize. Harriet joins in, a soft but sweet so-prano; Caroline too. Gradually I gain courage and slide in my own gruff but fairly tuneful tones. In the repeat, we grow confi-dent enough for some blues variations, becoming a passable choir, in love with our harmonies, unwilling to let the song go.

There follow "When All the Saints," in which Harold leads a dancing, clapping procession among the Fat Anna tables; "Ol' Man River;" "Fish Gotta Swim;" and a selection from *South Pacific*. We are making a helluva racket. As we slump into tem-porary exhaustion after "There is Nothing like a Dame," an elderly couple, not from the Centre, rise from their table, clap delicately, and the grey-haired man says, *"Danke schön! Sehr gut!"* They are putting on their coats, ready to go.

"Glad you enjoyed it!" calls Harold, at which they smile un-comprehendingly. "Are you here on holiday?" They shake their heads, and the woman says, "No English." They gather up their souvenir bags.

"I hope you enjoy the rest of your stay," Harold calls. Then, as they start to move off down the hill, he stands and shouts after them, *"And now get back to Nuremburg, you fucking Nazis! The Greeks don't want you here!"*

They turn, smiling and waving; and Harold smiles and waves back. He sinks into his chair, chuckling. The harried waiter places before him a plate of chicken and rice. Service is under-standably slow tonight. Harold rises again, takes up his plate, and lurches across to Demetrios's. He exclaims, "Would any of you like a bit of John? He's very tasty." There is a perceptible ignoring of him, a turning the back, a concentration on plates.

He staggers back, skirt swinging. Pasha, saying *"Pozhal'sto!"* leaps to his feet and his camera flashes. "I'll have the black spot with my muesli in the morning!" Harold says. "But I don't give a fuck. *Buggers."* He turns to face Demetrios's. Placing his hand over his heart, he shouts to a suddenly hushed throng: "You must excuse me but I'm rather drunk. I'm also terribly tired because I've been hiking in the mountains with my friends Nat and Mildred. We're expecting them along soon. You won't miss them, because Nat has a naked muscular thigh and a stump." He doubles up with laughter, and collapses. His head in Emily's lap, he goes on heaving with silent laughter.

145

"I think," says Natasha, "if there is any more Nat and Mildred, it will have to be *samizdat.* It's a little too strong for them, we were wise not to do reading last night. We've been showing some of them what we make, and a lot of them say it's pornographic."

Harold rises solemnly, staring across at her. "Of *course* there will be more Nat and Mildred, Natasha. Of *course.* You are incredibly beautiful." His head pitches again into Emily's lap. She strokes his hair.

Many are leaving Demetrios's. They glide past us without looking.

Caroline has found a different seat to escape from Pasha. Melancholy becomes frozen on the Russian's face; standing, he picks up his violin, and plays "When all the Saints," but in a dirgelike style. We try to clap and look animated, but it's a hopeless task. At last Pasha says, I go to bed, and with a last sad wave, camera in one hand, fiddle in the other, heads up the lane.

Everyone has gone, from both sides, except Harold, Caroline and me. Harold has recovered a little. The restaurant lights have been dimmed. Two waiters, and the gross form of toothless Fat Anna herself, slump at a table, politely waiting for us to leave.

I have never seen Caroline look so radiant, as Harold and I vie for her favors. Playfully outrageous, she says to Harold, "Do you want to fuck me?"

He considers the question very deeply, staring into his drink. At last he raises his eyes and replies, "Yes, I do. I do. And yet I don't. It's a complex question."

She laughs. She turns towards me. "And what about you?"

"Yes."

She laughs again.

We stagger up the lane, Caroline sandwiched between Harold and me, our arms supporting her. We harmonize quietly, drunkenly, *"Summertime, and the livin' is easy, Fish are jumpin' and the cotton is high . . ."* It's been a joyous evening, Harold says. Poor old Jonners, though. We trip over cobbles, almost go flying. She asks Harold if he will see her to her room. He seems uncertain. However, I take the hint and let go of her.

At the turning where Lucinda and I kissed, Caroline hugs me and turns her lips away from my kiss. Sod her! I think, stumbling on up, leaving them standing uncertainly together.

All the lights of the village and of the Centre out, it's very dark and starless. It is either now, or a *now* dreamt of later in the night, that I hear Harold's voice saying distantly, lyrically, "Mildred! How nice to see you! Nat! What's happened to your thigh?"

FOUR

The Educational Siesta

"I hear we missed a very nice spontaneous happening last night," Ezekiel says, as he and Teresa sink onto a mat in the Lotus Room. "We had a meal at Politas, in one of the back streets . . ."

"It's quite good there," says Peter.

"It wasn't bad." He glances towards me. "You must have been there just before us, Simon; you left this . . ." He plucks from his shirt pocket an Amex card and tosses it across.

"Thanks—thanks a lot!"

Teresa offers me an anxious, strained smile.

"But we should obviously have gone to Fat Anna's."

"Yes," says Peter, his Kojak skull and muscular, tattooed arms gleaming in the sunlight, "it was a good evening. It was the first time this course has really come alive." He nods at me appreciatively.

"We were very envious," says Elke. "I want to thank you for getting the singing started. You have a beautiful voice."

"Well, it was really Emily who—"

"You have hidden talents. Anyway, thank you."

"It was Emily who—"

"Tell me, is Harold a little crazy?"

"No, not crazy. Disturbed, perhaps. I'm sorry he got so drunk and—"

"There's no need to apologize for him. Of course he was upset about John going."

Brenda, Elspeth and the two English domestics haven't heard about his departure, and Elke explains what has happened. "It's a pity," she concludes; "a pity he couldn't see we weren't criticizing him personally. Although—" she smiles for the first time, rather charmingly—"I must say I shan't be sorry not to see those loose dentures anymore! He really should get them seen to."

There are subdued chuckles. The Greek domestic, Maria, shifts awkwardly on her mat, showing me her black tights right up to the seamed crotch. Elke asks if anyone has any important points to raise. Stephanos lifts a finger. "I have a favor to ask of you, Simon . . ." I took a call this morning from an English woman, a friend of Lucinda—she's here at the hotel down by the harbor . . ."

* * *

"Hello. I'm Maggie Sullivan."

I take her small, soft hand in mine. "Simon Hopkins! I'm so sorry." A slim young woman, she is like a slighter and more graceful version of Lucinda. Short black hair cut in a fringe, a gentle face, very attractive. A touch of Nefertiti, especially as her neck is slim and graceful. She is well dressed in smart jeans and brown suede jacket.

"Let's sit out on the balcony, shall we? They'll bring us some coffee."

We sit overlooking the harbor. It's my first time at the Hotel Eumenides; in spite of my delicate mission, I'm impressed by the hotel's quiet comfort.

"It must have been a great shock for you, Maggie."

She lowers her face; a tear appears in the corner of her left eye, and trickles. She wipes it with a tissue. "I was expecting her to meet me here for dinner," she says in a husky, shaky voice.

"When she didn't arrive, I tried to reach the Centre, but no one answered the phone."

"The office is closed in the evenings."

"Then this morning—I rang and—" She halts, overcome.

"Stephanos told you what had happened."

"I couldn't take it in. How did she die?"

I wait while a waiter brings a tray and pours our coffees. Then she listens, dazed, as I run through the tragic events. Stephanos has told me I may tell her the truth about her death, but that it would be better to say she has been buried at sea at her family's request.

After I have fallen silent, and placed a hand, trying to be comforting, on hers, she murmurs: "I don't understand it, I don't understand it. She rang me that very day. She was in good spirits. She said the group seemed nice, and she thought you could help her. There was one woman who got up her nose a bit, an American; she said she reminded her of her stepmother, but they'd had a talk and she was actually helpful, they were going to talk again. She was—oh, laughing and joking, and really looking forward to me coming over. She'd booked me in at this hotel. I couldn't get away on holiday until now, and anyway she wanted time to concentrate on her writing, which was terribly important to her."

"I know. It's very strange."

"And she certainly didn't take, or need, sleeping pills when we were together in London. Though maybe that was because—" she blushes, and blinks back tears—"we were together. If you see what I mean."

"Have you known her long?"

"We just met early in the summer. At a club in Pimlico. We hit it off straightaway. She even talked of possibly moving to England next year."

She cries; I look away tactfully, out to sea. The dazzling sea, which isn't wine-dark today—in fact I've never understood that Homeric epithet. Yet I can see the ships of Agamemnon unloosing warriors at the quay, where the small ferry for Skyros is taking on a few trippers.

She follows my gaze. "It's as idyllic as she said. We were going to have these few days here, and then go on to Skyros and

Skiathos. She was running out of money and I told her not to bother ringing again unless there was a problem. I can't *imagine* . . . You say there wasn't even a note for me?"

I shake my head, and she shakes hers, in anguish.

"She said she loved me. I think she did."

"I didn't know she was . . ."

"She was bi. So am I—I have a four-year-old son. I couldn't come away until his father could have him. Why, Mr. Hopkins? Why? Why did she do it?"

"God knows. We hadn't had a chance to talk in depth. Perhaps, as she'd been reminded of her stepmother by one of the women on our course, it's connected with her childhood?"

She opens a packet of Bensons, saying, "Do you mind? . . . I've no idea. I do know she was quite a lonely child. Her father was a well-known opera singer, Nathanial Gilbert—she gave me a tape of him performing operatic hits; so he was often away. And her mother had died in a car crash. Her father remarried. Oh yes, I remember Lucinda saying once she thought her stepmother was her dad's mistress while her mum was still alive."

"So one can understand resentment."

"Of course. But look, don't get the idea Lucinda was hung up." She smokes with quick, agitated draws, making me deeply envious. I pluck at the nicotine patch under my T-shirt sleeve. "She was very relaxed most of the time we were together, which was almost all of July. And in her letters and phone calls since, touring around the continent. I just don't understand. She sounded so *happy,* that very day she died! So full of energy! She said her—her sexual and creative juices were flowing." A touch of pink comes again into her pale cheeks. "I'm counting the hours, she told me, till you come."

"Well . . ." I sigh. "People do wear masks. Maybe the pressure to succeed, since she had a high-powered father. The pressure of having to prove herself, suddenly. Fearing failure. She was terribly competitive. Poised with her laptop computer. She did have those dangerous pills, and we do know she attempted suicide in her teens."

"Doesn't everyone?"

I stroll up from the hotel through the dusty village. It's quiet; siesta time is upon us. Waiters are already putting chairs on

151

outdoor tables; but I know that the "English breakfast" cafe will still be open, and I'm looking forward to ham and eggs. My workshop group, now sadly shrunken, will be joining me there. I set them to do more Nat-Mildred-Agnes writings in my absence.

Sitting outside one closed bar I walk by, surrounded by a phalanx of uptilted chairs, are Priscilla and an anonymous, unmemorable woman. Priscilla looks red around the eyes, and is clearly upset; her companion is talking to her soothingly, while massaging her thin, freckled neck. I stop to say, "Are you okay, Priscilla?"

She does not reply, but her companion says, "She's had a shock this morning, thanks to an Art Therapy exercise. She remembered that John, you know the old guy who's beat it, sexually abused her several times. Mostly while swimming. And she's his own daughter, for God's sake!"

I am momentarily startled by this announcement; but then realize she is referring to an *oekos* relationship. John was her mother.

"She *remembered* it?"

The woman nods. "In cases of parent-daughter incest, you can bury a bad experience almost instantly."

She goes on massaging Priscilla's neck. "You mustn't let him get away with it," she urges the back of Priscilla's head; "you've got to sue him."

"He lives in a council flat," I tell her. "He told me he's worried his daughter will have to pay for his funeral. His other daughter," I add hastily.

* * *

"Allo!"

I glance up from my yellowing plate. *"Allo!"*

Emily and Angus fling a folder on my table and plop themselves onto chairs. "Caroline and Harold are on their way," Emily says. "Natasha and Andrea send apologies. They're co-listening or fucking, I don't know which."

"We've had a *wonderful* morning's writing," Angus says. "We did as you asked, took up an idea and developed it. We chose the lamented Lucy's—whom we glimpsed in Elke's lot, covered in woad, it looked like. You remember she had dear Nat ringing a London police station and finding Agnes had been raped?"

"Yes."

"But the line was bad? . . . Well, we've taken that on."

"Natasha brought Priscilla's laptop computer," Emily adds. "They all dictated, and I bashed away." There are lots of mistakes, she apologizes to me in advance; but it's a long time since she learned typing at Bangor Tech. Angus lays his hand on her shoulder, tells her she was magnificent. Harold had wanted to bring in his bourgeois Margaret, he continues, and they'd all wanted the Japanese cannibal. Only—Emily takes it up—they didn't like the plot which had him probably eating Agnes before the opera. "So we moved into an alternative universe, where Agnes stayed in London and Kagawa went to Cardiff with his literary agent."

Angus has been studying the never-changing menu offered him by a young, slim waitress. "Same as this gent's; with lashings of the old butter, sweet girl." Emily translates into English and the girl vanishes inside.

"Talking of opera—Angus, you're an opera buff, what do you know about Nathanial Gilbert?"

"Lyrical tenor. Australian? No, New Zealander. Very good if not quite top-notch."

Harold and Caroline, talking animatedly, come striding down the road; a camera, swinging from a neck strap, bounces against Caroline's ample bosom. Concentrated on each other, good-humoredly argumentative, they seem to sense us by radar only. "You don't bloody invite a girl into your bed unless you're bloody willing to have a screw!" Harold exclaims.

"That's old-fashioned thinking," says Caroline. "My niece, who's a student, regularly shares a bed with a bloke but he doesn't expect to screw her! . . . Sorry!"—looking at us at last. "Yes, sorry!" Harold echoes.

"Who shared a bed?" I inquire.

"Who shared a bed?" Wide-eyed, Harold gazes around at his friends. "Who shared a bed? He doesn't know! The English tabloids are full of it! Agnes and Mike, of course! . . . You'll read about it. I'm starving—have you ordered?"

Caroline, saying she's hungry too, goes into the cafe. Angus, picking up my question: "He kept mainly to the southern hem. Died of a heart attack on stage in Auckland, about five years ago, while performing *Die Frau ohne Schatten,* that absolutely divine opera, with Kiri Te, that gorgeous creature and heavenly voice. What could the gods offer in Elysium better than to die on stage with Kiri Te?"

"Who died?" Harold asks.

"A minor opera star called Nathanial Gilbert."

"Ah, old Nat Gilbert! Another Nat!"

"Excuse me," I say, dabbing my sticky lips dry; "must make a phone call; I'll be back."

* * *

The crone at the phone shop is about to shut for siesta, but welcomes me with effusive bows. I dial the London code. Sian, my agent's lilting-voiced Irish secretary, comes through, then I wait a few seconds for Jim to come on the line.

"Simon! I hear you've been watching the sun rise over the Aegean! It sounds wonderful!"

"How did you know that?"

"Crystal Heseltine told me. She rang up and said she'd had a wonderfully poetic letter from you. She was intrigued to hear about *Infidelity.* I sent it over to her straightaway. I think it's fine. Deliciously funny."

I feel relieved and deflated at the same time. It was supposed to be quite dark and tragic; and I can tell from his urbane tone he doesn't think it's going to win next year's Booker. I had hoped for "brilliant, stunning, shattering," etc. Still, it could be a lot worse.

"Oh, I'm glad. You think it's finished."

"Yes I do."

"Actually I didn't ring about that. Do you have your opera guide there?"

"Of course."

"Could you look up Nathanial Gilbert, and read out what it says about his private life?"

"Nathanial Gilbert? I've heard the name. Hold on a minute." I hold, and in about thirty seconds his breezy voice says: " 'Born 1936 Dunedin NZ; Married 1961 Agnes Collinson, barrister, two daughters, widowed 1969; remarried 1970 Elizabeth Mildred Curnow. Died Auckland 1987.' Is that what you want? You don't want his performances?"

"No, that's fine, Jim. It's very interesting."

"I won't ask why you . . . Gilbert. Wasn't that the name of the girl who died at your place last week? It must have been very unpleasant for everyone."

"How the hell do you know that?"

"There's a piece about it in the *Independent* this morning. By that friend of yours I met once at the Groucho—Carla Brand. Writes very well. Suicide, wasn't it?"

"Fuck." I feel my heart racing. "What did it say?"

"Oh, that she took an overdose, and there was an extraordinary accident at the funeral; wasn't she chucked off a cliff, and didn't the coffin burst or some such thing? Sian brought it in and showed it to me; didn't have time to read it properly. It mentions you; quotes you, I think. Shall I go and get it—it won't take a moment?"

I feel faint, nauseous. This is too much. I don't like being between novels. Fiction is so much safer.

"No, Jim! Don't bother—I have to go; tons of work."

"Stephanos and Elke came searching for you," Caroline says when I return to the cafe; "and they're looking very hot and bothered. They're in the Metaxa Bar, they said to tell you."

"Don't rush off," says Emily; "you look pale, Simon."

"I'm okay."

"You shouldn't have tried the Gastric Dancing at the weekend; I'm positive that's caused a lot of the health problems. Even Elspeth says it can make you feel worse before it makes you feel better."

"I'll see you later." I set off up the dusty track of shuttered shopfronts. Elke and Stephanos do indeed look very grave and angry, poised over glasses in the almost-empty bar. Stephanos doesn't usually drink this early in the day. "Hi," I murmur, slipping in beside them. They look at me with silent reproach.

"I think I can guess what this is about, Stephanos."

He hands me the piece from the *Independent* that the London center has faxed through. As I read it I can feel their eyes brood on me as "Kagawa's" did on poor Agnes.

D. M. Thomas

Greek Tragedy
by Carla Brand

Skagathos Holidays, the New Age holistic center on the Greek island of Skagathos, which was started three years ago to provide (according to its brochure) "an experience of harmony, healing and meaningfulness," has suffered its first Greek-style tragedy. The body of Lucinda Gilbert, aged 36, of Dunedin, New Zealand, was discovered after a two-day absence from workshops. Yesterday former BBC drama producer, novelist Simon Hopkins, commenting on the tragic event, remarked that this was the first time he had lost a student through suicide.

A London representative of Skagathos Holidays declined to confirm or deny their tutor's account of Ms. Gilbert's death and bizarre funeral. According to the Wiltshire-based novelist, "The local fishermen refused to have a suicide tipped overboard in their waters, as it would bring on a curse; we therefore had to escort the body to the Acropolis, before dawn, where the coffin was pitched over. Unfortunately it hit something on the way down, and broke open."

Besides the Fiction Therapy workshop being run by Mr. Hopkins, the current holiday makers, who include a Russian tutor of striptease, are being offered a choice of Orgiastic Consciousness and Sumo Wrestling.

"I did write to this Carla Brand. She's a friend of mine and foolishly I trusted her. *Was* a friend . . . I did tell her what happened to the coffin, because it was so bizarre and she enjoys bizarre happenings. I told her in confidence; but in any case, as you said this morning, Stephanos, none of us did anything wrong. Lucinda's sister asked us to take care of it and we did it in the only way the islanders would allow. But I did not say it was suicide. Carla obviously misread what I wrote. My writing is pretty illegible anyway, and I was very tired and a bit drunk when I wrote to her. My pen was running out, and of course a

156

fax makes it fainter still. It's full of inaccuracies, this piece, Aco-polis instead of Acropolis, orgiastic instead of orgasmic."

"Sumo Wrestling," Elke says, nodding. "Where did she get that?"

"Carla takes a lot of drugs. What I wrote was a quotation: *'It's the first time I've lost a student*—Thucydides.' Thucydides used those word when a promising young historian he'd been tutoring wrote something that pissed him off."

It's a desperate lie, easily disprovable if Carla should choose to release either of my two letters, but I gamble on the second one having chastened her. Elke and Stephanos look almost as if they believe me. They are also clearly, like all post-literate, post-Gutenberg New Agers, impressed by my (quite spurious) learning. Stephanos: "Well, that's not so bad."

Elke: "We weren't concerned for ourselves, but we didn't want to get Dr. Sklaniatos into trouble. He signed the death certificate saying it was heart failure."

"He took a little risk," Stephanos chimes in, "to help us, and the islanders. To get it over with without a fuss. I know he's concerned. His brother, who works in a big hospital in Salonica, ran a test for him on some specimens from Lucinda—privately, I mean—just to be sure what happened. And his brother phoned last evening. There's no question: massive drug over-dose. Well, his brother will say nothing, and you haven't heard me say this." He glances from me to Elke, and back to me. We shake our heads. "It's very important everybody stick to the death certificate version." He must notice a change in my ex-pression, as he adds anxiously, "What did you tell this friend of Lucinda?"

"Well, I did tell her it was suicide. You told me to let her know what happened, Stephanos."

His eyes aflare, aghast: "I meant tell her what the death cer-tificate says."

"I misunderstood you. You said tell her what happened." I'm not taking the rap for this.

"This is terrible . . . Well, I will have to go and speak to her."

"You could say Simon wasn't aware the local doctor made a wrong first diagnosis and later corrected it," Elke suggests.

"Yes, I'll do that." He looks punch drunk. Problems multiply; he has had a fax from the London office saying Bethany Jarvis, romantic fiction writer, had rung pulling out of the last course due to start in three weeks' time. She says she's broken her leg, but they suspect she is fearful of scandal. "We have fourteen middle-aged ladies signed up for her, and now no writing tutor. We shall have to cancel, and we can't afford to lose those bookings."

"Can't you find a replacement writer?"

"Who?"

"Well, you won't get Martin Amis, but I could ring my agent and I'm sure, with a few phone calls, he'd find you someone."

A tiny glimmer of hope crosses his face. "It would be great if he could."

"I'll call him right now."

I am glad to spring to my feet and hurry back down the cobbled lane.

"*Yassou!*"

"*Yassou!*"

The crone nods me towards the booth. Sian puts me straight through to Jim, whose mind I can almost hear ticking over as I relate the problem. And it goes on ticking over; Jim is good at thinking on the line. After almost a minute's silence he says, "I was on the phone to Issei Sagawa just now. He's pissed off because no one will regard him as a real writer; the cannibalism gets in the way. His English is quite good. I know he'd like to explore more of Europe. What do you think? Shall I see if he's interested and if he's free in late October?"

My heart is fluttering joyously in my breast. "Please! I can't explain why, but it would be just perfect!"

"But how would Skagathos feel about him?"

"They're desperate."

* * *

The afternoon: my bed, a few drams of Metaxa. And Lucinda's ghost. The extraordinary coincidence of the family names—or *is* it coincidence? Isn't it likely that a few stray surreal words, in the exercise I gave them—on top of a resemblance to a hated stepmother she saw or imagined in the mild

Krystal—took her rushing back to a childhood turmoil? Over-whelming her? At least it becomes likely that my behavior was not the crucial catalyst, though it still may have tipped her over.

Banishing the painful thoughts, I turn to egg-yolk-stained fictions.

FIVE

A Diplomatic Atrocity

The sceptred isle (now un-isled by a channel tunnel), Blake's Jeru-salem, was sunk in crisis as a succession of scandals ripped through the governing classes. To mention only a few: the chair-man of the BBC had declared himself to be self-employed, as a way of saving a few bob on tax; three of the four children of the Queen had divorced or separated from their spouses, and the Prince of Wales could be heard on tape expressing to his mistress the wish that he might be her tampax; the princely fetishist pro-posed becoming a defender of faiths—*including Buddhism, Islam, Rosicrucianism, Mormonism, Marxism and Confucianism. A Cabinet Minister resigned because he was said to have sucked an actress's toes while wearing a Chelsea football shirt; another minis-ter fathered a love child (or bastard), then asked for another to be taken into account; the betrayed wife of a minister in the Lords shot herself; the Bishop of Durham said he didn't believe in Hell or the virgin birth or anything, really, very much; a Cockney-voiced soap star and a tabloid newspaper absorbed the talents of the High Court for a fortnight, to determine whether or not she had given her boyfriend a blow job in a lay-by; a tousle-haired, shyly charm-ing leftish Tory M.P., tipped for stardom, was found dead wearing stockings, binding flex and a plastic bag, and with an orange stuck in his mouth; female officers in the armed services who had left to become mothers were awarded hundreds of thousands in compen-sation, while soldiers who got killed or mutilated in the course of duty got almost nothing.*

The greying, grey-tongued, grey-suited Prime Minister was only exceeded in greyness by the greying, grey-tongued, grey-suited Leader of the Opposition. Behind and around them, on both sides, clustered "the ranks of the Grays," to quote Rider Haggard's King Solomon's Mines; *only these Grays were not regiments of brave Impis but, with very few exceptions, time-servers and ass-lickers. Almost alone in the government ranks Edith Hetherington, viva-cious, irascible and publicity-conscious, newly-appointed Minister for the Family, added a touch of the exotic with her flamboyant reds, greens and blues.*

Now her son Michael was chief prosecution witness and alleged victim in a sensational trial at the Old Bailey. Even without the high-powered political link, the case would have attracted huge media attention. The young man, a self-confessed gay, was virtu-ally accusing the defendant, Agnes Oldfield, of raping him. Com-ing after several much-publicized "date-rape" trials, this case was attracting worldwide interest. By the time young Hetherington took the stand, on the third day, most Britons were totally hooked.

Hello! magazine *had offered, and the accused had accepted, a second fortune for an exclusive if and when she was found not guilty. Her husband Nat, an unemployed builder, was being "looked after" by the* Mirror; *her divorced parents had been signed up by the* People *and* News of the World. *All three close relatives were in court every day, and their hurrying, furtive, well-guarded figures and faces became universally familiar. Ms. Oldfield's older sister Mildred, unmarried, Classics mistress at a girls' school, was holding out against the ubiquitous cheque-book. She too—much plainer than Agnes, with short straight hair and glasses—came loy-ally every day.*

When George Tosca, Q.C., acting for the defense, began his cross-examination of the tall, rather Rupert-Brookeish Mike Heth-erington, his opening recitatives were, as always, low-keyed, gentle,

161

agreeable. He seemed to accept the point that sharing a bed, and even some kissing and cuddling in that bed, no longer, with today's student morality of good-mateishness between the sexes, implied a tacit agreement that one or other could "try it on." He agreed—with perhaps a touch of irony—that it was "very hard on you, very hard indeed" to have Agnes Oldfield pressing her attentions on him. There was, indeed, a light chuckle in the gallery, since Agnes Oldfield was a gorgeous woman, and there wasn't a hetero guy in the land—judge and Tosca included—who wouldn't have given their right arm to have her press her attentions on them.

Hetherington made a good witness, winning the sympathy of most of those who hated his mother's (Tory) politics by taking his stand on the rights of women: "I believe a woman has every right to say no to penetration at any stage—even during penetration. And the law has taken that view too, recently. I enjoyed caresses with her, as a curiosity, but I told her forcefully I didn't want penetrative sex. She ignored me. Sir, I don't see why I, as a male, should have less right, or less protection from the law, than a woman."

"But come now!" The whippety little bewigged figure, feeling it was time to move into an aria, contorted itself into a dramatic gesture. "She didn't ignore you, Mr. Hetherington: she took the very broad hint of your erection! If a man doesn't want sex he simply doesn't get an erection!"

"I beg to differ, sir. One's body may make a purely physiological response, while one's mind is totally opposed. Just as, surely, a woman's vagina might become lubricated for sex, under stimulation by a rapist, but that would not be seen as implying her consent. Agnes—Mrs. Oldfield—performed an act which made it almost certain I would get an erection."

Tosca looked up sharply from his notes, staring at Hetherington over his spectacles. "What act?"

"She rimmed me. She bent over between my legs and rimmed me, sir."

Mr. Justice Breinton intervened to ask him what he meant by rimming. The young man explained; and incidentally provided most of the tabloids with their front-page headline for the next day's edition: I WUZ RIMMED! *"Perhaps because I'm gay, it had a very powerful effect on me physically. But I still said No, no,*

I don't want—" he hesitated—"penetrative sex. But she immediately rolled a condom on my penis—very skillfully, I must say—and got on top of me. I kept saying No, no!"

"But she's a woman, Mr. Hetherington. You're stronger. You could easily have thrown her off while she was trying to put the condom on you, surely?"

Biting his lip, looking upset, Hetherington shook his head. "I felt overwhelmed. Emotionally overwhelmed. This had never happened to me before. I thought perhaps she was going to give me oral sex, which I might not have objected to strongly. I felt terribly guilty at betraying Robby." He began to weep.

Waiting only briefly for him to compose himself, the barrister asked sharply, "Do you love your mother, Mr. Hetherington?"

Hetherington was startled. "Pardon me?"

"Do you love your mother?"

"Yes, of course."

"Of course. Among her many fine qualities, she is brave, wouldn't you say?"

There was an objection from the prosecution at this irrelevant line of questioning, but Tosca said he would be attempting to show that Mr. Hetherington's relationship with his mother was relevant in this case. The judge overruled the objection.

"I asked you," Tosca resumed, "if you would agree she is brave; but it's really a rhetorical question. She is in Sarajevo at this moment, isn't she?"

"Yes."

"That's a brave act. Do you know what she is doing there?"

"She and her Labor pair, Anne Fenwick, are investigating the mass rape, mutilation and murder of Moslem women by Serb troops."

Tosca nodded. "Don't you think it could be a comment on the essential frivolity of your accusation against Mrs. Oldfield that your mother has chosen just this time to be away, investigating truly horrific sexual crimes?"

"Objection!" But Tosca was already withdrawing his question. He was saying Edith Hetherington was a very formidable lady, and he wondered if having her as a mother had always been easy. "Do you recall, by any chance, speaking at a conference of young gays at Stanford University in California, some two years ago?"

D. M. Thomas

Hetherington looked slightly pale. "Yes. Yes, I think so."

"It was televised on local cable, in fact, wasn't it? Do you recall telling the conference you hated your powerful, domineering mother, hated her for her bullying and her embarrassing habit of sleeping around—sleeping around with half the Queen's ministers, and that you thirsted for revenge?"

A buzz had gone around the gallery. Hetherington looked down into his lap; licked his lips. "I don't think I put it in those terms."

And now the catching up of the motif, *in Tosca's inimitable way: "Well, I put it to* you *that your chance for revenge came, at long last. Your homosexuality has never perturbed her; she is a tolerant, liberal woman. But a highly publicized court case, such as this—how very embarrassing for her! And I'm sure you did feel upset after. You felt you'd let down your absent friend, your Robby. It was bad sex, from your point of view: regretted sex. But that doesn't make it a sexual assault, it doesn't make it rape—now does it?"*

"Yes. I didn't want it. It wasn't a game." His face was flushed, but his voice steady again. "I'm not trying to punish my mother. I can sympathize with Agnes up to a point; she was pretty drunk too, but really there was no excuse for what she did. She raped me."

"That will be for the jury to decide. No further questions."

Privately, afterwards, the prosecuting Q.C. said to young Hetherington, "There are rumors that the defense has a damaging tape of a phone conversation between you and your mother. Obtained illicitly from GCHQ Cheltenham. Do you know of anything that could damage us?"

Hetherington shook his head, but looked pale. There were so many phone calls, to or from his mother, that could be damaging. They had not had an exactly orthodox mother-son relationship.

* * *

Nat sat in an obscure wine bar not far from the Bailey with his minder from the Mirror, *a fat, bearded guy in the proverbial red braces, improbably called Rupert. Nat was telling him how, at first, because of a bad phone line, he had thought Agnes was telling him she'd been raped. He was in Wales with Agnes's sister, waiting for her to join them. It was a shock to find out she was the accused.*

164

"When she told you what really had happened, did she admit they'd had sex?"

He scribbled shorthand as Nat said, "Of course. We're always honest. We both kind of like wild games, they mean fuck-all. They were celebrating after their finals; he offered to drive her back to our flat, but on the way he invited her into his swish pad for a pizza and a piss-up. She got so sloshed she tumbled into his bed— his Aussie cousin was in the other room, down with flu. Agnes said he gave her a massage and then things got a bit hot; she was curious to see if she could get him going. They used a condom, that was all I bothered about. Him being a raving quean."

"Usually."

"Yeah!" Nat cawed a chuckle. "Well, Agnes could charm fuckin' John the Baptist into bed—and then have the Buddha and Quentin Crisp queuin' up to give her one."

Rupert smiled wanly as he scribbled.

"You can tone that down a bit," Nat said.

The reporter looked at his watch. "Better get back. That was great."

* * *

Nat crowded into the gallery slightly late; Mildred edged up for him to sit. He placed his cagoule on his lap. She never failed to be stirred by his lithe, prehensile presence, and again now she felt goose pimples run down her spine. She slid her hand under the cagoule to give his thigh a squeeze; and left her hand there, lightly. It was strange to feel the soft material of a suit; usually he wore jeans. His crotch was looser; she unzipped him; slid her hand in to cup his genitals. His cock hardened at once. "Toss me!" he whispered. She managed to free his cock, fully erect now. She smiled aside at her aunt Mavis, who was having a struggle to stop from weeping, and with her other hand Mildred squeezed her hand. Mildred loved the furtiveness of wanking Nat so quietly, gently, yet firmly, without anyone knowing. She was good at stroking him and jerking him off: the Classics mistress putting to excellent use everything she had learned from the filthy old masters, Ovid and Catullus.

* * *

165

Opening the defense by calling the ravishing though demurely dressed accused, Tosca asked, almost immediately, "Do you love your husband, Mrs. Oldfield?"

"Yes, very much." Agnes glanced up at the public gallery where Nat sat beside her sister and dear old Auntie Mavis. Nat smiled down.

"Very much. And is the sexual side of your marriage satisfactory?"

"It's excellent."

"So you love him, and have a very good sexual bond; yet you slept with another man that night . . . Could you explain why that happened?"

"I guess it was relief of tension, after the exams. And drink. And some curiousity because I knew Mike was gay. But there is really no conflict with my feelings for Nat—my husband—since we have an agreement that we may need occasionally to have adventures. Little ones."

Tosca said drily, "But this one didn't turn out to be so little, did it?"

"No!" The apparition of a smile, gone before anyone could be sure it had appeared on her pale austere face.

"At any rate, would you say that your relationship with your husband is still good, despite what's happened?"

"Yes. He's been wonderfully supportive."

"Indeed." Tosca pointedly glanced up at the still warmly smiling husband. "His support and loyalty are beyond question to anyone who sits in this court. Would you say he didn't object to your behavior that night?"

"He knows the sex meant nothing to me; and of course he knows I would never rape someone. He thinks it incredible anyone could imagine I might need to do that." She tossed her long black hair, proudly.

The diminutive Tosca took her through the events of the evening of the alleged assault, her account closely matching that of her accuser. Sexual intercourse hadn't been in her mind when she'd got into his wide bed. She was tense and couldn't get to sleep. Mike offered to give her a massage.

"It soon turned into something else. We kissed again, and he sucked my nipples. I began to stroke his penis, as I'd done earlier.

He had a partial erection at this stage. He lay on his back, passively, as I masturbated him. I asked him if he had any condoms, and he pointed to a drawer by the bed. I found a packet of Mates. I was kneeling over him and he started touching my genitals too. I was quite turned on. He still wasn't completely erect; I assumed this was because he wasn't used to a woman."

Tosca raised his hand, stopping her flow. "Mr. Hetherington told the court you rimmed him—gave oral stimulation to his anus. Did you do this?"

"Yes. I thought it might turn him on, as a gay man. And I could see it did. He sort of panted, and was very excited."

The Queen's Counsel asked her to describe their positions as she performed that act. She'd been kneeling between his legs, she said, facing him, then had moved his thighs up and further apart, so that she could get to his anus.

"Would you say it would have been difficult for him to have stopped you doing this?"

"Not at all! He had only to shove me away by pushing his legs out straight. But he didn't, he relaxed totally, and threw his arms back, sort of."

"What happened then?"

"I opened one of the Mates and put it on his erection. Then I moved myself over his thighs. He said I don't want to fuck . . ."

"He said I don't want to fuck?"

"That's right. Because of Robby, he said. His boyfriend, who was in Italy. But he'd grabbed my breast again, and was writhing his body. Everything about him contradicted his words, so I said, Well, I'd better force *you, hadn't I? I'd better rape you! And that seemed to turn him on even more. I got the very strong impression he wanted to be taken against his will, so to speak. He put his hand to my sex again, and commented how wet I was. That was when I put his penis in me."*

He had continued to protest, she said. —No, no, no! But clearly, to her, as part of the necessary fantasy of enforcement. When he'd come, she had rolled off him and he had lain beside her, peacefully, stroking her arm. She'd eventually turned away, to go to sleep, and she'd thought he was doing the same. The next thing she knew, she was being shaken by a woman police constable.

167

D. M. Thomas

* * *

"Mrs. Oldfield," the prosecuting counsel began his cross-examination, *"I'd like you to imagine you're in my position. As you may
be, one day. You are prosecuting an alleged rape. The victim, a
young woman, admits she enjoyed a kiss and a cuddle with the
accused, and got into bed with him to sleep; but told him very
firmly she didn't want penetrative sex, and he still went ahead and
did it. She went on protesting she didn't want it, but he took no
notice. Now tell me—would you say she has been raped? . . .
Please answer the question."*
*"Yes. But a man is bigger and stronger than a woman; the situa-
tion isn't the same."*
*"Well, let's imagine he's a weed, a wimp. She's a big strapping
girl, a Russian discus thrower, an Amazon, a karate black belt . . .
But he's manipulated her, he's exercised psychological power over
her—just as you did, I put it to you, when you performed a sexual
act on him which you suspected his submissive nature would find
irresistible. And yet he did still resist, verbally, didn't he?"*
"Yes, but—"
*"No, no, no! Isn't that what he cried out—so loudly that it
aroused and alarmed his house guest, his sick Australian cousin,
the cry penetrating through a solid wall! And surely, if we've
learned one thing in today's world of confused relationships, it's
that No means No, possibly the only absolute left in a world of
relativistic—"*
*She cried out passionately, "I was giving him what he wanted.
He wanted to be swept away, once in his life, with a woman, by a
woman. He* needed *to be raped." Tears sprang to her eyes. "You
don't fucking understand; how can you analyze that night so coldly
in a courtroom, twelve months later? Anarchic Aphrodite! You
can't pin her down in a sex survey or a legal brief!"*
"He needed to be raped! *No further questions"*

* * *

*Anarchic Aphrodite—a phrase which struck an unexpected note
in Agnes's testimony—was being studied and analyzed extensively
in Britain around that time. A survey of British sexual habits, published by Penguin Books, found among other paradoxes that, for*

168

women, sex got better and better over the years, and yet a quarter of women in their forties and fifties were having no sex at all, and most of the others were having very little. Divorce was rampant, and yet almost everyone had had only one sexual partner in the previous five years.

The children of Albion were learning to read, not from Pilgrim's Progress, as many had done in Victorian times, but from tabloid headlines such as TORY M.P. FOUND DEAD IN STOCKINGS AND SUSPENDERS. Seven-year-olds were being instructed about blow jobs, following a soap star's libel case; about why some men liked to be tied up with ropes while wearing women's underwear, with a plastic bag over their heads and a drugged orange between their teeth; and now, during the Oldfield trial, what rimming was. Some sex education teachers took the opportunity to move from rimming to felching: explaining that sucking sperm out of someone's bum was probably not a good idea in view of HIV and AIDS.

After the sex-related torture and murder of two-year-old James Bulger by two boys aged ten, two others of the same age were charged with raping a girl of five; and a man was found guilty of raping his daughter of eighteen months.

The Guardian traced Agnes's "anarchic Aphrodite" to a poem by W. H. Auden:

> Sad is Eros, builder of cities,
> And weeping anarchic Aphrodite.

By chance this led a screenwriter to a poem he thought perfect for a British film to be called Four Weddings and a Funeral, and ultimately to Auden's becoming, at long last, a bestseller.

* * *

Folly was on the march, just as surely as it marched alongside the battalions of young men moving up to the trenches at Ypres, Verdun, the Somme, and Passchendaele. It just took a different, sometimes more feminized form. And therefore, usually, a much more peaceable form, for which God if only She existed be thanked.

Kitchener's volunteer battalions had cosy, friendly names—

D. M. Thomas

Liverpool Pals, Oldham Pals, Grimsby Chums, Commercials,
Glasgow Tramways, etc. The new battalions ushering in the end of
the century might also have had similar folksy names—Media
Pals, Social Worker Pals, Privatized Utilities Gravy Train, Admen,
Lawyer Chums, Islington Wimmin, Limp Wrist Brigade, Counsel-
lors, etc. The great army stumbled on, not knowing where it was
headed.

And then there were the Balkans . . .

* * *

Edith Hetherington, sharing a sleeping bag with her Labor oppo-
site number, Anne, was asleep at a UNO military base outside
Sarajevo. It was around midnight. The night was quiet, the guns
for once silent.

A grey-stubbled French major gently shook her shoulder. "Ma-
dame Hetherington! Le téléphone!" She opened her eyes, took in
what he was saying.

"Thank you."

"In my office."

He turned and strode out. Edith wriggled out of the bag without
waking her lover. She hauled on trousers and boots, and headed
for the Major's office, a caravan.

It was the Attorney General ringing from Whitehall. He apolo-
gized for calling her so late. His voice was shaking. Edith's whole
body was shaking by the time he had spoken half-a-dozen sen-
tences.

"It will bring down the government," he concluded.

"Isn't there anything you can do to stop them using it, Bill?"

"I'm afraid not. It's relevant to the psychological line the defense
counsel is taking, by showing how Michael might well be sexu-
ally—uh, disturbed; and that he might well have wished to embar-
rass you with his own publicity."

There was a pause in conversation. The line crackled. She said
at last, "It's pointless saying I'm dreadfully ashamed of it; but I
am. I was, I'm sure, very mentally disturbed at the time. I'll be
disgraced."

"More to the point, so will—others."

"And I can do nothing to stop them playing it in court?"

170

"You'd have to do something very dramatic. Very dramatic indeed. I can't imagine what."

"I see. How long have I got?"

"A couple of days."

"Thanks for warning me, Bill."

The next evening Edith went into the hills and found the leader of a Muslim platoon. *"Bajro,"* she said, *"can I talk to you?"*

They walked together into some trees. They sat down, and she took a bottle of Scotch from her pack and two mugs. As they drank, quickly consuming half the bottle, she talked to him, pleaded with him; agitated, he flung his arms about, told her in his stumbling English he was not a brute like the Serbs, he did not treat women in that way.

A shell whistled overhead. They heard a faint crump as it landed in the devastated city.

Sad is Eros, builder of cities . . .

Bajro got to his feet and stumbled a short distance away; he stood by a tree, pounding the bark with his fist. She came after him, and stood stroking his arm. *"I am going to do it, Bajro. I have no choice,"* she murmured. *"If I am a victim and not merely a cowardly suicide, if my death is such that it arouses pity and horror and some respect for my courage—then that would help me and, much more important, help your people. It might be the spark that's needed for the West to do something at last. Please . . ."*

He beat on his forehead. *"I have a wife,"* he said.

"Then get one of your young unmarried men to screw me. The sex is unimportant. Only, afterwards, I would prefer you to be the one to—shoot me and the rest. As my friend, *Bajro . . . Show me no respect; a Serb rapist would show no respect. You can write something in Serbocroat?"*

Bajro nodded.

"Something like Keep out of our quarrel, English bitch. *Stick it in my pocket."*

Tears were running down into his black beard. He embraced her. *"I will do everything,"* he said. *"I'm not having one of my lads touching you. They're good lads, but they would talk about it. I will do it and no one will ever know. I will go back now and say you have gone. Meet me at the barn, the one below the village, in two hours."*

171

"Thank you."

"You will be our martyr when all this is over and we have our land, Edith."

The next day Bajro's platoon found Edith's mutilated corpse in a ravine near a Serbian gun emplacement.

* * *

Richard and Margaret blessed the day they found themselves sharing a park bench and started chatting. Their middle-aged romance flourished, and even Rachel, her daughter, liked the gentle, courteous ex-diplomat. Richard's niece, a professional singer, one of the Welsh National Opera chorus, sent him a couple of tickets for their new production of Jenufa. *As an ex-diplomat he had had more than enough of grand operatic occasions (the whole of Wagner's* Ring *in Bonn, he recalled with particular revulsion). He preferred Gilbert and Sullivan—as, he found, did Margaret; but he was fond of his niece and wanted to introduce her to his new friend. So they drove down to Cardiff one rainy June evening. The Radio Four News was still full of the world's reactions to the Bosnian atrocity. Richard, still a diplomatic "insider," to an extent, gave his expert views, and Margaret felt proud to be with such a distinguished, intelligent man.*

They booked into a hotel and walked to the opera house. To their surprise and pleasure they found themselves enjoying the tuneful and dramatic work.

In the bar during the interval Richard suddenly exclaimed, "Good Lord! I'm sure that's an old college chum of mine!" He indicated a tall, portly man who was in conversation with a small Japanese gentleman not far from them. "Do you mind if I—?"

"Not at all!"

Richard steered her through a gap. He grasped the tall, portly man's elbow, saying, "Excuse me, aren't you John Saunders?"

The man looked up, startled.

"Richard Davidson. Bristol University, 1958."

Recognition broke. "Good grief! Dick! How are you, old chap?" He spoke in an educated Welsh accent.

"I'm fine. I'd like you to meet a friend of mine, Margaret Rainsford."

172

"Pleased to meet you, Margaret. And this is a guest of the university where I teach: Mr. Kagawa."

A joyous light shone in Kagawa's eyes as, bowing, he pumped vigorously the hand of the middle-aged English lady.

At the end of the opera, Kagawa and his host joined Richard and Margaret. Richard—his warm eyes devouring Margaret's ample, well-controlled form—spoke of how they had seemed fated to meet. For years, they had lived near, shopped at the same Safeways, same market stalls—yet it had taken a park they hardly ever visited to unite them! Mr. Kagawa spoke of how he always seemed drawn to Dutch girlfriends.

The rain beat down against the bistro's windows. Richard said how dreadful the summer was; how he'd almost been forced to stop on the motorway, the rain had been so copious. Mr. Kagawa, answering Margaret's question, said he had flown from Heathrow with his agent. Agent had gone on to Belfast. "He have talk with Adams about book."

Feeling anger burn in him, yet not wishing to be rude to a foreigner, Richard controlled himself by bringing up the murder of Edith Hetherington. Indeed, probably no one in the bistro had not, at some point, mentioned the atrocity. Tempted to be indiscreet by the presence of a former student rival in the academic stakes, Richard passed on his inside knowledge. The defense in the trial of Agnes Oldfield had planned to introduce a tape which would have shown that Michael Hetherington had been totally screwed up by teenage mother-son incest. However, his mother's murder had effectively "killed" the tape. To play it at this time, when Edith Hetherington was a sacred figure, would do the defense more harm than good.

The whole subject made Margaret feel quite sick; and then there was this little Jap man gazing at her so intently through his slit eyes. She couldn't help thinking of what they'd done to our boys in the prison camps and on the Burma railways. She was glad when they had said goodbyes and were out in the steady cold downpour of a Welsh June night.

* * *

Mid-afternoon torpor. The Centre, deserted. I seek rest, fresh air and coffee, in the shade of a pomegranate tree. I'm

173

miles away when I find myself accosted. It's a ginger-haired man who wants to know how one sets about finding a publisher. A sociology lecturer at Cambridge Poly, he is writing a book about patterns of social deprivation in declining East Coast resorts. Intensely irritated, I try to be helpful. He speaks about Lucinda, how, rather to his surprise, Stephanos had asked him to come along to look at her body. "It was pretty unpleasant. I spotted the empty barbiturate bottle and said this might provide the answer; but I gather she had a heart attack?"

"Yes. Your name is—?"

"Bob." He thrusts out his hand; I shake it. The book, he says, is an expansion of his doctoral thesis. Dr. Bob.

He stretches, rubs his freckled stomach, thinks he'll go for a swim.

Stephanos, looking more cheerful than I've seen him for a week, comes jauntily out of the kitchen, spots me, and heads towards me. He rests his hand on my shoulder. "Simon, we had a fax from headquarters. Your agent found us a writer to re-place Bethany Jarvis for the course after next—a Japanese writer called Sagawa. You know him?"

A wild delight takes hold of me. "Not personally, no. But he's an interesting writer, and his English is very good. Will you tell your fourteen ladies who are expecting romantic fiction there's been a change of facilitator? I wouldn't say he writes romantic fiction."

"I don't think it will be necessary. I've checked and we're covered legally—all we promise is a writer. He writes comedy, no?"

"Not really. Who told you that?"

"Oh, I mentioned the news to Harold, when I bumped into him, and he laughed very much."

Shaking my head, I say, "Sagawa writes about food quite a lot."

"Ah, well, then he should appeal to housewives. Thanks a lot for your help, Simon!" He squeezes my shoulder, then lopes back inside.

My eyes close. I enjoy the silence, the solitude.

A soft, feminine voice calls me back from the edge of dream. It's Lucy. She looks haggard.

"Hello. How's the Art Therapy going."

"Oh, okay; but it's not what I want. You know that. I have to ask you something." A painful, fearful look comes into her eyes. "Someone told me you left your notebook around for people to read. Did you—did you say my writing was crap?"

"Absolutely not."

"You're sure?"

"Absolutely. I think, as I said, you need to be patient; but you're very promising."

"Oh, thank God!" Her body relaxes, and she breaks into a broad smile. "I didn't think they could be telling the truth." Her eyes search for warmth, for communication, in mine. "Do you still want to see me in Athens?"

"Yes. Yes, that would be lovely."

"Not before?"

"I'm sorry."

"Okay, okay; I'll be patient."

* * *

Back in my stuffy room, I write postcards to my father and my daughters. Then, on a wild whim, to Bridget, my second wife. The card I use shows Brooke's marble Skyrian tomb. "Remember the Malverns when, to tease your Irishness but also to show my desire, I quoted to you 'Breathless we flung us on the windy hill . . .'? On Friday a boatman called Socrates is taking me and some students to Skyros to see his grave. Nothing else in this fortnight matters to me. I'm on one island but want to be on another. The story of my life! . . . I'm reading his poem about his Tahitian mistress, and thinking of you. Your lovely firm body. If only I hadn't been a fool; if only we could begin afresh, afresh, afresh!—Love, Si."

I sit staring at it, and thinking also of how I misled Lucy. I know of course that all grief and all hunger, for all women, is hopeless grief and hunger for my mother; and that my writing is a desperate inoculation against the plague of time and death.

This card is too intimate to risk its being read by Dermot, my (much kinder) successor. My eyes stinging, I pull out a desk drawer, never till now opened, to see if there are any envelopes: and find through blurred sight some stationery but also, more dramatically, a baseball cap. Nestling under it is a handwritten note saying, "Good luck, Hopkins, in this shithole. O'Brien."

The cap and the note cheer me up. I wear the former when I descend in the early evening and meet up with members of my group at Fat Anna's. A couple of retsinas make me positively lively; it is Natasha who's in a fit of Slavonic gloom, over the death of myth in her country. (It doesn't emerge all at once; the rest of us make sure it's mixed up with old Doris Day numbers like "Deadwood Stage" and "Take me back to the Black Hills . . .") Her great-grandparents, she tell us, though they were poor, were sustained by their strong Orthodox faith, and the rituals of traditional peasant family life. Her grandparents, old Bolsheviks, had the myth of Communism, building the great earthly Utopia, two of Mayakovsky's "one hundred and fifty million." Her disillusioned parents had the myth of western freedom, just beyond their grasp, but one day . . . And meanwhile they read and circulated Solzhenitsyn and Mandelstam in *samizdat.*

"But I—I have nothing. Ab-sol-utely *nichevo!*" Her beautiful eyes flash a sad-angry glance around our table. "And that goes for all of us in Russia. At best—with *luck*—" a sarcastic grimace—"in twenty years we will be relatively prosperous social democracy, with mortgage and credit cards. At worst we will be fascist state, crippled by debts, starving, all Russia and Siberia contaminated by chemical and nuclear waste. Well, not even at worst—most likely. But even if it's the best . . ."

She looks around the tables, at Fat Anna's and across the lane, which are filled mostly with our New Agers; she shakes her head despairingly. Look at them, she says; look! at the westerners. "They want to share—*delit*—but it only means bore to death with some subjective idea. In Russia, in my parents' time, to share mean to tear one's last piece of moldy bread in half! That was a deeply spiritual event! Here there's so much hugging, and so little love!"

"O'Brien!" exclaims a fat one-toothed waiter bearing salads pointing at my baseball hat. "O'Brien nice guy, always a smile. O'Brien love Skagathos."

"Yes, he did."

"American."

"Yes."

"Sad about some woman."

"He was sad about some woman?"

"Yes. Women! Huh!" He rolls away grimacing, wiping his hands on a filthy apron.

Caroline: "Is Agnes a rapist, or not?" Natasha shakes her head vehemently, and says, "They had a big love scene, they kiss, they—what do you say?—pet, so from that point anything is allowed to happen, it's ridiculous even to mention rape." Harold agrees with her, but Emily and Angus are as adamant that she did rape him. "He said No, no, no!" Angus points out. "That's clear enough. If my lady said No, no, no, I wouldn't dream of assuming she wanted me to make love to her." The exchange becomes really heated. They want my opinion, but I decline to give it; my mind is running on Carla's newspaper story, and the likelihood that journalists will be ringing my home number; probably have already done so. Stupid of me not to have warned Marie; I must do so at once.

Saying I have to phone home, I leave the table, and hurry down the lane to the phone shop. On the way I catch sight of Lucinda's lover, Maggie something, sitting alone outside a bar, hunched over a drink. I go up to her and touch her shoulder. "Hello," I say, "you're still here." She looks up, recalls me vaguely. Yes, she says, she feels closer to Lucinda on the island; it's a little comfort.

"There are a crowd of us having a meal up the road: why don't you join us?"

"That's kind of you, but I'm happier on my own at the moment."

"Well, if you change your mind."

"Your manager, Stephanos, came to see me. So it was her heart?"

"Yes, I'm sorry I misled you."

"It's a relief. I think she said her father died of a heart attack, quite young."

"That's true, I believe."

"And he said the message that was found on her computer was directed at you, saying she couldn't go on with a piece of writing."

177

"Yes, I think she was probably just starting to tell me that when she felt ill."

Maggie nods, slowly. "It must have seemed, at first, like a suicide note. It's pretty awful, though—putting us through the extra anguish. I mean her family, as well as me. The way it's been handled seems so terribly . . . casual." She stares into the beer glass her arms enfold.

"Well, that's Skagathos." I press her shoulder sympathetically. "Go easy. 'Bye."

"'Bye." That beautiful Nefertiti-face. It seems—as Harold said of Emily, much less justly—such a waste.

The old phone-crone looks surprised to see me after dark. But a smile appears amid her wrinkles, and she lifts a yellow hand to invite me to go through. I am conscious of stumbling drunkenly as I pass trays of cheap trinkets, heading for the phone. Drunkenness makes me dial clumsily, and I have to go through the process again.

Our phone rings and rings. How annoying that she hasn't put the answerphone on if she's out! I could have left a message. It's too late to ring Dad, who goes to bed early. I drop the phone. Then decide to try Alan. Ask him to pass a message on—and also break the ice with him, without having to put it into words. Just by a friendly tone I can make it clear I forgive what has happened, and his having been to bed with Marie a few times this summer need not affect us, now that it's over. Pulling out my diary, I find his number. I dial and, after a few rings, hear his mild voice saying his phone number.

"Hello, Alan, this is Simon."

"Simon!" His voice comes across as a surprised, frightened yelp. I'm about to say something soothingly innocuous, like asking him about the football match the other night, when he bursts out: "I'm sorry. I truly am. I've been in a hell of a state. *I* thought it was over too. This'll sound like a load of shit to you, but believe me neither of us expected it the other day. She was a bit blotto after the Reunion and I thought it safer to drive her home. I stayed the night, but in the spare bedroom. However, I'm afraid, the next morning I didn't have to go in, it was Founders Day, and nor did Marie, and—we weakened. I felt really hellish when you rang, Simon. I thought, Christ, he's my best friend! Though I've been thinking that for the past year."

"The past year?"

"Well, maybe two, I don't know. God, I've been in a dream. You must bloody hate me, Simon. I hate myself. I've even started bloody smoking again. You heard my lighter click. She was sparing my feelings at the time, pretending to you I was someone else, but I knew she'd tell you when you next rang. I've been half-expecting you to call. I'm glad we can get it out in the open. It's sex, Simon; sheer sex. I don't believe she loves me. She loves my *kids;* she loves it when they're over here in the holidays; and she's so good with them, she'd have made a bloody marvelous mother. It won't happen again, I promise. She probably told you, we're taking your father up to town on Thursday; she bought three theater tickets, thinking you'd be home; as you're not, she asked me to join them and drive them up. But I'll back out."

"Why should you?"

"I'll have it out with her; I'll make it clear it's got to stop."

Trying to control the tremor in my voice, I tell him I'm using a public phone and am running out of money. We'll talk it through when I'm back.

"Yes, you're right; your friendship's important to me, old man. I know I've given a pretty awful demonstration of friendship, but I hope you can understand and forgive."

SIX

An Admiring Ghost

"What's the time?" I hear our lamp click on. Now the anger floods. "Jesus, do you know what time it is! It's two a.m., for God's sake!"

"I know. I'm sorry. I couldn't sleep. I had to talk to you."

"You're drunk, aren't you? For Christ's sake! I'm not lying around on a Greek island; I have to work in the morning!"

"I'm sorry."

"I've been exhausted this week; the bloody computer went haywire and I've had to receipt all the school fees by hand. I went to bed early thinking I'd get a good night's sleep, which I was doing until you woke me up. God, you're a selfish fucking sod! Well—come on—what is it?"

"Alan's admitted to me you were with him the other day when I rang."

"What?"

"I rang him a few hours ago, trying to get hold of you. You lied to me. You said it was Pargeter."

"I didn't say it was him. You asked me if it was him and I said it could be. It would have embarrassed both of you if I'd told you it was Alan; and what would have been the point? I'd have told you when you got back. It doesn't matter; it was a one-off."

"You told me it was over."

"Well, it is. It won't happen again."

"You're going to the theater with him on Thursday."

"So? I bought tickets for the National weeks ago, thinking it would be a treat for your dad. It would have been his wedding anniversary; he still likes to celebrate it. I'd forgotten you'd be away. You know how your dad hates being driven by a woman. It's very insulting, but he's too old to change. It's damn good of Alan to drive us."

"You'll sleep with him again."

With a sarcastic chuckle: "Oh yes! with Sam in the back seat watching!"

"When you've dropped him off."

"Even if we did, does it really matter? You're still in touch with that Carla Brand, you spoke to her the other day, I don't know how; she's had a piece in the paper. You're probably still screwing her occasionally; and I don't object to that."

"I'm not still screwing her. Even when I was it was only a few times. Alan said you've been involved with each other for two years."

"That's rubbish. A few months. Oh, we messed around a bit a year or two ago, but nothing much. A kiss. Look, it's over, right? Though if you go on like this I'll be tempted to bloody move in with him."

"All right, all right. What play are you seeing?"

But she has slammed down the phone.

I go on sitting in Stephanos's office, drained. My hand, wound with a white handkerchief, throbs, and red begins to show through.

* * *

"We had a break-in last night," Stephanos says, calmly enough; "there is not much damage, just pane of glass."

181

"Was anything stolen, Stephanos?" Elke asks. She is wearing her Save the Elephant T-shirt this morning.

"Some money."

"How much?" Ezekiel inquires.

"About eight thousand drachmas. It was Maria's wages." He speaks to the Greek widow in rapid demotic, explaining and (judging by her smile) reassuring.

"I was afraid," says Ezekiel, "it may have been some reporter from England, digging for information about Lucinda's death."

Stephanos, nodding, says that was his worry too, when he first discovered the broken window. He is sure it wasn't one of the villagers, who are absolutely honest; he can't imagine it's anyone from the Centre; most likely it's one of the back-packing tourists on the island. Cash for drink and drugs. We nod agreement.

I feel a tingle—almost sexual—of pleasurable guilt. To steal the money from the drawer was an impulse, an impulse to do something really degrading and unworthy. The kind of impulse and the kind of tingle that the young woman in the film *Indecent Proposal* probably felt when agreeing to sleep with Robert Redford for a million dollars.

I also felt it was owed to me, in a way. Eight thousand drachmas barely covers my phone calls to England; and it seems to me wholly wrong that we facilitators should have to pay for our calls home.

Stephanos doesn't intend to get the police in. He'll replace the money from a contingency fund for repairs and breakages. I suggest, unseriously, we could involve Pasha again; but Elke says, Didn't you know, he's left? Nodding, Stephanos says, Yes, he left yesterday; he was very bored; I refunded half his fee and managed to get his return flight brought forward.

Strangely, I feel a little hurt that he didn't come to me to say goodbye. I recall his short cotton sleeves, his melancholy eyes and violin. Then Elke says, "Oh! he left you a note, Simon; I completely forgot it." She fumbles in her shorts pocket and produces it. She stretches across with a grunt to hand it to me. I unfold it and falteringly decipher its Russian: "Dear Simon, I'm sorry I couldn't find you to say goodbye. It's boring here for me, and Caroline doesn't want me. I miss butter and meat, and have no money to buy it. Thank you for talking to me, a little, but you are very busy. I saw you kissing Lucinda that night. I couldn't sleep, I was feeling lonely and sad, so took a walk. I stepped back to leave you both in peace. But I was sure you had nothing to do with her death since I also saw you walk past me towards the Centre. I don't blame you for telling a white lie. Love gets us in hot water. Goodbye. Pasha."

"Okay?" asks Elke.

My face probably looks red. "Yes."

"He pissed me," Ezekiel says, "with his damned camera. On the beach, in our workshops—he wandered in whenever he felt like it; and at that very sensitive and beautiful moment here, on Sunday night."

Many are nodding agreement; Elke says, "I appreciate all of you for being so supportive of him. Thank you. So now . . ." She turns her eyes to Stephanos. "Anything else, Stephanos?"

"Only that more people seem to be getting sick again. Including Elspeth." He glances at the empty mat where Elspeth usually plants herself. Elke intervenes to say she is looking after Elspeth, who is quite bad. We murmur our sympathy. "We must make sure," Stephanos continues, "that everyone who's sick is being seen to, and probably it's better if one person takes responsibility to look after them."

I catch Teresa's eye; she does look strained and tired. I wonder if she's coming down with it—or have they been rowing? Could *theirs* have been the angry voices which, according to three or four at breakfast, disturbed their night's sleep? Unlikely—though he looks red-eyed and offish. I'd like to be alone with her. Co-listening. It's a long time till the evening.

"So, how are we all?" Elke asks. "Ezekiel?"

"I'm okay. I'm okay." He doesn't want to elaborate. He doesn't look okay.

"You look tired," Elke says; "I think you're working too hard, you're seeing too many people in private."

"Well, it's necessary. There are a lot of people ready to explode. Perhaps into violence. We can only hope to contain it."

He gives the impression we're sitting on a Chernobyl. His eyes look stary and haunted.

"Anyway, don't overdo it, Ezekiel." She glances towards Teresa. "And how about you, Teresa? The shamanic group seems to be going well."

"Yes; they seem to be getting a lot from it. I was going to ask, I have some certificates with me, for first-grade shamanism. They won't have done a two-week course but they're working very hard. May I give them certificates at the end of the week?"

"I don't see why not."

"Thank you."

"Simon?"

"I'm fine. Well, a few problems; domestic problems. But Teresa is helping me deal with them." She smiles across at me warmly, gratefully.

"You've hurt your hand," Elke observes.

"It's just a scrape. I walked up to the Acropolis last night, and tripped over a step." It's a half-truth; I was staggering around up there in the early hours, drunk, tormented by jealousy, raging at my blindness; and fell over on my way down, intent on breaking in to get at the phone. "I'm fine; we're a small group now, but they're writing with enthusiasm."

Stephanos looks at me, his hand lifted. "I meant to tell you, Simon, but it slipped my mind because of the burglary: you've lost someone else, I'm afraid. Andrea. And you"—he glances towards Ezekiel, then Teresa—"have lost Danny, her husband. I think they have some personal problem they need to sort out. They saw me at breakfast and said they're leaving later this morning."

My heart sinks even further if that is possible. I like Andrea. Now we are five. And Ezekiel and Teresa look decidedly sour at the news.

We wait for Elke to tell us how she is. At last she lifts her face, opens her eyes, and speaks. "I feel good. I enjoyed getting to know Harold a little better, Simon. We had a nice talk on the beach yesterday. He is not so crazy when you get to know him, you're right."

"How's Lucy settling in your workshop, Elke?" Ezekiel asks her unexpectedly.

"Oh—okay, I think."

"She has problems, big problems." He glares briefly at me. "I'm having to spend a lot of time with her to sort them out. She's a very vulnerable person, very easy to hurt. I think I'm helping her through, but we should all be aware of her." Again his eyes, almost wrathfully, seek me out. "Not everyone here on Skagathos has helped her all they might."

I need to create a diversion. "Someone else who could do with your help is Nat," I say to Ezekiel. He looks disconcerted. "Nat?" Others too look puzzled; though no one can know *everyone.*

"He's in Harold's *oekos* family," Elke says. "He has no penis. Harold was telling me about him."

"Whose workshop is he in?" Ezekiel asks. "Yours, Simon?"

"No, I'm not sure who he's with." There are glances around the room, invitations to claim Nat. Ezekiel: "Can anyone describe him?" but it's late, time for the workshops, and Elke says—as I murmur privately, "Ask Harold"—thank you very much, have a good morning.

* * *

Andrea and Danny have visited the Calypso terrace to say goodbye. They won't say what has happened, but something has disturbed their harmony, that's clear. Andrea has hugged me, and said she wants me to keep the book I've borrowed, as a keepsake.

Natasha has Priscilla's laptop with her. They want, all five that are left, to continue what they're starting to call *Bosnian Sacrifice.* I'm happy to leave them to it, and descend to the breakfast terrace. Screams come from Orgasmic Consciousness. Elspeth sits under the pomegranate tree, looking pale but convalescent. She offers me mineral water as I sit by her, asking if she's better. She blames the attack of dysentery on her negative feelings towards her father's health; she has got too used to seeing his death as inevitable and—even if that should prove to be the case—as a wholly bad thing. "Whereas it's a part of life's cycle; he will become wheat and rainwater." She sips water and nibbles at dry bread.

She clicks on her portable stereo and I hear, softly, the Borodin piece that I think of as "Hold my hand, I'm a stranger in paradise." Elspeth sways her slender body; I can see her tiny breasts bob a little as she bends forward and her low-necked vest gapes. She stretches back, eyes closed, swaying to the music.

Then nibbles again. "There's aluminum," she says, opening her eyes, "in this bread. My stomach's telling me not to eat too much of it. It can lead to Parkinson's and other diseases. It must be in the soil where the wheat was harvested. But it's okay, it's okay." Goes on swaying to the music, rubbing her stomach. "There's some phosphate too; that's good. We're eating our ancestors."

Her father, the sub dean, is a wonderful man, Elspeth says; if only he would try gastric dancing. In other ways he's always been open-minded. "He fought hard for women priests and gay priests, even before he came out himself five years ago."

"My brother is gay. He lives on Castro Street in San Francisco."

"Oh, really? Well, Salisbury isn't quite San Francisco. I'm sure the cancer is a result of too many years repressing his nature. He's a transexual. He was in the midst of having a sex-change operation when this damn cancer came up. He should have been putting flesh on his chest and hips, and the doctors couldn't understand why he was losing weight. Now he's neither man nor woman; a half-man."

Poor Dad, wheezing and coughing, hardly moving in the little ground-floor flat we found for him. Elspeth is asking me about him. "We try to entertain him. Trips to London for the theater, which he likes."

"That's nice."

Tomorrow night. Marie sitting by Alan in front, speeding up the motorway. A sick lurch. Alan-in-Marie. Sounds like a Breton church. Dammit, he was *my* friend.

"Your mother? . . ."

"She's dead."

I look away. I can't talk about her. "My brother's managed to stay healthy."

"That's good."

"Perhaps because he never took drugs, or poppers, or whatever they're called. Certainly not from being monogamous. Colin's had thousands of lovers. But in his last letter—it was quite touching, really—he said he's at last learning commitment. A couple of times he's invited one of his sexual partners at the bath house or the bookshop back to his apartment for a coffee. And one of them even stayed the night."

"I think they should be allowed to marry," Elspeth says, swinging her legs onto the bench and raising one saronged knee to lean on.

"So do I; as often as they want."

Her eyes closed, she sways rhythmically. I think she is swaying to the Borodin. Then she opens her eyes. "Peter made me eat some of the aubergine and mozzerella casserole you're going to have for lunch. It's very healing. I'm feeling better every moment. It loves me; I can feel it."

"That's good. Well, I must go back and see what my group have written. See you later."

     * * *

The morning after the opera, in the Cardiff Hilton, Issei Kagawa was getting dressed when his phone rang. He sat on his bed to pick the phone up. He heard the wide-awake tones of his agent, Larry Stanton. "Hi, Issei, I just wondered how things have gone."

Stanton prided himself on taking good care of his writers, but also not wasting any opportunity. So, after depositing Issei with his university hosts, he'd spent a productive hour in a wine bar talking about a possible book deal with a famous Welsh rugby league player. Then—off on a flight to Belfast for more business.

"Lecture go very well, Larry. Lots applause."

"Good, I knew it would. And how was the opera?"

"Good too. Fat lady sing good."

Stanton chuckled. "Only one *fat lady?"*

"How your trip?"

"Very useful, thank you. Didn't get much sleep; I've been reading Gerry's manuscript. It's fucking good, the guy can write."

187

Kagawa's eyes fell on the front page of the Independent, *delivered free with his full English breakfast. Somber picture of the PM saluting Edith Hetherington's casket as it was carried from a plane at RAF Brize Norton. Kagawa told Stanton about meeting an ex-diplomat and his wonderfully fat lady friend, and the amazing story about the dead Minister and her son. Disbelieving at first, as he picked his way through the grenade explosions of Kagawa's English, Stanton gradually became more and more excited. "My God, Issei, it* could *be true!" Gazing out at the rainy Falls Road, Stanton skillfully matched Issei's words to other rumors he'd dismissed as incredible. "I know a UNO colonel who owes me a favor. I'm going to get this Captain Bajro out of there. Call me when you get back to London. Hope you're enjoying Wales."*

"This nice trip. Only not so good as France. No talk shows, no autographs, no book signs. No proposals for marriage."

"There will be, Issei. When your book comes out in English. I promise. There'll be droves of women, plump and white-skinned, offering their hand, and anything else you fancy!"

* * *

A couple of days later Stanton sat, in a private lounge at Claridges, drinking coffee and talking earnestly with Bajro, bewildered and swarthy and black-bearded, dressed in jeans and a sweater that Stanton's attractive blonde secretary, Jean, had bought for him at M & S. Stanton had expected to have to bring in an interpreter, but had been pleasantly surprised, on collecting the soldier at RAF Brize Norton, to find he could speak passable English.

"Just run through what happened exactly, Bajro; once more."

Bajro did so. His stumbling on two of his men, in the act of cutting the breasts off the dying woman. Her gasping out to him that this was what she wanted, and giving as her reason that it would help Bosnia. It was very much as he had told the English colonel.

"It doesn't sound quite right, Bajro."

"No," Jean said; "I can't imagine a woman who's having her breasts cut off being able to gasp out anything."

188

The Bosnian hung his head. Tears welled from his eyes. At last he confessed, stumblingly, that it was he who had had sex with her—not raped, it was what she wanted, to provide evidence for a UNO autopsy; he'd shot her, and only then mutilated her and written the message in Serbocroat as she had suggested.

"This is an amazing story!" Stanton exclaimed. As Bajro went on weeping Jean stroked his arm gently. "You have a family?"

"Yes. Four children."

"They'll never have to want for anything again. Bajro, you're going to be a very rich man. Isn't that right, Jean?"

"That's right, Bajro."

He looked puzzled for a moment, then horrified. "I did not agree to come to England for that," he said. "I came to plead for justice for my people; and to tell what a brave woman Mrs. Hetherington was. I did not come to write a book, or to become rich. I must go back to fight." He started to rise. "You are very kind, but it does not feel right to be here."

"You wouldn't have to write the book," Stanton said; "we would have someone to help you. What we call a ghost. Please, Bajro, sit down; let's talk about this at least. There's no way you can get back until tomorrow."

Bajro subsided into the easy chair.

Stanton nodded at Jean and she said, touching his arm, "We know how you feel. It does you credit. But a book, your book, with extracts in the press, would do more to bring justice for your people than anything else."

Stanton nodded. "Tell it as it is. Anyone can fire a gun."

Bajro took Gauloises from his jeans pocket; Stanton struck a hotel match for him. "No," the Bosnian said; "I must fight. What use would justice be, in six months, a year, when my people will be destroyed by then?"

"You can give talks. Though I wouldn't advise saying much more about the Hetherington business; the press distorts things; wait until it's written."

"No. I go home. Tomorrow."

"But you have such a magnificent, tragic story to tell, Bajro," said Jean. "It would be a crime not to reveal it. The film rights would be bought up . . ."

"Oh, for a huge sum," Stanton said. "Didn't I read in a file that you studied film at Sarejevo University?"

Bajro's hard, tired eyes softened. "Yes, I study the movies. Twenty years ago or was it a century? I love the movies."

"Movies," Stanton pressed, "can have an overwhelming effect on public opinion—you know that. It could change the whole way we in the West see your situation."

"Which actors do you like, Bajro?" Jean asked. "Can you see anyone playing your part, for example?"

He deliberated. At length he said, "I liked Stanley Baker in Zulu. *I see that film many times."*

"Well, Stanley Baker's dead," Stanton said. "Anyone else? How about Clint Eastwood?"

Bajro's lips almost framed a smile. "Ah, well, Clint Eastwood, yes!"

"Oh boy!" Jean exclaimed. "That would be wonderful! There is a resemblance! He's a little taller; but with a beard—oh yes, he's the one!"

"And what about the heroine?" asked Stanton. "Who could play Mrs. Hetherington?"

"Meryl Streep?" asked Jean. "What do you think, Bajro?"

Bajro said he thought she should be English.

"Emma Thompson?" the secretary suggested. "But she'd probably refuse for political reasons. She did call her a bloody Tory cow, I seem to remember."

"This is stupid. I must—"

"She wouldn't refuse," Stanton interrupted. "It would be a fabulous role, especially opposite Clint Eastwood. But you're quite right, it's stupid to start casting; what matters is that audiences all over the world will be able to see the rape of your country. But first, there's the little matter of the book. . . ."

"Do you have anyone in mind to ghostwrite it?" Jean asked her boss.

"I thought of Tom Foster."

"Yes, he'd be good."

Addressing Bajro, Stanton explained: "Tom Foster's a young journalist and travel writer. He wrote a wonderful essay about a client of mine, Issei Kagawa, for Vanity Fair. *Incidentally you must meet Issei—he's here in London right now. Foster's a genius at drawing out details, forgotten memories; and he knows the Balkans well. I think he'd be perfect to help you with the book. Jean, why don't you take our friend out shopping, and buy a* Vanity Fair; *show him Foster's piece and help him with the English. I must go, I have to phone Gerry Adams. Stay with Bajro; have a drink with him, take him to the movies, relax him."*

She glanced at her watch. "How about Issei?"

"Issei is fine; he's with his Dutch publisher who's come over to see him; they were having lunch and then they were going to see Alive, *somewhere in Camden Town. You don't have to worry about Issei."*

Rising to his feet, he laid a hand on Bajro's shoulder. "I have to go, old chap, but Jean will look after you; she'll provide you with anything you want."

* * *

The microwave that held their steak-and-kidney pies started to beep, and Tom Foster leapt up from the table. He switched the dials to turbo on a low heat for five minutes, since he'd reached a crucial point in the conversation. A neat, trim, controlled young man, he slipped back into his interviewing role, saying, "How were you feeling, Bajro, while you were making love to Edith?"

Bajro took a gulp of Mackeson's. In the six weeks he'd been in England he'd become very fond of Mackeson's. He thought. Tried to remember.

"I was feeling torn to pieces. But she want me to enjoy. She want to enjoy herself, her last moments on earth. And we were friends, had share many beer. She cry. I cry. But we are tender. She say, Enjoy, Bajro. But I don't enjoy. Not enjoy. But the sex—you know—sex is sex, I not had sex with my wife for many weeks. It's terrible to think I could feel desire, lust, at that moment, knowing what I had to do."

Foster stared, wide-eyed, for a few silent moments; said, "That's brilliant!" and started to tap on his laptop.

"Could you say how her eyes looked at you?" he asked, tapping.

"I don't remember, Tom."

191

D. M. Thomas

"Would you say they were loving? Tender? Beseeching?"
"Tender, yes. Tender."
"So you could say, She gazed up at me tenderly?"
"I guess so."

SEVEN

The Suburban Bolero

"Watch our Mother Night sew the stars together." Teresa sits with me at nightfall on the upper terrace, holding my hands, our heads tilted skywards. "That's what my Navajo guru says to me. God, it's so beautiful, isn't it? I only wish I could make Ezekiel ease up and see how beautiful life is. I wake up in the morning, feeling glad, and I see his mournful face and it pisses me."

I nod sympathetically, feeling a tremor of pleasure.

"I'm so relieved I have you to talk to, Simon." She looks away, out to the darkened sea. Beneath our terrace the colored lights that hang between the olive trees have been turned on, and the helpers are setting the tables for the evening meal. I hear, out of the darkness, faint, inconsequential, Harold's voice crying out 'Nat's stump!' followed by laughter.

"I may not be able to co-listen with you tomorrow," she says, gazing into my eyes again. "He's so jealous of everyone. He was even angry with me down at the beach last night because I was having fun. I looked for you, thinking you might like to come too; where were you?"

"I was wandering around on the Acropolis."

"Oh, that's right. We were having a good time—Eddie, Natasha, Danny, Rhona, a few others; but then Ezekiel just stalked off. He hated me enjoying myself. It was just, you know, great friendship and fun, with a nice group of people. I'm so sorry Danny and Andrea have left, they were really great."

"And he doesn't like us co-listening?"

A headshake. "It's probably weak of me to give way to him, but . . . Well, if he and I fall out too openly it'll be bad for our workshop. So I think I must be *compliant.*" She screws up her mouth in disgust. "Don't mistake me, he's a lovely guy, I'll always be very fond of him. But our Greek rendezvous hasn't quite turned out as I expected."

I squeeze her fingers, wearing my mask of sadness, murmuring, "I'm sorry."

She sighs. "I hope I'm clear of cancer but you can never tell. I intend to live the rest of my life to the full."

"You had such wonderful vitality, such joy, when you first came," I murmur gently to her. "It was intoxicating to all of us. To me, anyway. But it's been dimmed. It would be terrible if you lost it because of Ezekiel."

"That's what I feel. Thank you!" She tugs strongly on my fingers, then relaxes her grip, takes a deep breath, flings her head back and looks up at the sky. I follow her glance. More stars have been sewn together by Mother Night.

There is a pause, a moment of balance. As at the turning of the tide—Artemis, one might say, co-listening with Poseidon— we stay as we were, yet change. It's no longer I who am holding her fingers, but she who is holding mine. I who gaze out to sea, troubled.

"I rang Marie last night. And Alan too, actually. They're still involved."

She grips my hands, her eyes melting with tender compassion. "I'm so sorry."

"I'm very jealous too. About Alan anyway; not over casual flings. I know that almost certainly they'll be sleeping together tomorrow night. I can see it too clearly. She'll be on top, riding him. She's very dominant, you see. Quite an emotional bully.

Like most South African whites, even the liberal ones. Or especially those. Alan's a mild fellow, rather passive."

I gaze up again at the spangled darkness. *Oft in the stilly night*—McCormack. Bridget liked it. Since writing the card, I can't get her out of my head.

The dinner gong sounds. "Jealousy's an awful thing," she says. "I guess Andrea was jealous last night; of me and Danny; which was silly, there was no reason to be. We were all just having fun. There's a technique for riding jealousy," she says; "You have to push yourself to the limit. I learned it from a shamaness in Arizona. I'll teach it to you."

On the way down, after she has outlined what I should do, she checks me by the wall which falls away sheer, a hundred feet, to a dry riverbed. Normally I keep well clear of it, as I have no head for heights. But tonight she makes me look over. My head spins. "Remember, you take it to the edge," she repeats. Her eyes, dimly seen, have an excited glitter. "It can be good— on the edge!"

Ezekiel is earnestly ensconced with Lucy on another, safer part of the wall. He is nodding as if in sympathy as she pours out her complaints—about me, almost certainly. Though yesterday she was friendly, I'm sure she feels bitter when Ezekiel prompts it. I feel threatened and intimidated.

* * *

Midnight. I'm with my shrunken workshop group on Calypso, under the stars. By the light of a lantern I'm sharing with them extracts from the Brooke biography. Teresa also has a late-night session; from her amphitheater we can hear the primitive drumbeat and a wail of voices singing that they are one with the earth.

"Let's go and duff up the shamans," Harold suggests.

"They're all going to get certificates at the end," I say; "old Bob and Arnold and Priscilla and Fred . . . they'll be grade-one shamans." The drumming gets louder; the wail becomes a howl. Turning to Emily, I ask her: "Are you going to let a bunch of fucking Zulus outsing a Welsh lesbian choir?"

At once we are the veldt, we are Rorke's Drift nestling among the sinister hills, where the massed ranks of the Zulu hordes are thundering spears against shields and chanting in a

195

frenzy, whipping up their bloodlust for the final assault. I'm Stanley Baker, weary, wild-eyed, streaked with sweat and blood, urging my men to one last-ditch stand. And Emily, resting her rifle on the sandbag, all but spent, croaks out, "They've got a very good bass section, but no top tenors, that's for sure . . ."

The shamans are chanting and drumming; I'm exhorting "Sing! Sing!" and "Men of Harlech" emerges raggedly, but with growing power and defiance, over Skagathos, over the veldt. Only Angus and I know a few of the words, and Natasha knows neither words nor tune, but we manage to belt out the old ballad loudly and lustily enough to unsettle the shamans. At least, I hope so. There is, so I have gathered, a genuine needle between the writers and the therapy groups. Some of the latter, who have read photocopies of our Nat writings lying about, have complained about our negative and aggressive forces unsettling the Skagathian calm.

Well, as Angus has said: fuck them!

But tonight, they conquer. Our ragged singing fades away; their more sober chanting and drumming continue, quieter again. Natasha excuses herself to go and swim with her boyfriend Eddie; Emily too goes off—perhaps to sleep with Harriet, who knows? Angus is drunk and almost asleep, his head hanging between his knees. Caroline has slumped to the ground, and has laid her head in Harold's spread, skirted lap.

Angus, his eyes closed, sways his head as if in colloquy with the drumming, and murmurs: "If only my woman, my *donna,* were here! . . . But then, what would be the use,"—he sighs— "she would give me nothing, nothing!"

"Tell me about her."

"She is a tree-woman, all green and shimmering with light in summer. She is like those lines in Pound: *Daphnis with her thighs in bark / Stretches towards me her leafy hands . . .* She is almost sixty, stout, and quite wrinkled; but those are mere externals. Soon I shall be with her; and yet . . . as far away as ever." He opens his eyes, raises his head. "It's chillier."

A cold breeze blows. Half the stars are blotted out by cloud. "Yes. Time to call it a night."

* * *

Almost twenty-four hours later, following journeys by ferry, air and train, I am letting myself into my Marlborough semi. On Skagathos, I can trust Teresa to visit my sickroom and tell the others I'm very poorly. I'm quite sure no one has seen me walking into our drive in the dark; all our middle-aged and elderly neighbors are crouched over their TV's or already tucked up in bed. Marie has left the kitchen light on. Our black cat Winnie wraps herself around my legs, purring.

I consider and discount the possibility that the adulterous lovers will go back to his flat, our house being much closer to where Dad lives. After taking a beer from the fridge, I go into my study, smell the polish, switch on the desk lamp. A pile of letters. I sit in the swivel chair and say hello to various women. The pregnant bronze Black Madonna; my bathing-suited mother with me on Weston sands, already showing weight loss; Alison's delicate line-drawing, concealing almost all her antagonism of Sonia, her half-sister; Niamh in armor, a cropped and auburn-haired Saint Joan, in the school play.

I riff through the letter hoard, tossing aside the depressing brown envelopes and the trash mail offering me fortunes. There is an impressive-looking airmail with an Iranian postmark, and a London letter scrawled with my editor's artistic script. I open this first. Crystal has hand-written it . . .

Dear Simon,

It's always a treat to get one of your sporadic letters. I envy you your idyll. I just wanted to let you know, as soon as possible, that I love *Remembering the Forest* (though I think I prefer *Infidelity);* I found it overwhelmingly powerful, a colossal achievement. My warmest congratulations! Of course I'm jumping the gun, no one else here has read it yet, but I've no doubt they'll feel the same.

I would love to have dinner with you. Of course we must have a real celebration when the new book is signed and sealed, but why don't we have an informal private dinner somewhere soon? Call me when you get back.

Affectionately,
Crystal

197

D. M. Thomas

My spine is still tingling with the pleasure of Crystal's letter when I slit open the other, azure envelope and read . . .

Dear Mr. Hopkins,

I have been command to write to you to inform your novel *Transplanted Hearts* has be shortlist for Shalimar Prize. As you shall know, this distinguishing prize is for best and most spiritously enhancing book from non-Islamic country. The exact amount of prize varies per year, but is always suffice to relieve author of all finance anxieties for many years.

Before the last judgement takes place, I have to ask you one question. Should you be award prize, we would have be sure that you shall not use occasion to propagandize on behalf of author Salman Rushdie, but on contrary express sympathy of Islamic position. May we have your assure on this?

I look forward to hear from you.

Your sincerely,
Ibrahim Rafsanjani

The joyous shiver in my spine runs on. How maddening not to know the sum! And how many are there on the shortlist? But perhaps the others will be terribly moral and refuse to give them their assure. I've no doubt I can assure them sufficiently, saying I don't approve of works that wantonly denigrate great religions. Needn't even mention Rushdie's name. Anyway, bugger him, he's got millions.

Taking the first train out in the morning, it won't be difficult to be back on Skagathos in the evening. I can circle the village and walk down, as if from my sickroom, to Fat Anna's, where everyone will be happy to greet me.

They should be back soon. I switch off my desk lamp, feeling shivery with excitement and apprehension. I pull aside the curtain and stare out at the moon-glimmered patch of patio, dull shrubbery and high fence that forms my event horizon for three-quarters of my waking life. Either typing feverishly or twiddling my thumbs. If my mind could become computer software, it would find little difference.

I climb the stairs. All lights out, I sit on our bed. At last a car; it pauses, swings into our short drive. Doors click shut; Marie's

faint voice. I withdraw into my lair: our spacious built-in ward-
robe, its sliding door not fully shut.

* * *

The act of fucking is a blur of screaming and moaning and
jangled springs. He pulls her up from the missionary position
until only her head and neck are on the bed, and hammers
down, as if his immense tool is a road drill.

Afterwards, breathing, along with the musty smell of my old
sweaters, Marie's L'Air du Temps mixed with the fishy whiff of
post-coital sex, I watch in shock as my mild, academic friend
tortures her back and shoulders with a knife. She whimpers
each time he nicks her and then bends to suck the blood.

Bolero is playing quite loudly on CD, so that the neighbors
won't hear her occasional scream among the whimpers. There is
actually little fear of that, since Frank and Mavis, next door, are
hard of hearing.

"Thank me, bitch!" he orders.

"Thank you, sir."

"Kaffir cunt . . ." He puts a trace of Afrikaans in his voice.
She screams.

"Enough," he says at last, laying the pen knife on the bedside
table. She turns on to her back, moaning; grasps his hand and
presses it to her mouth. Winnie, named for Mandela's wife,
leaps up onto the bed, tail erect, and Alan kicks her off. She
miaows, vanishes.

They lie embraced, outside the duvet, quiet now. He smokes;
I see the tip glow and fade.

"I shouldn't have gone that far," he murmurs. I think he must
touch her with the end of his cigarette before stubbing it in my
Dartington glass ashtray, as she gives a hiss of pain. "Simon'll
see all the cuts and bruises."

"I don't care, Alan; everything's different now. Please, let me
move in with you. I hate this hypocrisy."

"No. I don't want you all the time, sweet bung hole. Besides,
I'd lose my job, and so would you. That's not the main thing,
though—we'd lose what makes it special; I don't want a
harassed Mum with nappies. When are you going to tell Simon
you're pregnant?"

D. M. Thomas

"When he gets back. If you won't have me I should *never* have told him about us."

He chuckles. "You mean he might not want you?"

"Oh, no, that would be welcome. Vanilla sex, with Simon, is so boring. No, it just makes it awkward between the three of us, that's all."

"He'll come round. I know old Si. He'll endure any humiliation. You having my kid. You still fucking with me. Seeing you cut to ribbons and knowing it turns you on. Anything."

"That's what you wanted, isn't it? His humiliation. That's why you made me tell him. You're a swine, you know that?"

"I know that. And you love it." In a softer tone, he murmurs: "I enjoyed being with you tonight. Like a couple—and openly."

"Really?"—A girlish, fluttery voice I've never heard, any more than I've heard the masochist's tortured whimpers.

"Yes."

"It *was* nice. I think Sam must have sensed we loved each other and there was something going on."

"Oh, I think so. From the way he told you to sit in front for the drive home. I'm sure he knew my left hand wasn't always on the gear stick. But equally I don't think the old boy minds. I shouldn't think he has any illusions about what it's like to live with his son."

"Probably not."

"I think he enjoyed himself, don't you? It was good. I've only ever seen the film of *Macbeth* before, so—"

"Shh! you mustn't say the name, it's bad luck."

An hour later, with one movement of the knife, I cut their throats while they sleep embraced.

EIGHT

A Gastronomic Movie

Spanish Nights reaches its end with the closing chords of *Bolero,* and soon after I hear Elspeth's faint floaty voice thanking everyone for a good early-morning workout. Not wishing to risk a mug from the rack I've pissed onto, I carry down one I've had in my room for several days. A gnat floats on the coffee dregs.

I'm almost blown off the steps as I descend. Ezekiel and Teresa are just coming through the gate, plastic macs billowing behind them. I say "Hi!" and enter the kitchen behind Teresa. Flicking water from her face she says to me, "Well, did you ride on the witch's broomstick?"

Somehow the rainwater etches the lines on her face. She really has aged in the days since her arrival, and is less attractive.

I nod. "Yes, it's fantastic! I never thought I'd be able to dream lucidly; but as you said, if you catch yourself just on the point of waking up, you can—ride the broomstick! I had a fantastic orgasm!"

"That's great!"

"It was so totally real! Of course it probably helped that I could hear the wind and the rain; a very English sound!"

"I guess it would!" She gives my arm a squeeze and, saying she'll catch up with me later, turns back to Ezekiel. More caped and hooded figures crowd into the kitchen.

Since it's impossible to eat our breakfast outside we must carry our plates and mugs into the crammed Lotus Room and eat as best we can. We do so almost in silence, depressed by the weather, both in itself and as a portent of what is fast approaching for most of us: the autumnal English gloom.

Stephanos stands, his thin brown legs out of keeping with the grey, rainy sky outside the window. He begins the *demos*. He's sorry about the weather; but it should clear by the afternoon. No, he doesn't think there's another, longer *meltemi* on the way. He warns us to be on the lookout for reporters from England. There was a very inaccurate report in the English press about Lucinda's death. Partly it was understandable, since there was an impression at first that it could be suicide; but now we know different. We should be careful what we say.

Also, this is the day when sometimes we get a few of the people holidaying on Skyros coming over, looking at this smaller but more picturesque island. Stephanos smiles ironically. It would be nice to be pleasant to them if we meet them in the village, and invite them to call in at our Centre. We can tell them, if we like, to come next year to Skagathos where they'll get much better food and general value for money.

He sits and Elspeth rises. The willowy facilitator says as it's so dismal we should sing a cheerful song; so could we please stand up, hold hands with the persons nearest us, and sing the simple Greek song she's about to teach us.

After we've finished singing rather dolefully, Stephanos asks if there's anything else anyone wants to say, and Harold stands. His very appearance, in Caroline's elasticated skirt over his boots and socks, draws amusement. Yet it's noticeable that this skirted, grey-stubbled, skin-peeling Harold is more, not less, masculine than the smooth-featured man who arrived on Skagathos. He announces very soberly: "This is a message for Fred, Arnold, Priscilla, Bob and others involved in the group sex: due to the bad weather, it will take place in this room, at two as usual." He sits, to sporadic and uneasy chuckles.

On the way out I pass Teresa again and say, "Do we co-listen later, or—" a glance towards Ezekiel, who's chatting to Elspeth—"not?"

"Better not, Simon; I'm sorry; he's already in a bad mood because I was here late with my shaman group. I disturbed his sleep coming in, he says. No mention that the night before last *he* was out and about, in a foul mood, till four a.m., keeping *me* from sleep." She pulls a face.

"I'm sorry too. I'll miss our session."

"So will I. Maybe tomorrow."

I would have confessed to her my misgivings over the savagery of my lucid dream. They're lying there, drained of blood. Dad will come eventually, worried she's not answering his calls. He'll see blood dripping from the kitchen ceiling, as in *Tess*.

But no, they're still alive. And this evening they take Dad to the National.

       * * *

A girl I haven't spoken to so far, a tall, awkward, earnest girl called Sandra, is reading Shakespeare's Sonnets in paperback. I take the chance to speak to her. Her name has been bandied about as someone very depressed; and I've not so far seen her smile. But when I talk to her she does show a glimmer of a smile, as she says how much she loves poetry, how she liked reciting at school. She went to Oxford Poly to read English, but had to leave owing to a breakdown.

I tell her, lying through my teeth, how much I enjoyed the folksong she sang at a *demos*. Actually she was dreadful, pitiably shy. She thanks me, says she really would have liked to recite a poem, but our group (and my presence especially) put her off. She's enjoying the Reiki, yet wishes she'd had the courage to take the Fiction Workshop.

She has heard Harold and Angus talking about a trip to see Rupert Brooke's grave on Skyros, tomorrow afternoon; would it be possible to join us, as she loves Brooke? Of course! I say, You'd be more than welcome. I take my slim Pocket Brooke out of a folder and let her glance through it. How about reciting some of his poems at the grave, I ask her? Rather to my surprise, and almost alarm, she agrees, after a show of reluctance. She will be a bundle of nerves, but her counselor has said she must accept challenges. She goes off, bearing Brooke, glowing. I feel a certain glow myself. Even if she recites the poems badly, what the fuck does it matter, so long as it helps restore her confidence?

Our group can now sit comfortably in the storeroom, breathing in the smell of onions, apples and—the nonsmokers being inclined to be charitable to Natasha and Harold—smoke. We discuss the labyrinths of fiction. Harold wonders how a writer ever gets out of the maze of his own imagination. We ourselves have reached many dead-ends and *cul de sacs.*

Priscilla's laptop is here; with more pages that have been group-written. Does God sit before a word processor, Natasha wonders; or with a laptop on his knees; or her knees; tapping out history, creating a more and more impenetrable maze? Wondering whether to save and continue, Emily pursues the metaphor, or abandon edit?

What's much more terrible, Angus says, and more likely, is that there is *no one* with a laptop. The almost endless, winding story stutters itself out haphazardly; each of us appears as a minute character momentarily, and disappears. And the story and its style get drabber and drabber as entropy takes effect, the running-down battery; the computer runs on JOHNMAJORJOHNSMITH software . . . This would be worse than the well-known monkeys typing away and eventually producing Shakespeare's Collected Works. That would by now be quite impossible; at best the monkeys might produce the Collected Speeches of Bill Clinton.

* * *

The atmosphere at the Centre is gloomy and irate. The house that once saw banquets and orgies involving Mayor Lansky, other hoods and various broads, now has fifty gloomy people huddling in the kitchen drinking elderflower or mint tea. Pressed against my back is a plump grey-haired woman who is talking querulously with a ginger beard about (I gather) an awkward member of their *oekos*. "You're his *father*, for heaven's sake, Dennis," she says, "and he's treating you like shit!"

Entertained by this, at first I don't hear the quiet voice say "Bonjour, Simon." She calls my name louder and I turn to my left.

"Oh, hello, Jeanne! How are things with you?"

"Pas mal; not bad for a fading Frenchy!" She smiles wanly.

"Ah! Jeanne, I write stupid things like that, just as an *aide-memoire*. It was really to remind me that you were—a mature Frenchwoman. To distinguish you from, say, Lucy or Andrea, who were younger. I didn't mean you were *fading!* Good heavens! You're one of the most attractive women here."

"It's okay. I *am* fading."

* * *

The screams and orgasmic noises from the Ezekiel-Teresa workshop are loud enough to be disturbing when our workshop is in the storeroom. However, we have become inured to them by the end of the morning; we are engrossed in discussions of the exploding Kagawa and Bajro texts. Conscious also of how many plots involving the Welsh cottage we have simply abandoned.

But now we become aware of different sounds; acrimonious voices, female then male; a woman sobbing. We look round at each other, wondering. It's lunchtime and I bring the discussion to a close.

As we emerge into the grey and drizzly air, I see a group of people from the orgasmic workshop clustered around a stranger—a short greying semitic-looking woman, in a black trouser suit, who sits wiping her eyes, obviously deeply upset. Hands are patting her hunched shoulder, stroking her frizzy hair. I sidle up behind them, curious. Dr. Bob the sociologist says to her, "Thank you for sharing that with us."

* * *

Lunch at my Greek-English cafe. I reflect on the weird incarnation of Sara Morgenstein: which only emerged after Ezekiel and a weeping Teresa had emerged from their orgasmic den. Harold and I agreed we admired her *chutzpah* in flying (unshamanically) all the way from Vancouver to confront her erring husband. But it's more than that, it's obsession, obsessive jealousy, and I understand that only too well.

An elderly lady drinking tea at the next table gets into conversation with me, announcing she's from the Skyros Centre. She asks me if I can help her with a crossword clue from Skyros's holistic magazine *i to i.* "A classic upset—if you go topless you'll burn." Five letters, last one M. "Ilium," I tell her. Normally I'm hopeless at crosswords, but it's lucky my mind has been running on Helen of Troy.

In heavy-knit sweater, corduroy trousers and sneakers, she's turning, like so many old ladies, into an old man. The lady from Skyros, I mean, not Helen of Troy. Though it may have happened to her too; the more beautiful a woman is, the more she tends to scorn feminine beauty when hers has waned.

She's loving every minute on Skyros; it's so well organized and such fun. She's sad that the weather is bad today; very few have come over to Skagathos. Though at least it has stopped raining. "I'm Flo," she says, offering her hand.

When I tell her my name she pretends to have heard of me, confessing she is a fan of the detective story, and particularly of Ruth Rendell. "She's a wonderful tutor—works to all hours. Today's our first real break. It's thrilling to have the chance to get to know her a little. All of us are devoted to her."

"Is it a good group?"

"Oh, yes! We're a very mixed group, from different parts of the world. Most interesting people." They're all quite keyed up, she says, because tomorrow they'll get their stories back, and will be invited to read out loud. "Fancy having a story read and remarked on by Ruth Rendell!" she exclaims, thrusting a liver-spotted claw against her chest. "Oh my! But some of the others are very, very bright."

"You have someone who started with us. An American lady."

Her old face lights up. "Krystal! That's right! Yes, she started later than the rest of us. Oh, Krystal's a great character! Full of fun!"

I hope I don't show how unlikely that description sounds. I say cautiously, "Yes, she seemed very nice; but we probably didn't get the best of her because she really wanted to write detective stories. I was glad she had the chance to move over."

She takes a packet of cigarettes from her handbag and asks if I mind her lighting up. I shake my head. "Well, she has an awfully useful background for a detective writing workshop."

"Does she? I don't recall."

"Her husband was in the CIA. *Goodness,* some of the things he was involved in! It would make your hair curl! Mind-altering experiments, that kind of thing. He taught her hypnosis, she wanted to try it on me for my smoking, but I'm afraid I declined. I'm seventy-six, and you've got to die of something."

"Well, that's true."

Her son's just given up, and she's proud of him. He too used nicotine patches. "Have you any children, Mr. Hopkins?" Three daughters, I reply; all overseas at the moment. The youngest at Trinity College, Dublin. How wonderful! she says; and do they have writing talent? And her friend Annie has a granddaughter at university—and so on.

I summon my bill. Flo spots Annie in similar heavy-knit sweater, corduroys, sneakers, waddling out of a jewelers' opposite; and rises to signal to her. "Oh, there you are, Flo!" says the newcomer.

"This is Mr. Hopkins." I half-rise to shake hands. "Annie's in our workshop. I was telling Mr. Hopkins what fun we have. He knows Krystal. Krystal was here for a couple of days."

"Krystal's lovely!" Annie agrees, just as a slim Greek man with a black beard appears and says, "I'm sorry, ladies, we must get to the boat; there could be a storm."

"Oh, what a pity!"

Harold, passing at that moment, comes over and slides a couple of pages out of his T-shirt, saying, "A snip from next year's Oscars."

"Thanks. This is Flo. And Annie."

"Hi, Flo and Annie!"

They look somewhat taken aback by the wild-eyed, stubbled man in his skirt, socks and lace-up shoes, but return his greeting with impeccable English politeness. "We have to get the boat; Nico says there could be a storm." Flo shakes my hand again.

"It's been so nice meeting you, young man! Would you like my paper? It's only three days old."

When they have disappeared down the road, Harold says, in answer to my invitation to a drink: "Mustn't stay; have to try and see Socrates about the trip. Just wanted to say—" his face wearing a roguish grin—"we admired *your* chutzpah too, in fucking Teresa last night on the wall right where old Mayor Lansky used to dump unwanted guests."

My face expresses my bewilderment.

"You mean it wasn't you? Oh, shit! We were *almost* sure it was you. He looked like you, as far as we could tell in the dark: thin, medium height, not too much hair on top." This, he explains, was after I had left them on Calypso, following Men of Harlech. "Caroline and I stayed on till the whole place was quiet and empty, as we thought. But when we staggered down the steps we saw Teresa and Anon humping away on the wall. We beat a hasty retreat, I can tell you, and came down via a hedge and the road. By that time they'd vanished too. We knew you fancied her, so we thought . . . Don't worry, I shall clear your name. See you later, old boy."

The darkened sky lightens again. I sit on with an orangina, my mind maddeningly on tonight, at home—even when I scan Harold's script.

* * *

HANKS (on stage reading): *Nominees for Best Actor are: Dirk Anderson, for* UFO over Vermont; *Hank Sheen, for* Bosnian Sacrifice; *Dusky Hogmann, for* Dark Desire; *and John Radar, for* The Golden Dude. (Big screen, split into four, shows the relaxed tuxedoed nominees.) *And the winner is . . .* (slits open envelope and takes out card) *Dusky Hogmann!* (Tumultuous applause; screen shows the three losers, clapping wildly, their faces alight with joyous smiles; then Hogmann striding between the tables, clasping eager hands. He leaps onto the stage, is hugged by Hanks, and takes the Oscar from him.)

HOGMANN (after a long, reflective pause, during which the audience grows hushed): *Any one of the nominees would have graced this stage. Hank—I want to say to you particularly, what a truly great actor you are.* (Applause, whistles; camera picks out

Hank Sheen, smiling, saluting.) *That great scene, the scene with the equally wonderful Juliet Harrison, when you are making love in the forest outside Sarajevo and you know, you both know, you must kill her: for me it's just about the finest cinema since* Citizen Kane. (More claps.) *You should be up here instead of me, partner! But okay, the dice fell to me . . . A decade or so ago, in Paris, a young Japanese student did something very strange and terrible. Anyone who has seen* Dark Desire *will know what he did. It wasn't evil, and it wasn't a crime, because it rose out of madness. Temporary madness. And that madness was the result of rage, smoldering rage, unconscious rage, not from his lifetime only but many lifetimes. Rage at the* real *evil, the* real *crime: centuries of exploitation of colored people by whites. Culminating in Hiroshima and Nagasaki. It was the same rage that drove two peaceful Californian boys to kill their parents who had brutally abused them; that drove a gentle African American to mayhem with a gun in a New York subway; drove a quiet lady called Mrs. Bobbitt to emasculate her violent husband . . . This award is not for me; and not even for the people without whom I couldn't possibly have won it—Greg Southerby the director; you're beautiful, Greg . . . Jennifer Peters my brilliant friend and co-star; Lena Collins, Henry Luke, Crosby Thorn, and so many more. This award is for the writer, Issei Kagawa* (applause: screen shows Kagawa and wife, with friends, at their table); *not the least joy of taking part in this picture is that it's enabled me to get to know Issei and Siri, his beautiful wife, and we have a dear friendship. But I know Issei would agree with me that this award belongs to every poor exploited Hispanic, Afro-American or Oriental, to every sexually abused child, to every gay person struggling to live productively in the midst of prejudice; to every handicapped person; to every woman enduring the daily pinpricks of discrimination. It's an Oscar for every lesbian. For every person with a weight problem. In the words of Federico Garcia Lorca, this is for all the poor beautiful dejected ones. I'd like to thank my mother, who was poor and beautiful, but never dejected for long. I'd like to thank my first high school drama teacher, a gay man called Pete Lewis. This belongs to him too. Jesus, I never expected to be standing here clutching one of these. Hollywood, I love you; you have a great, generously beating heart. Tom, you moved us so much when you described all*

209

the gay men walking the streets of heaven. Well, it reminded me of when my poppa first brought me to see LA, when I was ten or eleven. I couldn't believe a city could be so big! I got tired, walking the streets. And my poppa said, Keep goin', son; if you keep walkin' you'll come to Paradise! . . . I've found out what he meant. Thank you. (Leaves stage; applause.)

NINE

An Erogenous Clock

The rest of the day is a delirium; I am aware only of Alan and Marie making love. This time it is gentle love, as I'm sure it is in reality. It tortures more than the knife pricks I imagined.

He is bigger than me . . . She told me that, teasingly, sexily, during our passionate August. At once saying size didn't matter; if it did, she'd never have left N'dosi, her black lover . . .

It's morning, the sky a brilliant cloudless azure. Whatever they did—it's done, and I feel relief and release. Elspeth, leading the *demos,* guides us in colonic massage, a clockwise gyration of the pelvis to encourage a bowel movement. Several people, herself included, are beginning to suffer from constipation following their dysentery. It's hard to think of shit underlying the slender, fluid, sari'd exterior, her hands scooping and pushing down.

When she's finished, she invites appreciations and messages. Brenda announces, to murmurs of concern, that Elke has a very bad back which some pre-breakfast Reiki hasn't yet cleared up, and the artists must work on their own today. As Brenda sits down, Harold stands, skirted, booted. If any expect another joke about group sex they are disappointed; he speaks seriously. "The Fiction Workshop are running a trip to Skyros this afternoon. To the grave of the poet Rupert Brooke. We've room for a few more on the boat, if any of you are interested."

"It's a very peaceful, very beautiful spot," says Stephanos.

"Some of the Skyros people I met yesterday have been there," Harold continues, "and they found it—as Stephanos says—very beautiful, peaceful and moving. Brooke was on his way with his regiment to Gallipoli in 1915; they landed on Skyros for training; Brooke said if he were to die this would be a beautiful spot to rest in. He had sunstroke and a mosquito bite, developed a fever, and died. His men bore his body up through a dry stream to this beautiful olive grove and buried him there. They had to struggle to dig a hole in the dry ground. Later the Greeks made a marble tomb, and on it there's his famous sonnet which starts 'If I should die, think only this of me, That there's some corner of a foreign field that is forever England.' "

He looks queryingly in my direction as he sits down. I nod and get to my feet; eyes swivel towards me.

Brooke, I tell them, did not have the time to become a major poet but was a true poet. "He represents a tragic generation. My grandfather was killed on the Somme. For me, Brooke's grave is a symbol. The chance to visit it was one of the main reasons why I accepted the invitation to Skagathos. Just before his death—"I open the paperback biography—"he referred in his journal to the peacefulness of these islands. Let me read that passage to you: *There are moments—there have been several, especially in the Aegean—when, through some beauty of sky and air and earth, and some harmony with the mind, peace is complete and completely satisfying. One is at rest from the world, and with it, entirely content, drinking to the full of the placidity of the loveliness. Every second seems divine and sufficient. And there are men and women who seem to do what one so terribly can't, and so terribly, at these moments,* aches *to do—store up reservoirs of this calm and content, fill and seal great jars or pitchers during these half-hours, and draw on them at later moments, when the source isn't there, but the need is very great."* I close the book; there are appreciative murmurs. "Isn't that what we're doing here? Seal-ing up jars and pitchers of serenity for when we need it?" I sit down.

"How much will it cost?" white-haired Fred asks. "Some of us are getting a bit short of the readies."

Harold rises to reply. "It's three thousand drachmas altogether, and the boat can take up to ten people. So, depending on numbers, between three and six hundred drachmas—a quid or two. The price of a fucking ice cream at home."

"How long will it take?"

"An hour on the water," says Stephanos, "an hour's walk there and back. Maybe three hours all said."

Ezekiel and Teresa raise their hands. "Count us in," says Ezekiel. Also tall, plain, shy Sandra, a few seconds later.

"I've managed to persuade Sandra to read some of Brooke's poems at the grave," I say, nodding pleasantly in her direction. Heads turn towards her and—scarcely tanned by the Aegean sun—she blushes to the roots of her short mousy hair. The people closest to her stroke her and make encouraging noises. Seeing my Pocket Brooke on the table in front of her, I ask if I may borrow it back for a moment, to read something. I read out Brooke's poem about things he especially loves. It rouses clucks of approval.

A Dutchman or a Belgian—our paths have not crossed so I'm uncertain—stands up to say it's encouraging the cult of war to go to Brooke's grave. "Piss off!" Harold says. "If it weren't for brave English soldiers like Brooke you'd be twitching under Hitler still, you wanker!" There is shocked laughter—Harold is smiling, so it's hard to know if he's seriously angry. But a few people, including Lucy, Priscilla and Arnold, speak briefly in support of the Dutchman or Belgian. Priscilla snipes, "He had no fucking business coming here with his weapons of death." There's a decidedly autumnal edge in the atmosphere for a few moments, but Ezekiel speaks some calming words. We can honor a young poet, victim of man's tragic stupidity, he urges, without honoring war.

"That's all very fine, Ezekiel," exclaims Lucy, "but in practice it's impossible to honor a warrior without honoring war."

There is a hum of agreement with her. Harold: "I find this

D. M. Thomas

distasteful. I think there's some homophobia going on here, under the surface."

"I didn't know—" begins Priscilla.

"His first, and probably most passionate sexual experience, was with a male. I thought everyone knew that. He wrote a wonderful, famous account of it. Of buggering his young friend. You just don't want to honor a gay poet."

"No, no, that's totally untrue!" Priscilla's voice has a slightly hysterical edge to it. "I'm not in the least homophobic."

"Nor am I," exclaims the Dutchman or Belgian.

"It does change the circumstances," Priscilla adds. "You should have told us he was gay. In this case I have no objection. Back home I've been protesting Clinton's broken promise to allow gay servicemen."

Harold says those planning to go should meet at the beach taverna at two. The boatman is called Socrates, and his boat is the *Medea.* "Wear a hat," Stephanos advises us, with a nod up at the pure blue sky; "it's going to be hot; the grave is in a secluded grove, a sun trap. Also you will burn on the water; take care . . . Anyone else wish to speak?" He scans the assembly. ". . . Well, it's your last day on Skagathos. I'm hoping the water will soon be on. But in any case you will have nice hotel in Athens, as on the way out, to rest up for a few hours and take a shower. Tonight we eat here and say our farewells. Please have your bedrooms stripped by six in the morning, and carry your cases down to the pick-up point by six thirty. Tamsin will be going to Athens with you. Enjoy your day."

As the *demos* breaks up, Teresa strolls across to me, smiling. "Ezekiel realizes he's been sulky. I had a good talk with him last night. *He's* the one who's involved elsewhere, after all! He wants to get to know you better. We can co-listen tonight, when we get back? I've lots to tell you."

"Me too. Do you know if there's a staff meeting?"

"No. Elke's real bad; she may not be able to leave tomorrow. She fell out of bed during the night. She says she's not used to such a narrow bed."

* * *

214

Calypso. I read to them some more Brooke. Somehow it strikes a chord in all of us. Blue-vaulted silence. I want to write. I want to write about those sealed jars. And the way Skagathos has stolen away every carnal desire. I no longer have any urge to sleep with Caroline or Natasha; and with Teresa, it's as if we've already gone through a fifteen-year marriage. My temptation is quiet.

The others want to write too. I've advised them to cut free from their recent fiction and bury deep inside their own sealed jar. We become absorbed. Nobody hears the donkey bray, or the screams from orgasmic consciousness. Even when Harold farts long and loudly, and Angus murmurs, "Be not afeard, the isle is full of noises," no one smiles or shows any loss of concentration. The sun bakes us, and the air shimmers.

We look up only when the black-suited, collarless, stubbled old mayor calls to us and gesticulates from beyond the fence. We take it the water is on again.

"Thank Christ, now I can shit," says Emily, but again without a change of expression or evoking any response; the writing goes on.

* * *

Returning to my room to shower before lunch, I am intercepted by Stephanos. "A fax for you, Simon." I read it climbing the steps, my heart sinking. "Dear Simon, Many thanks for your fax; glad you're enjoying your workshop. This is to let you know I lost no time in reading the new novel and I like it. There are a few things that need tidying up, but it's very amusing and charming. The only thing is, before I pass it on to other readers I have to say I don't think it's the sort of book that will have a very wide appeal. Perhaps not even as much as *Transplanted Hearts,* which as you know didn't do as well as we had hoped. We have had to clear some of the stocks due to lack of warehouse space; you should have been informed of this and I'm sorry if you weren't. I don't think we could offer you as much for this one as we did for TH; we certainly could not offer more. I will be sorry to lose you, but will quite understand if you can get a better offer from another publisher. Perhaps you can

215

D. M. Thomas

discuss this with Jim and he can let me know if it's worth my while passing this book on to others to read. All best, Crystal."

* * *

Fuck it. Fuck her. I'll have to crawl, eat humble pie.

* * *

Opening the door and entering the dark corridor, I bump into Maria, the shit-clearer, carrying bucket and mop, emerging from the bathroom. She backs away, with a faint smile, to let me enter my room. So close to her, I catch a scent of heavy black clothes and sweat. In this half-darkness it's like a different world. Maria's is a face of many wrinkles, her somber eyes bear a signature of suffering and labor; what we've been doing, this fortnight, and what I do constantly, seem mere self-indulgent play; her eyes rebuke my self-pity. She turns away.

Hovering half in and half out of my bedroom I say to her, "Please, wait; I want to thank you." She doesn't understand; I remember she hasn't a word of English. I pick up a thousand drachma note from my desk and hand it to her. *"Efkaristo,* Maria!"

"Efkaristo!"

Embarrassed, she turns away again; yet hovers, as if uncertain if I want something from her. The uncertainty, the rare moment of privacy in a stuffy corridor, disturbs and inflames me. It is worth the probability of a humiliating rejection to try to have her. I can do with some comforting, some mothering. My voice trembles as I say, "Please, Maria . . ." I take her arm gently and draw her fully into the bedroom. I place on the bed a ten thousand drachma note. She frowns. I run my hand over the rumpled, unchanged sheet on which I have lain alone for twelve nights. Her frown clearing, she makes an exclamation, waves away my note, and grabs the sheet to take away.

She thinks I want it washed. "No, Maria!" I take back the rolled-up sheet. I rub my chin. How to explain? Especially something so indelicate.

Now she grabs *my* arm and, flicking her head towards the exit, pulls me. Having abandoned her bucket and mop, she opens the door to the outside and leads me down the stairs.

216

Harold, about to climb the stairs, recoils in surprise. He holds towards me a few pages, saying, "I've started an autobiographical novel, like you suggested."

"Great! Could you put it in my room?"

"Of course."

I follow Maria out of the gate and down into the village. At times I have almost to run to keep up with her, and I am breathing heavily, sweating. She runs with a pronounced stoop, as if carrying a burden. The sky is now the color of her thick grey-violet tights. One or two spots of rain fall. We move left, into a side lane I have never walked before. On one side are some poor shops and on the other a drop to a barren, goat-cropped gully and beyond that a dun-colored hillside, on which a bulldozer is carving out a flat area. It's where, I recall Stephanos saying, a luxury hotel is to be built. Even Skagathos is changing, though less so than Skyros, where Brooke's grave is soon to be buried under a new naval base.

I glance at my watch as Maria tugs me along the rutted lane.

I follow her into a souvenir shop, crammed with postcards and kitsch. A portly middle-aged man with a red beard and hair steps forward. Maria speaks to him volubly; he nods, concentrating. Swinging around to me, he thrusts out a hand, saying with only a trace of accent, "Hi! I'm Mike—Maria's brother."

Taken aback, I murmur, "Hi. Simon Hopkins."

"Yes, she told me. You just caught me; I was just about to close for siesta." He points to a shelf where there are baseball caps like mine. "Very popular in Skagathos this summer! Nice Americano bring these for Maria's children, but they no want them. They like football—like me. Spurs, Manchester United. So I sell."

"You speak good English."

He grins proudly. "I was married to Englishwoman for a time, and lived in Hounslow. I learned electronics there." He points around the shop at various ethnically colorful plates that have been turned into clocks. "I made these. You buy one, perhaps? Wait; I get ouzo."

I am about to say no thank you, but he has vanished, and returns moments later with a bottle of ouzo and three glasses. He pulls out two chairs and invites Maria and me to sit. I say

217

I've got to go soon, we're taking a boat trip to Skyros. He shakes his head disapprovingly, glancing outside. "The weather's not too good; it will be very windy out on the sea. Who is taking you?"

"Socrates."

He smiles, sardonically I feel, and rolls his eyes at his sister. Maria smiles in the same sardonic way. "Good fellow, but the *Medea* rocks like hell! If the weather's not so good you'll—" He mimes an attack of vomiting. "No, drink your ouzo. Maria says you offered her money, but she doesn't know what for. You explain, please?"

I can sense the blood rushing to my face. I start to stammer out that she's misunderstood, but he interrupts to say: "She thinks maybe you were offering money to fuck her but she wasn't sure; she didn't want to make embarrassing mistake. Was she right? Do you want to fuck her?"

"No, of course not; I—"

"Really, it's okay!" He squeezes my arm, pours us more ouzo, despite my attempt to cover the glass. "It happens. Maria is no oil painting, but she's sexy, somehow. You wouldn't be the first. She has four children; it's not easy to live. Be honest! Is that what you meant?"

"Yes."

He beams; and says something in Greek to Maria. She babbles and throws her arms around.

"She like you. You can use my flat upstairs." He points at the ceiling. "But first, we must do business. It will be fifteen thousand drachmas. Including my commission. As long as you like. All afternoon and evening." He barks another sentence at Maria, and she responds with a longer stream of sentences.

"She says twenty thousand. She's short this week; she hasn't been paid by Stephanos yet, because they had a robbery. You can have everything, everything you've ever wanted. Blow job, buggery, water sports, you name it."

"I'm sorry, it's too much. I'm running out of cash."

"It's okay—you have credit cards?"

"Well, yes. American Express. Visa."

"Then that's fine! I take Visa. Look, you like this clock?"

He hooks the plate off the wall, and turns it over to show me

218

the electronics. "All my own work!" he boasts. "You like it? Normally this is ten thousand, but you can have it for five— twenty-five thousand, and that's a bargain! Twenty-five thousand for all day with Maria and a gift to take home for your wife!"

I examine the plate. It *is* rather a nice design. But twenty-five thousand is quite a lot of money. "Look, ten thousand, cash, to lie naked with her and kiss." I really only need to be held and comforted.

He looks sour; waves at me angrily. "That's stupid! You think it's fair to rouse my sister and then leave her unsatisfied? No, twenty-five thousand for Maria and the clock. Take it or leave it."

"Visa, you say?"

"Yes, Visa, of course."

I'm sure the bedroom upstairs, plain and anonymous except for a framed photo of an English-looking boy and girl, has seen many men from the Skagathos Centre. No matter. I slip out of time. We melt together perfectly, somehow marrying the fleeting passion of youth with the playfulness of carefree maturity. I hear, now and again, a gust of wind outside the window; at one moment I seem to be observing a downpour of rain, and even a flash of lightning; then again blue sky, bright sun; but all this might easily be within me. Or within us: because the borders are dissolved, this afternoon, this evening.

Her smile, her eyes, seem to be telling me to ignore the sordidness of her brother's haggling. The silkiness of her black slip, the suavity of her lips and her sex, seem somehow to slide inside me, in my flesh and in my soul, creating a warm tenderness, a floating joy. I feel that she feels this too, that it's something rare, never to be forgotten, special.

Her legs wrapped around me, I drift into an endless rowing rhythm, entering and moving back; slow, lazy, exquisite. She feels it too, her eyes closed, her lips slightly parted in a kind of Madonna smile. Normally I like to talk during sex; it feels strange not to be able to communicate. I risk the word *"kalon,"* having a vague idea it means beautiful. She opens her eyes, her warm brown pupils gazing up into mine, and murmurs, "Gazza."

It's a kind of question. I chuckle, and repeat, "Gazza, yes!" And when she follows up with "Bobby Charlton?" I agree with that too.

Such joy, after the drench of sperm, the last withdrawal, to be buried in the dusky, sweaty plenitude of her breasts . . . My mouth moves from her nipple just long enough to murmur, drowsily, *"Kalon!"* And then, crazily, the foreign words "I love you!" Her arms tighten round me, and she says, nodding, "T'atcher."

* * *

Her brother finishes taping the awkwardly shaped package and gives it to me. "You got your Visa card?"

I hand him the Visa, he runs it expertly through the machine, and I sign. "You come another day," he suggests, handing me back the card. I explain that it's our last day and he says, "That's a pity; she like you, you shouldn't have waited. Next time you could have had twenty percent off." He shakes my hand vigorously and unlocks and opens the door.

Dusk is starting to fall; the air has freshened since noon and I take a deep, healthy, tobacco-free breath. Maria has brought me new vitality. Post-siesta music starts to jingle from one of the bars. I stand lost in thought for a moment; then my arm is firmly gripped, and I look aside and see Stephanos's mild, smiling face. "Hello!" he says. "Were you soaked?"

I don't know what he means, look at him perplexed. Guilt makes me rush to the wrong conclusion. He knows I've paid a lot of money to fuck Maria. He means soaked as in soaking the rich.

No, of course he sees the package under my arm! I shake my head.

"That's good; I thought you might be. It's a beautiful spot, don't you think?"

Remember I'm quite dazed from my experience, and still enchanted by it; so that, once again, I think Stephanos must be talking about that island of the Hesperides between Maria's thighs. But, not being absolutely certain, I stand perplexed. "Brooke's grave," he says. For a moment or two it makes no sense, like a phrase of Swahili; the boat trip had completely vanished from my mind. Then guilt and regret rush in.

"Oh! I didn't go. I'm afraid I called in here to look for a present for one of my daughters, and got talking and drinking with Mike."

"He's an interesting man. Maria at the Centre is his sister."

"Yes. She's here, as a matter of fact." I nod my head towards the shop.

That's good, he says; he's forgotten to give her her wages, and he was going to hand them to Mike to give to Maria in church; but now he can give them to her personally. Touching my parcel, he says he hopes I wasn't overcharged. I shake my head. He asks if Mike knew I was a member of the staff, as that entitles me to a discount, and I say I think so.

It was quite a big storm, he says. He hopes the boat-trippers weren't on their way back when it came on as they would have gotten soaked.

I make my way back, stepping carefully because the path is wet and slippery and in places there are small torrents tumbling down from step to step. More and more remorseful, I look out to see if I can spot any of the boat-trippers in any of the bars, but without luck. Well, what the hell—I chose life rather than death. As the rising lane becomes narrower, the music left behind, I feel a great tranquillity. I nod a greeting to the black and cowled crones sitting on their doorsteps, hairs sprouting from their pointy chins. They smile gummily at me, and bow. There's such courtesy here; and Brooke was right about the harmony of the mind, amid the sea, white stone, flowers and blue sky.

A wild thought takes possession of me, gradually. If things go awry at home as a result of Alan or Carla—or even if they don't—why shouldn't I move here, and propose to Maria? I could never ask for more beautiful sex; I felt terrific peace in her arms after. I smile at the memory of "Bobby Charlton"; there's something to be said for a silent woman, especially if she's the wife of a writer. Raised in the Greek tradition, she would serve me unquestioningly. And her children. Ay, there's the rub: those four children. Yet, even if she's younger than she looks, say in her forties, they're growing up, largely self-sufficient; and the Skagathian children—there are some in front of

D. M. Thomas

me, shyly offering to sell me decorated stones—are so beautiful and polite!

One of them might even be called Achilles!

It seems to make more and more sense. My modest royalties would probably make me one of the richest men on Skagathos. No more of that damned school! When I arrive at the Centre, there is already the beginnings of a festive atmosphere, with men in slacks and women in dresses: for Skagathos a positive Ascot of high fashion. A couple of nondescript women whom I still haven't spoken to suddenly look astonishingly attractive—though I think the change has more to do with the erotic after-glow of my hours with Maria. Good, tender sex bathes everyone in its spell, for a while. I hurry up the steps to get to my room and to change my clothes.

On my bed I see the Pocket Brooke, and the pangs of re-morse shoot through me again. I borrowed my book back from Sandra, promising to bring it with me. I've betrayed her. Beside the slim paperback are some handwritten pages, and it takes me a moment to remember Harold brought me the beginning of his novel, which bears the title NAT'S STUMP . . .

* * *

When I was five my uncle, who was called Nat, took me into our back garden shed and buggered me. I remember a muscular, hairy thigh pressed between my own bruised and scabbed little legs, to force them apart; and then a burning pain that shot right through me.

It was such an overwhelmingly dreadful experience that I spent the next ten years having nightmares about it and hoping it would happen again. We lived in a poor neighbourhood, in the East End of London, and one would imagine it wouldn't be too difficult for a boy to find an abuser. But such was the case with me—I was treated alas with the greatest respect and consideration on the part of relatives, friends and teachers. Of course, Uncle Nat was not around for those ten years. The myth was that he was abroad, in Africa. In reality he had been banged up in Brixton for armed robbery.

Then he returned and lived with us again. By us I mean my mother and my sister Veronica (Vonnie). And one day he caught

222

me wearing my mum's clothes, and persuaded her that I should be taught a lesson. If I wanted to dress like a woman I should learn what being a woman felt like. In her presence he buggered me for the second time.

I have always, until just recently, believed my life was ruined by these early experiences. And yet, when I lie on my bed thinking of those things that make life worth living for me—such as Bessie Smith, Wilfred Owen's war poetry, the Book of Job, wanking or fucking to fantasies of anal rape, Paul Robeson singing Ol' Man River, *or Woody Allen in* Manhattan *lying on a sofa thinking of what things make life worth living for him, leading up to Mariel Hemingway's sad-beautiful young face telling him he has to have a little faith in people—then I realize they mostly arise, immediately or distantly, from pain, injustice, oppression, abuse, pogrom.*

From that moment on, I decided to go looking for Nat's stump . . .

* * *

(All a bit vague so far, me old matey, but it's a start. Hope I didn't disturb you last night with that awful ruckus. After you left the bar last night, Elke and Brenda turned up and I offered them a Metaxa. Elke asked me if I'd come back to the Centre to help move her beds apart, ready for the next "leader!" It hardly seemed a fitting job for the middle of the night so I assumed she was keener on putting things together . . . She joshed about what she and Rollo got up to before he had the runs, and very soon she was demonstrating. I didn't mind her giving me a blow job but did object when she tried to suck my nipples. Which are terribly sensitive and I asked her to stop. The randy old bugger wouldn't, and I pushed her away a bit too firmly, unfortunately.)

* * *

I strip off, and start doing a bit of packing—making sure the plate-clock is embedded in dirty shirts. I find the still unposted card I wrote to Bridget, my mad, feary wife from the banks of the Liffey. Decide to tear it up. Tear up and throw away also that cheerful, stunning fax from Carla. Her silence may be eloquent of displeasure at my breezy response. I feel a general disquiet and guilt.

I dim the shadows with Metaxa and memories of a black, glistening nest of hair.

TEN

The Socratic Catastrophe

The red lanterns glow; the tables are being set for supper; the crowds mingle. *Bouzoukis* play, cameras flash to preserve Skagathos forever. There are women showing a hint of cleavage, and thereby creating an erotic charge, when for two weeks they've displayed all, without a charge of any kind, on the beach.

Rhona, a waiflike bosomless woman I've dismissed previously, now seems, in her little black classic dress and earrings, a woman I might desire if I were not filled with thoughts of Maria. Rhona has her shaman certificate, but realizes there's a long way to go. Stephanos interrupts, annoyingly, our chat. "Excuse me: Simon, I'm a little worried. Your trippers should have been back a couple of hours ago."

"Natasha's here," I respond; "there she is, over there, so they must be back."

"No, she didn't go. She wasn't feeling well. I rang the beach taverna, and the boat isn't back."

I feel the quiver of tension, fear, excitement, in my stomach.

225

"It was a real bad storm," he says. "Socrates is a good, reliable boatman, but his boat is old. My God, we can do without another catastrophe; that would finish us." As we discuss what steps he will have to take if they don't arrive soon, I reflect that another catastrophe wouldn't do *my* reputation any good either—to have lost almost an entire workshop of eleven people, by one means or other, in less than a fortnight. Stephanos looks increasingly grey and ill; I can see he is starting to become convinced the nightmare is a reality. And he says, "I'd better go and ring Skyros."

I move apart from the crowd. I feel my heart beating rapidly. I must prepare what to say to the English press. I start to compose my statement.

"They were a wonderful crowd of people. Brooke died on St. George's Day, on Shakespeare's birthday; remembering the sweet English air of home, the laughter of English friends. There would be, he wrote, 'a corner of a foreign field that is, forever, England.' I wondered at first what my Skagathos friends could be said to have died for, what meaning one could ascribe to their lives and deaths. Nothing so simple as patriotism. One doesn't die for vegetarianism, or even the earth. One might die for Christianity, but not for Reiki or Orgasmic Consciousness. However, they all gloried in the human imagination . . ." Something like that.

Small talk with people I've scarcely met, my attention on the door through which Stephanos disappeared. I long for a cigarette. I become deaf to all around me.

I recall saying to the group, while discussing tenses, "There are certain events that are so appalling—the Hiroshima bomb, for instance—that they seem, at least in retrospect, predictable, inevitable; they happen ahead of time, and I can imagine a novel written entirely in the future tense." So, now . . .

Stephanos will head towards me, his bronzed face ashen

I shall have to stay on. Grieving relatives will arrive, along with forty people expecting a holiday, a dreadlocked Rastafarian poet, a psychodramatist and a tree shamaness: for it's too late to cancel the next course. Incredible confusion, Stephanos leaping around in a frenzy. "Welcome to Skagathos. Unfortunately it's a little crowded because . . . Let me tell you about

226

the plumbing . . ." Reporters will arrive, and a couple of television crews. Among the journalists will be, to my great surprise, Carla, with our daughter strapped to her back. A couple of English tabloids will print photographs of Carla, baby and me standing together outside a church, following a memorial service for Socrates and his passengers. There will be so much publicity Carla will think it pointless to keep quiet anymore, and will admit that we were lovers and Nadine Anne is my daughter.

When I return home, I shall find an empty nest; Marie will have moved in with Alan. The school will say it might be best if I resign. Carla will invite me to share her cramped, damp flat in Herne Hill. There's even sheltered accommodation for my father quite close. Yet the idea of two fiction writers, sharing a computer and a toddler, fills me with horror. The temptation to move to Skagathos and Maria will become irresistible.

Natasha is touching my arm to attract my attention. She thinks *I've* come back from the trip, and apologizes for missing it: she felt a bit queasy at lunch, and thought a voyage unadvisable. She feels okay now, and is sad to have missed it. "Was it enjoyable?" she asks; and without waiting for a reply draws me to a seat; has something to confess. As from a great distance, my eyes straying, I hear the Russian beauty say she has never lived in Magnitogorsk; it's simply the title of her first novel, written when she was twenty, about a woman who does a protest striptease on top of a blast furnace, then leaps to her death. I attend to her closely now. "I'm a writer, you see. My book is coming out in English and several other languages, including Russian, next year. It's already been read by two million Russians, in *samizdat.*"

Her eyes are half-pleading, half-teasing. She clutches my arm. "Forgive my white lie, Simon; I am no stripper, but I kind of identify with my heroine. It was arranged for Pasha and me to win the quiz show because we were commissioned to write article about the western New Age. He was photographer. When he'd taken enough snaps, he went—back to his precious meat and butter."

"So he was not police or KGB?"

"He was police photographer, once upon a time. He's a really nice guy; we've worked on several projects together."

"But you seemed so . . . antagonistic."

"All part of the act. I'm sorry. I did not want to say about me being much-read *samizdat* novelist because—well, people might have felt insecure about their writing. Even you, Simon, though I read *Transplanted Hearts* before coming and I think you are good."

"Thank you."

"I told the others, in confidence, two days ago. So now—I am so sorry! So tell me about the Brooke grave."

"I didn't get there. Actually I'm rather worried—"

But before I can explain my name is called out, I turn to see Stephanos smiling and pointing towards the gate. Teresa, in shorts and a top, is coming through it, followed by Ezekiel and Emily. Teresa pushes through the crowd to me. "Hi, Simon! Where did you get to?"

"I'm sorry; I took a walk on the coast and got marooned by the tide. We were just getting worried about you."

"Socrates said we should wait until it was calmer." She glances at her watch. "And we were going to co-listen: sorry!"

"It's okay." I'd forgotten our arrangement.

Harold pushes his way through to us. "Where did you get to?" he asks accusingly. "We wasted good grave-visiting time waiting for you. It was very moving. So utterly peaceful."

"It's a long story." I want to tell him I too experienced something beautiful and moving; I want to break into "Maria" from *West Side Story;* I want her again; I want to be with her; all wives and loves fall away behind; Maria is what I was meant for. I'm about to draw him aside when he forestalls me by saying anxiously, "I don't suppose you had time to look at the beginning of my novel?"

"Yes. I like what you've written."

"Oh, that's great! Well, it's a start."

Guiltily I ask where Sandra is. His face sombers; she was very upset not to have the book, to read from. She had practiced for hours and hours. All she could do was read the sonnet carved on the tomb; she did that beautifully. But she complained on her way back of a headache, and has gone to rest.

"I let her down," I mourn. "I begged her to do the readings,

228

as a boost to her confidence, and then I had the book myself and didn't come. Fuck!"

"Well . . . Yes, I guess you did; but I'm sure it was something you couldn't do anything to avoid." As they had extra time, he says, a few of them hitched taxi-lifts to Skyros village. "I bought you a couple of postcards. I didn't realize there was a statue of Brooke."

The face of the nude bronze seems closer to a Neanderthal's than to Brooke's feminine beauty. "Modeled by a Belgian male prostitute, according to the guidebook. When George V visited the island, they put a fig leaf on the statue. If Charley-boy came now, they'd drape the island with tampons."

"Shouting hurrah for the Tampax Britannica."

I reveal that I know about Natasha. Harold says, "It became obvious she could write us into the ground. She's carried the rest of us for the past week—even in English she's been shit-hot."

* * *

A half-moon shines; Elspeth's Moonlight tape is playing; the remains of the last vegetarian meal have been cleared away. Everyone's fairly drunk. Stephanos slurs his words as he thanks me for my contribution, and says he'll be glad when the next four weeks are over and he can relax. In the winter he does a little fishing with the villagers and molds a few pots. It's even nicer on the island, he says, when all the tourists are gone. His enthusiasm sparks off again the yearning I have to leave behind the febrile emptiness of England. "What happens to someone like Maria?" I ask casually. "Is there work here for her?"

He shakes his head. "Life is hard for her, especially in the winter. Her husband died of cancer three years ago, and she has four children. That's why"—he clasps my arm warmly—"I am grateful to you for helping her. I was a little annoyed with Mike; as a facilitator, you should have had a discount; but I hope she give good value? I've heard before that she does."

* * *

Natasha and Priscilla have withdrawn to sit in an alcove, and seem engrossed. Angus pours out to me his sorrow over his

229

woman, his married Catholic madonna, never to be possessed. Caroline confesses that she is extremely fond of Harold, but something holds him back from commitment. She senses I'm distracted, but would never imagine I am picturing myself in a little white house overlooking the sea, with Maria cheerfully sweeping or cooking somewhere near, careful not to interrupt me by shouting too loud to four football-playing teenagers. It seems, actually, logical that this should happen.

I exchange addresses with Teresa, and she says she and Ezekiel are going down to the beach for one last swim; do I want to come?

"Thanks. I'll catch up with you later."

I join Emily, alone, reflective, surprisingly feminine and lovely in a long white toga in a haze of lanternlight, moonlight and bougainvillea. Harriet has left early, she says, to team up with friends for a walking tour in Crete. We sit then in silence, not needing to talk; sensing a similar sadness in each of us.

* * *

Teresa engulfing us in a huge beach towel, rubbing us dry, and Ezekiel holding my balls. "Simon," he says, "this is good of you. It feels good; it's taking away a lot of my jealousy."

Teresa, letting the towel fall, stroking each of us on the back: "I told him there was no need to be jealous of you."

The hiss of the exploding surf; the ghostly Milky Way line of white; the moon flying.

"I can see that now. I've got to lighten up. I went kind of crazy, Simon, when she fucked Danny."

"You shouldn't have," says Teresa, giving him a hug. "That was a wonderful warm, bright, magical night—just like this one—and the whole heaven and earth was fused together. You know what I mean, Simon?"

"Yes."

"Okay, I was making love to Danny, in a sense, with the spray sweeping over us like God's own sperm, yet really it was with Ezekiel too, and—well, everyone. It was celebrating life, nothing more. And it was helping Danny use what he'd learned in our workshops."

"I can see that now," he murmurs. "I had no business blabbing about it to Andrea and upsetting them. I hope they're okay."

"I think they're basically an okay couple," she says. "I think it was just the shock of you hammering on their door in the middle of the night that threw her so badly." She turns her face towards me. "She'd left the beach party early; she wouldn't have known anything if this idiot hadn't gone charging around the village, waking God knows how many villagers up, to find out where Danny and Andrea were staying. Why did you do it?"

"I was upset. I shouldn't have hit him, it was inexcusable." He kisses her cheek, and almost smiles; immediately he darkens again, just as the moon vanishes behind cloud. "But then there was Arnold." Turning his face towards mine: "You must know about that; some of your workshop saw them together."

"For Chrissake, Ezekiel," Teresa snaps, "this is ridiculous! I told you, that was a shamanic exercise, to try to give Arnold the experience of flying. He's so earthbound. There was almost no penetration. Do you think I'd *want* to make love to Arnold? Enough to do it on a wall overlooking a vertical drop that would mean certain death? Come *on*, now!"

"You're right. It *should* be possible to treat sex more lightly. Si, holding your balls will help me to, I know. Unless you've had experience with a guy, as I haven't, our equipment can seem kind of *awesome*, don't you think? More so than pussies, because we're used to pussies. I've always thought, if a woman has somebody's cock up her it must blow her mind. But I can see now the male genitals can be just smooth and silky and heavy; nice, but no big deal. Thank you for letting me have this experience."

As we begin to stroll, Teresa in the middle, up the beach road, he says, "The whole month has been a great experience. I've gotten close to everybody. Though it'll be good to get back to theaters, cinemas, my IBM and Internet. Have you noticed, Simon, how in the past few days everyone's been hungry for news from outside? Like that rape trial that's going on in England? Do you know if it's over, by the way?"

"England? Yes."

"The trial."

"Yes again. Guilty; two years imprisonment."

"Really? Oh, well, that sounds about right. Intriguing case, woman raping gay male. But I was saying, people are beginning to need a wider reality; these days you can only drink from a pitcher of quietness for so long. I've truly enjoyed this, but now I want the movies! I want to see that *Dark Desire* everyone's talking about here."

He has to join his wife in Athens next week, to sort things out. That was the only way he could get her off the island. She's planning to sue Teresa for using black magic to lure him to her. When I express incredulity, Ezekiel says he hasn't always been as well balanced as he is today. It's because Teresa persuaded him to come off lithium and use the juice of the mariposa lily instead. He feels so much better; but a West Coast jury might be swayed by orthodox arguments.

His wife, he says, has also persuaded Lucinda's friend, staying at the island hotel, to sue Skagathos Holidays for negligence. "Sara's a very persuasive, domineering woman," Teresa observes; "if you do see her in Athens she'll eat you for breakfast, sweetheart."

"That's nonsense, Tess."

"You're scared of her. I still think it was you who broke into the Centre and tried to call her in Vancouver, the night you rampaged through the village looking for Danny. I think you would have begged her to have you back, that night."

"For Pete's sake! Are you saying I'm a thief too? There was money stolen, remember."

"That was to throw Stephanos off the scent."

"For fuck—"

She breaks our slow stride and his exclamation to kiss him. He gives a relieved chuckle, and murmurs, honestly, he didn't, and she says, okay, but if I were you I wouldn't give her the chance to browbeat you.

"Maybe you're right."

The road steepens. We pass a statuesque, timeless, moon-blanched donkey.

Three moon-fleered figures loom, descending towards us and

passing. Natasha, Priscilla, Eddie. Past almost before we recognize them. "How's the water?" Priscilla calls back in a high, tremulously excited voice. "It's real good!" calls Ezekiel. "Enjoy!"

ELEVEN

A Black
Sea-Dog

The hollow horse, in which the Greeks stowed away to gain an entrance into the city, is sponsored by Coca-Cola and has its logo on it. ICI doesn't want us to show the horse during the presentation of the trophy. They will tolerate the winning captain wearing a small Cola logo on his shield, but that's all. There's a lot of confused argument among us about this. *I* don't think the BBC should be mixed up in advertising and sponsorship at all; but I'm old-fashioned.

Masterson presents the trophy to Odysseus. The trophy is Helen. She speaks a few words herself, very Home Counties. She doesn't *look* like a replica, though Masterson knows (and actually Herodotus knew) she is. There's another war going on in Egypt, and the real Helen is there. ICI took a gamble, that that war would be finished first, and lost.

There are still street fights going on here, and Masterson is in his uniform of the Gloucesters, leading his men against the guerilla fighters. I see the geometric cemetery of white crosses, stretching away across the plain; an awesome sight, I tell the viewers. But Odysseus says casualties were light. "My men dug a far bigger mass grave than was needed, in the event; and we have thousands of body bags unused." His face is scarred, blood-streaked; he wears a camouflage jacket and the blue beret of UNO. He asks me if I will send a fax to his wife, explaining that Sky Sports has invited him to comment on the later stages of the World Cup, and this will delay his return. With him, suddenly, is Pele, the great Brazilian star . . .

Something like that. I can't vouch for its complete accuracy. I know I'm enjoying being part of a team again, as with a parched mouth and thumping head I come round on the ramshackle Skagathos ferry, in the pre-dawn murk, seeing the cliffs low on the horizon.

As those cliffs lessen, and the cliffs of Skyros appear, I think of Maria. Stephanos has promised to pass on to her ten thousand drachs to buy presents for her children, and to tell her that I shall keep in touch. But I feel I should have seized the moment—and stayed.

Athens. Dusk, turning to moonlit darkness. After resting at the Hotel Ceres—or in some cases shopping—we have threaded through the Third World city—so noisy it seems to Angus like the guns opening up at Gallipoli—to an open-air restaurant in the Plaka. Though above us the cradle of civilization is lit up, for a while, waiting for wine to arrive, we sit in a kind of half-gloom. "The black sea-dog or Black Sea dog," as Angus calls it. Harold wonders if the gods on Olympus feel, as he does, an impotence at having started so many plots that they can't continue. He's thinking of Nat and Mildred and Agnes, of course. He wonders what's happened to the Agnes who thinks she's pregnant; the one who has a man's foot stuck up her pussy and who says on the phone to Nat, "It's WONDERFUL!" that Mildred is feeling okay . . .

This raises our spirits and a laugh. Emily imagines waiters and waitresses suddenly doing a Potteresque dance routine around their table, singing, "'SWONDERFUL! 'SMARVEL-LOUS! YOU COULD CARE FOR ME!"

Natasha asks what Potteresque means. She has not heard of Potter. She isn't amused by our drollery. She has, she says, a terrible choice to make: "Freedom or enslavement. East or

West. Priscilla has fallen a little in love with me, stupid woman, and wants me to teach and study at her university. I can go back to Russia and freedom. Nowadays it's totally free there; you can say anything, believe anything. Only I was not used to freedom, and for the past two years I have a block. Well, since Priscilla has been my co-listener I have felt a craving to write, because she has maddened me with her censorships. You know, her university has five hundred Sexual Harassment Officers! So like our old Political Officers, when anger made me creative! Yes, I think I must go there. Next month. To the West. I choose enslavement for the sake of my writing."

And she will break Priscilla's heart by falling for some hunky black basketball player; just as she has caused Eddie heartache, telling him it's been lovely but bye-bye. He has gone off backpacking in Arcadia.

Et in Arcadia Eddie, booms Angus.

A waiter arrives bearing salads and cutlery. Smiling at Natasha's irony and Angus's joke, I'm looking absently at Lucy, who walks past our restaurant towards a neighboring one, with a few others including Bob and Tamsin, Elspeth and Brenda. All but Lucy wave; her haunted eyes stare at me with hatred. I recall I half-promised to have dinner with her in Athens. My smile must make it worse for her. I turn away from her gaze. Emily too turns back to face Natasha after a wave at the passersby. She says, "Priscilla mentioned it to me. I had a coffee with her at the hotel just before she left for the airport. She seemed sure you'll come, Natasha, and is obviously over the moon about it. I get the feeling she wants to bask in your reflected glory."

Natasha frowns and asks what that means.

"All the publicity you're going to have when your book comes out; you're going on a big book tour in the spring, aren't you?"

"A book tour!" Angus demands, his boom straddling a question and an explanation; and the others echo him, all craning towards Natasha. She frowns; mutters that Priscilla has too big a mouth. What does a book tour entail? asks Harold: how many cities?

"I think it's something like twenty."

"Twenty!" exclaims an awed Caroline.

"Something like that." She frowns again, as if it's of no moment, a great bore. Asked to detail them, she says, "Oh, San Francisco, Los Angeles, Denver, Dallas, Houston, Detroit, Philadelphia, Boston, New York of course . . . I don't remember them all."

Everyone, with small variations: "That's marvelous!"

". . . And Canada. Toronto, Vancouver . . . All in one month, it will be killing."

"Are you doing a book tour in England?" Harold asks, his eyes huge with desire and envy.

"I don't think so. Maybe; *Magnitogorsk* doesn't come out there until next autumn. But English publishers are more sensible, I think. Simon would know about that."

"Have you ever done a book tour, Simon?" Caroline asks.

"Tenby Public Library, Stroud Arts Centre, a pub in Bridgewater," I say more or less truthfully, but with an ironic smile.

Natasha nods: "I'm right, you see. The English are more sensible. I didn't want to say anything about the tour, stupidly I was afraid Simon might think I was trying to *khvastat'sa*—be showoff. It's not so." She stretches her arm to stroke my hand.

"You're so wonderfully modest," says Harold. "All the same, you're obviously going to be a big literary star. The name Natasha Rodlova will soon be a household word."

A shake of her lovely head. "No. Natalia Kaganovich. Rodlova is from a very short, very unhappy marriage."

"Kaganovich . . ." I muse. She nods and hangs her head. "Pasha was giving you a clue, saying my father was Politburo apparatchik. Not my father though, but a great-uncle." She shivers. "Horrible brute, old Uncle Lazar."

I recall at last, dimly, from three or four years back, a news item in one of the weeklies saying that one of Stalin's archmurderers was related to a promising female dissident writer.

* * *

As the wave of star worship subsides a little, our conversation shifts to the home world, the differing fates to which we return. Caroline has rung her son, and found he's been suspended from school, for nothing more than smoking a joint in the toilets.

237

Harold, phoning his sister, has found she has won fifty quid in the lottery.

I commiserate or congratulate with my eyes, while sipping wine and chewing squid. My thoughts are adrift. I too made a phone call at the hotel; I heard my father wheezing worse than usual, almost drowning a frenetic Rugby League commentary from his TV. Yes, he enjoyed his theater trip—he's always liked J. B. Priestley—and Alan's a very nice chap; unfortunately he drove home a bit fast, and that brought on one of Dad's breathless attacks. "Marie was a bit worried; she stayed the night on the sofa bed; I said it wasn't necessary, I'd be all right, but she insisted. She's a grand girl, Simon."

"You're right, Dad."

"Get her some nice perfume in Duty Free, and I'll pay you for it."

"No need for that; I was going to anyway." *L'Air du Temps.*

"Well, then, as you don't smoke anymore, son, buy a carton of Silk Cut for Alan. That's what I saw him smoking. I never got a chance to thank him proper. It was very nice of him to drive us to London."

Eating swordfish and drinking claret, I reflect on my mixed reaction of relief and disappointment. Though, of course, Marie and Alan could just as easily have got together the next night. More easily in fact, they wouldn't have been so tired. That slight shiver in the spine. Though I have the feeling that, while they might yield to a moment's weakness, they would draw back from a prearranged meeting.

The fact is, I'm not sure what I want. I would be clearer if I'd had a second meeting with Maria.

A large, quiet dinner party near us is on the point of departure, and I find myself—in the midst of eating, talk and reverie—being greeted by an unknown woman with lank grey hair. "Hi, Simon!" she says "How was Skagathos?"

The stranger's intrusion irritates me, but I smile back. "Oh, fine."

"This poor man had to put up with my nattering on the flight over," she explains. It floods back—our animated conversation over vodkas. I grieved deeply that she was bound for Skyros. Can't remember her name.

"How was Skyros?"

Her slightly equine face glows. "Magical! I was just talking about you, strangely enough. I met someone at our hotel, a Japanese writer called Issy something who shares a London agent with you, he said."

"Good grief! Issei. He's not due to teach in Skagathos for another two weeks."

"That's right, but I think he feels nervous about it, so he decided to book in for this fortnight as a student. I think he's doing psychodrama. He ate with us, you've only just missed him. Anyway, must go. When you're next coming to Bath, give me a ring. You've got my number?"

"Yes." Though undoubtedly I've lost it. She melts, with her companions, into the dark. "Fuck!" says Harold. "Sagawa! We probably passed him."

Caroline places an anxious hand on mine. "Simon: if you do use our Sagawa material for any reason, you will please change his name, won't you? I'm terribly afraid he'll sue me, because I started it off."

Emily: "Do you really think a cannibal is going to sue you?"

Harold: "One can never be too careful, these days."

We concentrate on eating and drinking. The air is balmy. The Parthenon glows. Jokes, laughter, memories. Elspeth approaches from the next-door restaurant, floaty-haired and -skirted. *"Allo!"* parrot-squalks Emily. Elspeth, laying a gentle hand on my shoulder, asks us not to get up; taking the earlier, Heathrow flight, she's only come to say goodbye. I stand and hug her, thin, ethereal.

She will be met by her father, she assures an avuncular Angus, who also half-rises and hugs her. Mentally I see the feminized, transsexual, terminally ill sub dean, shivering at Heathrow in the middle of the night.

Caroline asks if her meal was good. She screws up her mouth. "I had squid. It was nice but . . . I had to eat it too quickly; also I think he must have suffered a lot before he was killed. I'm going to have to concentrate hard during the flight to try to help him."

"Play your *Moonlight* tape, that's very calming."

"I will." She touches my shoulder again, and Emily's; then is gone, floaty, translucent, weightless.

Harold rises; raises his glass. "A toast to Simon!"

"To Simon!"

"Some of us were a bit pissed off with you," Harold says, "when you left your notebook around for us to read—if we were curious; and of course some of us were. But then we realized it had to be deliberate, and was designed to give us a jolt. My stories *were* twee; and in saying I was the Noel Coward of Hemel Hempstead you were too kind."

Natasha: "It was sweet of you to say I'm fuckable, Simon."

Caroline: "I was too moral to look, Simon; or maybe too cowardly."

Harold: "Jonners was hurt, that you found his stories 'boring, boring,' but well . . . you were probably right."

Dessert, coffee, liqueurs. It's chillier; we don jackets or cardigans; the moon's obscured by cloud. Angus eulogizes his *donna,* whom he will be seeing in a few hours, in a Rome holiday apartment, where she's with her husband. Angus knows he is a pawn in a never-ending marital chess game; but he does not care; he loves her to the death. Natasha flings an arm around him, and tells him what a dear man he is! what dear people we all are! She is going home to write her article for *Liudi,* an offshoot of the American magazine *People,* and will have nothing but good to say of us.

She hopes Pasha's photos come out well. She can't promise Harold that Ezekiel's bum, in the death ritual, will be on the magazine's cover. She will send copies to us, of course, with a translation. Probably by then she will be in the States.

We lapse into quietness, waiting for the bill. An old man, rather Gallic-looking in a black beret and dark glasses, hobbles past our table on his way out. He is one-legged and on crutches. Perhaps a war-wounded. Harold, noticing him after he has passed, swivels on his seat, flutters a hand to call him back, and cries weakly: "Nat! Nat!"

* * *

Candida passes me over straightaway to her husband, Jim. "Ah, Simon, they did give you the message; my pigeon Greek worked. I rang Marie and found out you were briefly in the richly named Hotel Ceres. Candida and I are watching a Korean remake of *Battleship Potemkin;* absolutely splendid."

"We have to leave for the airport in five minutes: is there a problem?"

"Nothing huge, I hope. But I thought you should be warned, in advance, there's a rather nasty piece about Skagathos, you, and Ms. Gilbert's tragic death, in tomorrow's *Sunday Telegraph.* I've heard about it through one of our neighbors, who works there. The piece is by Andrew Scott Holsworth."

"Tell me the worst."

"Basically that you joined in an attempted cover-up of her suicide, trying to claim she died by natural causes. And that you deeply distressed many of the extremely vulnerable people there by leaving your notes on them lying around for them to read. It quotes some supposed rude comments."

"Such as?"

" 'Boring little fart,' 'Jewish dwarf,' 'Pussy Galore.' Those were the ones our neighbor remembered. Oh, and suggestions that you rather like the ladies—as if that were a crime."

"Do you know anything about this Scott— . . .?"

"Holsworth. He's having a well-publicized affair with Jan Gregson, who as you may know is the sister of Carla Brand. So there could be a connection there. The affair broke up both their marriages, I believe." In brisker, cheering-up tones, Jim assures me the piece sounds too malicious to carry much weight; indeed, since the *Telegraph* is a semi-Fascist paper, I could even gain kudos from the attack. The book readers and opinion formers will sympathize with any attempt there might have been to protect the privacy of the unhappy young woman and her family. 'Jewish dwarf' etcetera could be a bit damaging but Jim can't imagine I ever said any such thing. We would have to see if there are grounds for libel; though the lawyers usually go through these things with a fine-tooth comb. The only thing I could see might be actionable is a quote, supposedly from some anonymous student you scared off the island, to the effect that you screwed practically every non-Greek on Skagathos. But again I haven't seen the text; it's no doubt very carefully worded."

241

In the pause, I hear an explosion: presumably the *Potemkin*'s guns firing.

"Don't worry unduly. Today's hot news is tomorrow's shit-paper. Marie didn't seem particularly disturbed; she sounded in very good spirits. Busy knitting garments for her anticipated second nephew in Durban, she said."

"Yes."

"I didn't know she was a football fan—I heard Match of the Day in the background."

"She's not; she probably just left the TV on while she went to wash her hair or something."

"That gorgeous hair: yes. Preparing to welcome her Odysseus home. Have a good flight. We'll speak on Monday."

I fill out a return luggage label, then sit staring at it until the words turn into hieroglyphic. Rather than listen to televised football, even distantly and through wet, shampooed hair, Marie would dye her hair pink. Yet, on the whole, I feel glad that their affair continues. He's there, now, in her probably, and I don't mind. It's best. Carla is clearly in a rage with me; that means a letter from the CSA, demanding impossible sums—or perhaps a private demand from Carla's sister or parents—is only a matter of time. Marie's vengeance on me will be worse than Clytemnestra's—unless she herself has a guilty conscience.

I didn't know she was knitting for her sister's expected baby. Alan was right in seeing his kids as an important factor. She hardly ever mentions them. Which means they're the key. Good sex, with a man eager to communicate and share, instead of one who, a second after coming, is wondering how to make a subordinate character more interesting . . . And two nice kids who come to their dad every school holiday and need mothering . . . It's really no contest. Sex and intimacy and potential stepchildren—make for a very deep plot.

No wonder her old threats, of returning to *Sath Efrica* have ceased in the last couple of years, just when one might have expected them to increase.

She needs a normal, caring husband, with children; and I need pitchers of quietness filled by the silent Maria.

The phone's trill breaks through my absorption. It's Tamsin, impatient, telling me the coach is ready to leave.

242

All the same, it's disturbing, knowing he's there, a last night in our bed; as comfortably familiar as her old trainers, yet secretly thrilling as her silk basque (and I know now who bought it for her) under her business suit.

* * *

The vast departure lounge is packed and gloomy, like the banks of the Styx on the first day of the Somme. All the flights are delayed; an hour after our departure time, midnight, our plane from Gatwick has only just landed. I glimpsed, through a glass screen separating us from arrivals, a tall and stooping woman in flapping cord trousers and clogs who I am sure was the tree shamaness from Barnsley.

Harold is stretched out flat on his back in front of us. Glancing up to where *Paris* has been wiped out, he murmurs, "Dear old Jeanne has gone." Rome too has gone; Moscow is boarding.

Caroline starts to giggle, her flabby bare midriff rippling. She's thinking, she says, of those fourteen genteel ladies who, in a fortnight's time, will expect a lady romance writer and will find a Japanese cannibal. "He'll say"—trying to control herself, wiping her eyes—"he'll say . . . he'll say to Stephanos, coming down from Calypso on the first day, I'm sorry, I've got to leave, I 'ate the 'ole workshop!"

Harold rolls around on the floor. I'm doubled up, choking. At the same time, knowing there's more than a touch of hysteria in my laughter.

I should have stayed on Skagathos; sent a fax to the school telling them to get stuffed; put up at the hotel, then thrown myself on Maria's mercy. I don't think she'd reject me; for her too, I'm convinced, it was far more than a giving of "good value." I have a sudden urge—despite all that's in England or already unstoppably checked in—to announce that I am staying in Greece. I am, actually, on the very point of standing up and astonishing my friends when Harold returns me to good sense by demanding, "Where the *fuck* is our plane?"

I decide to go on a walkabout, to try and settle my agitated thoughts. Match of the Day. Silk Cut. Chanel.

Picking my way through the sprawl of cinder-crisp, half-naked, torpid tourists, I confront suddenly a well-known, darkly attractive face. She doesn't know me from Adam, until I introduce myself and we shake hands. The waiting is very tedious, we agree. We're both looking for the coffee machine, and together we go in search, find it, and get our coffees. We lounge awkwardly against a pillar, sipping. "Did your students do some good writing?" she asks.

"Tremendous! And yours?"

She wouldn't say tremendous; there were a couple of imaginative stories. One was about Rupert Brooke, who I might or might not know is buried on Skyros. I nod. "What was it about?"

"His death. A post-modern version. A Methodist minister wrote it. In his account, Brooke and Asquith, the Prime Minister's son, were both in love with another young officer, Shaw-Stewart. Asquith found them *in flagrente,* and stabbed Brooke through the heart with his sword. A *crime passionel.* It had to be hushed up, of course, and Churchill at the War Office helped to create the myth of the gallant soldier-poet."

"That's a good plot."

She nods. "It was publishable, with some revision, but Ken said he'd be much too embarrassed to do anything with it. It sounded so very *likely,* don't you agree? At least for our time." She takes a Silk Cut. "Thanks." Accepts the match flame; draws in. "The other good one was a rather *un*likely spoof on New Age holidays by a hyped-up American widow. —Ah, I think she was with you first."

"Krystal."

"That's right. She wrote an account of a midnight co-listening session between a rather Oedipally obsessed girl, who brags about being groped by her tutor, and an old, lonely, drab widow—sort of Krystal's shadow figure, you might say. She has one gift, for hypnosis; and she bumps off the girl by persuading her she's her mummy giving her candy, whereas it's really sleeping pills."

It was farfetched, she continues, but clever, and the psychology was quite well observed. The widow wanted to do just one extraordinary thing in her life; and found the murder a sexual stimulus. "One of my old dears, Flo, asked her what a multiple orgasm was!" She grins, exhaling smoke. "When Krystal told her, Flo said in her day women never even had *one!* They were a good group."

My smile feels frozen. "Of course," I say, "an island like Skyros would be a good place for a murder. New Agers don't recognize evil."

"That's right! Krystal made that very point." She drains her coffee container, crumples and trashes it. "Well, it's been nice meeting you." A nod, a smile, a turnaway.

I wander back to my friends. "Natasha's gone," says Emily, nodding up at the monitor.

These our actors. Into air, into thin Aeroflot.

Krystal's story. I'll think about it later. It demands a wide-awake, sharp mind, not this floating Lotus state. Think now, dreamily, of that more likely crime of passion. Brooke. Asquith. Shaw-Stewart. Churchill. The *jeunesse dorée* of the last golden English epoch. The last generation to fight and die with Aeschylus on their lips. The last to believe that obscenity should be, literally, off-stage. "Hearts at peace under an English heaven" and all that. It *is* a bloody good plot, damn this Methodist minister chap to hell.

Caroline is passing round some photos she had developed this afternoon. I take a few to look at, out of politeness. I'm not attuned to holiday snaps at the moment. But the second one I look at, after a last-night group shot, makes me stare at it intently. I recognize Maria, climbing a lane of steps; she's smiling for the camera; and is bent over, since she is carrying what looks at first like a big glassy-eyed fish trapped in a net slung from her shoulders, borne in front of her. Then I see that the "fish" is human. Caroline observes my shocked look. "That's Maria," she says; "a villager who cleans at the Centre."

"Yes, I know."

"And that's Nikos, her son. He had meningitis when he was a baby, and is practically a vegetable. My landlady told me. I met them one morning, when Maria was taking him to her mother's to be looked after while she worked. She asked me to take his picture, otherwise I'd never have intruded; I promised to send it to Stephanos."

"Poor little boy!" says Emily, glancing at it.

"Poor *big* boy. He's only eight, and already he's very heavy, as you can see. Maria has to do everything for him, turn him at night when he cries—which apparently is a lot of the time, put him on the toilet, and carry him in that contraption up to her mother's every morning. And she has three other small children. If you can believe it, she's still in her early thirties! She could be carrying him like that when *he's* in his thirties. She has no life; she lives for Nikos, my landlady said; and you could see it in her eyes when I took that photo. She wanted me to take it; she thinks he's as beautiful as a young angel."

"It's very humbling," says Harold, "when you see such devotion. Only you women are capable of it. It's hard to think of a *man* with that kind of laptop! Don't you think, Simon?"

Nodding, I manage to comment, despite the iron weight in my chest, that she often nodded off in our staff meetings, and I'd assumed it was because she was wearing heavy clothes and didn't understand English.

* * *

We sit waiting to board the plane.

"You seem a long way away, Simon. Are you glad it's over?"

"No, not glad, Caroline; but I need to write. I have to return to fiction. I can't afford too much reality."